Tangled
Promises

by

Linda Trout

Tangled Promises

Cover Art by *Kim Mendoza*

The Wild Rose Press, Inc.
PO Box 708
Adams Basin, NY 14410-0708
Visit us at www.thewildrosepress.com

Publishing History
First Crimson Rose Edition, 2020
Print ISBN 978-1-5092-3094-5
Digital ISBN 978-1-5092-3095-2

Published in the United States of America

Dedication

To the plotting class at WTAMU Writers' Academy,
who helped me lay out the overall premise of this book
and kept pulling me out of the quagmire.

~~

To my family and friends, who keep encouraging me to
write faster, and never giving up on me.

~~

And to my critique partners,
Jackie Kramer, Marilyn Pappano and Susan Shay,
who helped me whip the story into shape.
I don't know what I would have done
without all of you!

~~

To my wonderful editor, Ally Robertson,
whose patience and guidance means the world to me.

~~

To my awesome husband,
who gives me the strength to pursue my dreams.
You are my hero. I will always love you.

Other Wild Rose Press Titles by Linda Trout

Grave Secrets
Last Hope Alaska

Chapter One

Jake Bennett could spit from one end of Rock Ledge to the other. With no traffic lights and two stop signs on Main Street, the town didn't leave much of a footprint on the landscape.

Today, moisture hung so heavy in the air he was unable to see more than a few feet in front of him, much less to the city limits. He hated fog. All it did was provide work for ambulance chasers and tow truck companies. That's the way it was in Chicago, and he figured the people in backwoods Arkansas were no different.

As of two weeks ago, he was part of the backwoods himself. Sheriff for a nothing county, living in a nothing town, and pathetically grateful to be there.

He pulled the door closed to the furnished two-bedroom house the town had offered up as incentive to take the job, as if it could compare to his place overlooking Lake Michigan. Here, the floor creaked, the plumbing groaned, and the windows stuck. The house had to be fifty years old and the furnishings reflected it, but it was sound and clean. Two blocks from the sheriff's office, the free living quarters almost made up for the poor salary.

Bypassing his pride and joy '68 Firebird, he slid behind the wheel of the city-issued SUV. The vehicle had all the bells and whistles an officer could ask for,

Linda Trout

including a computer. At least they were keeping up with technology. He made his rounds through downtown, then the outlying areas within the city limits. Nothing looked amiss, not that he could see much with the low visibility, so he headed to The Tangled Rose café.

After he climbed from his vehicle, he stopped and listened, the dense moisture creating a buffer for the normal noises he'd come to associate with the small town, its ebb and flow vastly different from the big city. An automatic wrench screwing the lug nuts from a tire in the garage resonated down the street. Bell's on one of the church towers chimed the hour. A horn honked right before tires screeched. There wasn't an accompanying thump, so at least a mishap had been averted. For now. His luck wouldn't hold, though. If he wanted anything to eat, he'd better get with it before what promised to be an active day materialized.

An old-timey bell above the door jangled when he walked in the café. Something about the sound made him feel as if he'd stepped back into another era...the 60's or 50's maybe. The back wall had been painted a light green with a mural of a rambling, wild rose bush, complete with thorns, taking center stage. The Arkansas Razorback logo, the Rock Ledge Panthers logo, vinyl records and pictures of movie stars from previous eras were scattered across the other walls. A shrine to a fallen soldier—the owner's husband—sat in a small nook.

The sizzle of frying bacon, the aroma of coffee drifting in the air along with hot grease reminded him of his local hangout in Chicago. His jaw tightened. How long before he'd be able to return to the job that

2

defined him? Not a day too soon as far as he was concerned.

A few people were seated in the dining room, including Mayor Frank Davidson. Jake gave a quick nod as the other man squinted at him briefly before turning his attention back to his breakfast and the newspaper spread before him. Since Jake had first pinned on the badge, the mayor had been cool toward him. It chapped to be on the receiving end of another unfounded judgment.

It hadn't taken long, though, before he'd learned the mayor had wanted someone more local for the position, specifically his nephew. Deputy Clay Larson was a good cop, but didn't have the experience to be in charge. From all appearances, he was perfectly happy in his current position. In his mid-twenties, he was eager to learn and the two men worked well together. Which made Jake's job much easier.

The sweet and very pregnant waitress who greeted him each morning sat behind the register. Normally, Holly would be lumbering around pouring coffee, joking with everyone as they came in. Today, she made no effort to leave her perch on the barstool.

"Morning, Sheriff." She grinned weakly as she rubbed her ever-expanding stomach.

Jake dropped his hat on a peg near the door and headed toward a spot at the counter. He sat there for a while as she stared out the window. "Everything all right?"

She jerked, as if she'd forgotten him. "Hmm? Oh, yes. The baby's letting me know he's there. Probably the change in the weather."

He narrowed his gaze, studying her closely. "If you

need anything, you let me know. Okay?"

She gave a tiny laugh. "I'm supposed to ask you that. But thank you, I will."

Since he didn't see any other waitress, he stood, went around the counter, and helped himself to a cup of coffee. Before he had a chance to get back to his seat, the owner came out of the kitchen with plates in both hands. When she saw him, she came to a sudden halt.

Melody Rose was of medium height, curvy, and with red hair so fiery that it tempted him to touch, to see if it burned. Her green eyes should be twinkling with a million lights but were shadowed instead, and her mouth that was made for smiling was thinned in a pursed line. She wore the café's uniform, a pale pink dress and an apron with roses on it. He'd wondered why she didn't wear jeans, but the extra attention to little details seemed to bring in the customers. That and the quality of the food.

"I'll be with you shortly." Her flat tone left no doubt she was displeased with him helping himself.

She continued on to serve a couple of farmers. Swinging back around the counter, she dropped a menu in front of him. He didn't bother opening it. "I'll have the special."

She had just reached the door to the kitchen when she paused and turned toward him. "Seriously?"

"Sure. Why not?" For the first time since he'd met her, a sly smile spread across her face, transforming her lips into a mischievous grin.

"You got it," she said with so much sweetness it made him wonder what he'd done to himself. His stomach rumbled so he figured it didn't matter as long as he got fed, the food was hot, and there weren't any bugs running around in it. Now if he could only teach her how to make a good pot of coffee, he'd be satisfied. Although, he doubted her other patrons would appreciate her switching from her so-called good—make that weak—blend to what real coffee should taste like. He preferred his strong enough to jolt a person out of a coma.

With a whoosh, Melody disappeared behind the swinging door. Jake thought he heard her giggle as she turned in his order. He looked toward Holly, but she only shrugged with an apologetic expression. Yeah, he'd regret this.

Eight minutes later—he checked his watch—he had a plate sitting in front of him. This time she waited for his reaction. *Quiche.* He'd hoped, against reason, that steak and eggs was the special. The added fruit and toast aside, he didn't think this meal would satisfy the hunger cravings of a gnat.

He took a bite, ready to wash it down with the weak coffee. He didn't need the coffee.

"Hey. This is pretty good." He shoved a large bite into his mouth. He'd had quiche back home, but this had a whole different flavor to it. He liked it.

Her eyes widened and her jaw went slack. "Uh, most men prefer something a little more traditional, like bacon and eggs."

"Yes, well," he said between bites, "they're missing out." He glanced up to find her eyeing him.

She straightened and plastered a smile on her face. "Glad you like it."

He'd been a regular since he'd come to town, and that was the friendliest she'd gotten with him. The cop in him wondered why. The man in him didn't care. "My compliments to the cook," he said as he raised his fork in a salute.

"I'll tell him."

Before he could take another bite, his radio squawked to life. He'd begun to wonder if it even worked. Apparently so.

"Bennett." He held the device close to his ear.

"Sheriff, Larson here. We have a problem."

"Go ahead, Clay." Jake noted that in addition to the mayor's now avid attention, everyone else in the café had turned to listen.

"There's been a plane crash on Randi Johnson's property. It sounds bad." Gasps and scraping chairs distracted him as the deputy's words echoed through the room. Several people stood, including the mayor. Silence hung heavy as they waited for details. Jake refocused on the mic.

"How big of a plane?" Not that it made any difference except in the number of rescue personnel needed.

"She said it looked like a commuter. I'm on my way there now. I asked dispatch to call Roger Hunter in to serve as backup." The young deputy sounded calm and not panicking. Good. Jake needed a solid team and for everyone to do their jobs. Having the reserve deputy there would help.

"Get all available rescue personnel out there, ASAP. Have dispatch call in from surrounding towns, then notify the FAA. They'll contact the NTSB. I'll meet you there."

"Got it."

Jake didn't wait for Larson to disconnect and was two steps toward the door when the mayor's voice boomed in the quiet room.

"Are you capable of handling this, Bennett?" The mayor's tone held an underlying threat. The man would probably never stop looking for an opportunity to get Jake fired and Larson appointed as sheriff, whether the deputy wanted it or not.

Jake had no experience with plane crashes, but he did have numerous years of protecting people from danger. He would do what he'd always done: rely on his instincts. They were damned good.

He faced the man and swallowed the retort that sprang to mind, forcing his tone to an even, professional level. "Capable enough, Mr. Mayor, that the county hired me after only a phone interview."

Frank narrowed his eyes.

"I'm going with you," a feminine voice said close behind him, interrupting the exchange.

The café's owner had pulled on her sweater, her jaw set in determination. He started to shake his head when the mayor piped up again.

"You can't let her go out there! She's a woman. No telling what you'll find."

A slender man about Jake's age, wearing a white apron smudged with food debris, stepped through the swinging door leading to the kitchen and glared at the mayor. "Shut up, Frank. You go on, Mel."

"Yeah, we've got the café covered. You go check on Randi," Holly added.

"Fine. Let's go." Jake didn't have time to debate the issue and ushered Melody outside. Several people were already on their cell phones and a few men were pulling on their jackets. The previously peaceful café had erupted into a noisy den.

Linda Trout

"Remind me later to buy your cook a beer."

She glanced at him and grinned. "Yes, Roy pretty well speaks his mind and no one is brave enough to stand up to him."

People were afraid of Roy? He wasn't what you'd call a big man. Of course, a person's size didn't define who they were or their character. Jake reached the car and opened his door, his mind already back on the task at hand. He had wanted some excitement.

He'd gotten it in spades.

****

Melody stared at the sheriff's car, unable to move. She took a deep breath. *I volunteered for this. Now I've got to do it.* Only her legs didn't cooperate. Closing her eyes, she offered up a quick prayer for the people on the plane, and for Randi. Nothing could happen to her best friend. Not today.

Not on the anniversary of her husband's death. *Please.*

The sheriff started the engine, snapping her attention back to the present. "What are you waiting for? Get in."

Melody squared her shoulders, then climbed into the car. While buckling her seatbelt, she glanced up to see a shotgun in a holder between the driver and passenger seats, inches away, and she almost bolted. Her determination to check on Randi the only thing keeping her in the car.

"Which way?" He'd put the car in gear but hadn't taken his foot off the brake yet.

"What?" She was still focused on that gun. Or rather trying to *not* focus on it as her heart pounded against her chest.

8

"I need directions to the Johnson place."

Of course. He hadn't been here long enough to learn his way around so she quickly told him how to get there.

"Thanks." He flipped on the lights and siren as he pulled into the street.

Two years ago, on a day much like today, there had been other sirens, other cops and paramedics, another disaster. Except there had only been one casualty. Michael. Well, two if you counted the fellow vet who had shot her husband at point blank range before taking his own life. Her world had shattered as she watched the love of her life die. To this day, she hadn't figured out how to let go of the past, to let go of that horrible day and move forward.

Refusing to go down that path right now, she focused on the road and on recognizing landmarks so she wouldn't miss the turnoff, then glanced over at the man beside her.

He had to be a little over six feet, but his aura of authority made him seem taller. Most law enforcement she'd seen wore their hair cut high and tight, like men in the military, but Sheriff Bennett let his hair grow a little longer on the top. The excessive humidity had his hair curling, giving him a boyish appearance. Except there wasn't anything boyish about the man. He had a hard look in his eyes, as if he'd seen more than his share of mankind's inhumanity.

"She's okay." His raised voice penetrated the deafening noise of the siren and broke into her thoughts.

His comment surprised her. "What?"

"Your friend. She's okay." He threw her a quick

glance before returning his attention to the road.

She studied his profile, ignoring the computer, shotgun, clipboard and other items that separated them. Unconvinced she asked, "How do you know?" His jaw clenched, and Melody regretted her harsh tone. After all, he had only been trying to reassure her.

"Ms. Johnson is the one who reported the crash. If she'd been hurt, she would've told dispatch."

Relief flooded Melody as the butterflies in her stomach flew away. She took her first full breath since hearing the news of the crash and she slumped back in the seat. If anything had happened to the woman who felt like a sister, she didn't know what she'd do. She nodded her thanks, then realized he couldn't see her while concentrating on his driving. "I appreciate you saying that. Randi lives alone so I'm worried about her."

"Tell me about her place." His softened tone was more of an honest inquiry instead of a demand for information.

Was he trying to make small talk? After the way she'd treated him since he'd arrived in town? Guilt crept over her. Poor man. He probably thought she was an absolute shrew. Which, in a way, she had been simply because of the gun on his hip.

"She has twenty acres. It's wooded and rocky."

He threw her another glance. "Outbuildings?"

"I think there's an old barn somewhere, but no large buildings near the house." Randi had moved to Rock Ledge to take care of her ailing grandmother, and after she passed away, had stayed, making it her home. Inheriting the property probably a deciding factor.

Jake nodded, but didn't respond to her comments.

That's when she realized he hadn't been trying to distract her, but to gain information about what he would be facing once at the crash site. Regardless, it had worked. She had stopped wringing her hands.

"How much farther?"

His question pulled her attention back to the road. They were close to the turnoff. "Slow down. We'll be turning left not too far past this next bend."

Melody hated the fog. It had been foggy like this the day Michael died. Reason enough to stay home with her head buried under the covers, if you asked her. But you can't run from reality. She inwardly sighed, then sat forward, straining to see the road.

"There." She pointed to a small dirt road. He slowed and turned.

Apprehension ate at her. She hadn't wanted to deal with anymore death, yet a short distance away was a downed airplane with who knew how many dead. To her surprise, there were already several cars lining the single lane road. Jake swore under his breath at the sight. She agreed with him one hundred percent.

The fog made it hard to tell, but she recognized a couple of the vehicles. The good ole Rock Ledge grapevine must have been going nuts, but most of the people already here had to live close by. They probably had heard the crash and rushed over. She was sure they wanted to help, but would they be in the way? The volunteer fire department hadn't even had enough time to mobilize yet.

At least there were flashing lights up ahead, most likely Clay. As they neared, Clay came out of the tree line and flagged them down. The man looked a little green around the gills, even in the fog.

The sheriff turned off the siren and parked the car, then glanced at her. "Is the house close or can you tell? I can drive you all the way if you'd like."

She unhooked her seat belt and got out. "No, that isn't necessary. It isn't far so I can walk."

"Sheriff! Over here," Clay called, pointing to the right and through the woods.

He looked over at Melody. "You sure you'll be all right?"

"I'm sure. And don't worry, I'll find my own way back to town later." The last thing she wanted was to be in the police car again.

He nodded, then took off, not giving her a reply. The man had more critical things on his mind besides seeing her to Randi's door.

Melody stood cocooned in the dense moisture. Faint sounds of men shouting and moving about in the woods drifted through the trees. The stench of jet fuel permeated the air, yet another reminder of the tragedy just out of her sight. Bile rose in Melody's throat. She could feel death, like the day Michael died, as if it were part of her…as if it followed her. Which was absurd.

Tires crunching on the gravel got her moving. With visibility so poor, it would be easy for someone to accidently hit her with their vehicle. A cold breeze swirled the moisture, forming an arm without substance that teased and taunted her.

Mocking her.

Slowly, she began making her way toward the house. She'd driven this road hundreds of times over the years and thought she knew it like the back of her hand. But in this weather, it would be easy to become disoriented. All she had to do was turn around once and she might head back in the direction she'd come without realizing it.

The sensation of losing her bearings, of not knowing where she was, seeped into her pores and reminded her of how she'd felt right after she'd become a widow. How would she know which way to go, who to turn to now that her best friend, her confidante…her rock, was no longer there? She stopped, placed a hand on the side of a car. The grief and absolute loneliness that had assaulted her that day came back in a flash. She closed her eyes, willing the emptiness away. Taking a cleansing breath, she straightened and moved on.

The brush to her right rustled. Unable to see much she stopped and listened, wondering if it was one of the workers or an animal that had been flushed by all of the activity. She braced herself for whatever was coming at her at a rapid clip. Then a man with shaggy brown hair stumbled out of the foliage. Blood dripped from his forehead, he cradled his left arm and his clothes were dirty and torn. A crash victim survivor! When he saw her, he paused, looked around, then headed in her direction. He used the hood of a car to steady himself as she rushed to his side and took his good arm.

"Help." His voice was hoarse, as if he'd breathed in a lot of smoke.

"Stay here. I'll get help." She peered into the woods, hoping to see or hear someone.

"No…" He sagged onto the car.

Something metallic hit the gravel. She automatically reached down and wrapped her hand around the object before looking. When she did, her blood froze in her veins.

She held a gun, the barrel pointed toward her. As if

she'd touched a live wire, a shock jolted through her. Her fingers tensed, gripping tighter until the metal bit into her skin.

"Give me that," the man growled and yanked her upright. Only she couldn't seem to let go of the gun.

The nightmares she'd had for two long years pressed in on her. The images of the Veteran who'd pointed a gun at her husband, then pulled the trigger as she stood nearby flashed in her mind's eye. Was this how her own life would end?

Would she finally be put out of her misery?

Chapter Two

Following close behind Larson, Jake reached the wreckage and stopped short.

He'd seen plenty of gory crime scenes. This was different. The plane's impact had dug a deep crater in the red Ozark clay, tearing the fuselage into several pieces. Crackling fire burned parts of the plane and the surrounding undergrowth. The stench of burning flesh, along with the smell of jet fuel, filled the air. Bodies—some intact, some not—were scattered throughout the debris. Rescue workers—locals from the looks of them—were rushing around, trying to find victims still alive. It didn't appear as if they were having any luck. His gut clenched even tighter. If there were survivors, they had to find them fast and get them to safety.

Or get the blaze put out.

He studied the area. Thick with oak and hickory trees, and strewn with jagged rocks, the area looked like you'd expect a mountain top to look. Impassable via normal vehicles. He ground his teeth. How would the firemen get their trucks in here?

The destruction, along with the heavy haze swirling about, reminded him of a disaster movie. Only this was no movie. Those were real bodies, real blood. He almost lost his breakfast. Had the property owner seen this? If so, he would hazard a guess she'd have nightmares for a while.

Jake started to turn away.

"Do you see that?" Without waiting for a reply, Larson continued toward the exposed interior of the plane, easily navigating the rocky terrain. Less sure-footed, Jake followed him to a quasi-intact back section—with multiple people still strapped into their seats—to one particular body. The man's neck appeared to be broken and a set of handcuffs dangled from his left wrist. The other bracelet was open. Larson dug in the man's pockets, pulled out an ID and handed it to Jake.

Acid churned in his stomach at the sight of the empty handcuffs. He flipped open the wallet. "A US Marshal."

"His weapon's missing," the deputy supplied.

Letting out a string of curse words, Jake kneeled, studying the area, trying his best to ignore the other bodies and debris around him. It didn't take long to find a blood trail. "What's over there?" He pointed in the direction the trail led.

This time the deputy cursed. "The house. And Randi Johnson's there alone."

Jake shoved to his feet and tossed the wallet to the deputy. "No. Mrs. Rose is with her...or is supposed to be. Come on. We have to find that fugitive." He took off with long hurried strides, trying to keep the blood trail in view.

Before long, the trail veered to the left, back toward the road. He cursed the fog and the dense forest for making this harder. The man could be anywhere by now, but instincts told him the escapee was still near. And still a threat. Jake broke through the trees. Through the fog, he saw the fugitive.

Pointing a gun at Melody.

His last assignment as a CPD detective came rushing back at him with a force that almost brought him to his knees. He'd been guarding a witness in a high-profile murder case. Everything had been status quo…until it wasn't. One minute it had been a quiet evening at the safe house. The next, all hell broke loose. Jake would have sworn the knock at the door was his relief. But the minute he threw the deadbolt, the door shoved open, catching him off balance. Before he had time to react, the witness had been murdered and Jake had taken a bullet to the chest. His vest saved his life.

The shooter had gotten away and since the man had worn a mask, there was no way to identify him. Blamed by his captain for the death and therefore the conviction they had wanted, Jake had had no choice but to resign. Things might have been different if the media hadn't splashed his picture all over the front page of the newspaper and smeared his name. Jake had always felt the captain had spoon-fed them misinformation. But again, there was no way to prove any of it.

He refocused on the current situation. He'd lost one person at gunpoint. He didn't intend to lose another. Not today. Not ever again if he could help it.

Melody stood frozen, the man yelling at her. Jake pulled his gun and advanced on the pair, Larson moved to the side with his own weapon drawn. Jake wondered if he'd ever had to shoot anyone before and hoped the young deputy could handle whatever happened next.

The prisoner saw him and wrapped an arm around the back of Melody's neck, pulling her toward him. The gun pressed against her body.

"Stay back or I'll kill 'er. I swear I will." He

swayed on his feet, sweat beaded his forehead.

Jake kept his voice calm, even though he wanted to roar in outrage. "You know she can't help you."

"I don't know nothing except I'm getting out of here and I'm taking her with me as insurance." He tightened his grip around her neck. Melody let out a small cry of pain.

With Melody in between them, Jake couldn't get a clear shot. The stalemate continued with neither man giving an inch. The fugitive glanced behind him, looking for an escape route. The man's breathing became ragged, probably from his injuries. This whole situation could go south any minute.

"Let her go," Larson called.

The man jerked and twisted toward the deputy, turning Melody with him. He glanced from Jake to Larson and back. Jake saw when the man gave up hope—and knew he would go out in a blaze of glory, taking Melody with him. As the man moved his arm as if to fire, Jake pulled the trigger of his own weapon.

The escapee dropped to the ground. Jake ran up, expecting to see the gun on the ground. Instead, Melody held the weapon in what appeared to be a death grip, still pointed at herself. Clay checked for the man's pulse, then shook his head to confirm he was dead. Jake turned to her.

"It's okay. You can give it to me now," he said, keeping his voice soft. Placing his hand over hers— over the gun—he leaned in close. She didn't reply and he realized she was staring at the man on the ground. He moved his body, blocking her view.

"Mrs. Rose…Melody, it's over. Let me get rid of this." Gently he eased the weapon out of her grasp and passed it to Larson. He tilted his head toward the dead man, indicating for the deputy to take care of the situation and to secure the scene. Deputy Hunter arrived and Jake knew they would soon have everything under control.

He took Melody's elbow and headed toward the house. So far she hadn't said anything, letting him lead her blindly. Which wasn't like the strong woman he'd seen at the diner. Her breathing became shallow and thready. Her hands began to shake in short, jerky movements, followed by her entire body. Jake stopped and wrapped his arms around her trembling body as she buried her face in his shirt. Her hands continued to flutter against his chest. A low keening sound from her broke his heart.

Her knees gave way and she sagged against him. Jake scooped her into his arms and carried her far enough that the fog enveloped them, distancing them from the sights and sounds of the crime scene. She leaned against his chest, her soft body reminding him she was all woman.

Jake stopped at a pickup whose tailgate had been left down and sat on it, holding Melody on his lap. His behavior was unprofessional, but he couldn't just dump her someplace to pull herself together. He'd witnessed a lot of traumatized people over the years, but to see the pain of this always in control, tough, take no guff from anyone businesswoman put a little crack in his cop-armor. Besides, he liked the way she felt in his arms and pulled her a little closer.

Her shoulders shook as she silently cried. It wasn't long before the front of his shirt was soaked. He didn't speak—what was there to say?—so he sat and gently rocked her until her tears were spent.

Sniffing, and with her face still pressed against him, she said, "Thank you."

Jake laid his chin against the top of her head, inhaling the smell of almond shampoo with a hint of bacon. What man could resist that combination? "No problem. Just doing my job."

Which got him a wobbly laugh. "You earned your pay, then."

He'd had no choice except to kill the man and would do it again if put in the same position. Protecting the innocent was his main responsibility. They sat in silence for several more minutes.

Finally, she took a deep breath and pulled away, her face puffy...her nose red. "I hate guns," she whispered.

Jake didn't know if she'd meant to say the words out loud but decided to respond anyway. "I'm not too fond of them myself."

Eyes wide, her mouth dropped open. "But..."

He shrugged, tilting up the corners of his mouth. Neither spoke. Neither moved. Things were becoming way too intimate. He must have tensed his muscles because she blinked, as if coming out of a daze.

"Well. I should..." She looked a bit confused.

"Uh, yeah. I need to check on my deputies."

She slid off his lap and to the ground. "I have to ask. Who was that man?"

He stood but didn't put any extra space between them. He liked her almond/bacon smell. "A fugitive. I don't know his name yet but he was escorted by a US Marshal."

Hesitating, she asked, "Is he alive? Did he make

it?"

Subtle wasn't in Jakes' genetic makeup. "He's dead. Can't tell if it was from the crash or not."

She gave a slight nod, meeting his steady gaze. "Thanks for not being like the others and tip-toeing around me."

He wondered what she meant, but decided not to ask. "You okay, now?"

"No." She leaned her head back and gave little laugh. "But I will be."

Taking her elbow, he steered her toward the house. "This time I'm making sure you get inside."

"That's not neces—"

"Yes, it is." Once they were at the house, he took her up the front steps and knocked. As soon as the door opened, Melody threw herself into her friend's arms. He wasn't sure who was consoling whom, but from the haunted look on Ms. Johnson's face, it was a toss-up.

He cleared his throat to get their attention. "Stay inside. Keep the doors locked and don't let anyone in you don't know."

The friend looked a bit confused, but Melody must have understood.

"Sheriff—" Melody started.

"Jake," he corrected her. After the last half hour, he figured they were on a first name basis.

"Jake. Thanks for letting me fall apart in private."

He gazed into her eyes, then touched a finger to his hat brim and left. Not only did he have a plane crash to deal with, now he had a dead criminal on his hands. He had known the fog would bring problems. He just hadn't anticipated how many.

****

Melody felt bad, but apparently not as bad as Randi. Dark circles rimmed her eyes, and whatever makeup she'd had on earlier was gone. It dawned on her that Randi might have seen a lot more death and destruction than she had.

"How did you hear about the crash?" Randi asked as they settled on the couch.

"You have to ask? This is a small town. But mostly because the sheriff was in the diner when the call came in. I insisted on coming along. Probably a good thing 'cause he never would've found his way out here." And she never would've had a gun pointed at her, then fallen apart in the arms of a man she wanted nothing to do with. Although, it did feel good to have strong arms wrapped around her again, so maybe she was close to the point where she could move forward with her life.

She almost snorted. That wasn't possible. Not and continue living in Rock Ledge. She was the widow of their hero. The townspeople would tar and feather her if she even looked at another man. Nope. She was stuck, pure and simple. Melody swallowed her pity party to concentrate on her friend. "Are you okay?"

Randi clamped her lips closed as a couple tears seeped out of the corner of her eye. "Oh, Mel, you have no idea what I've seen. I went down there—"

"Randi, no."

She shook her head. "I wanted to help save people. But it was useless. I don't think anyone survived."

"There was at least one," she said flatly. She studied her hand, the one that had held the gun.

"Thank goodness! Will they be all right?"

Melody raised her gaze. "No. Jake shot him."

Randi furrowed her brows. "You mean the new

sheriff? But why?"

Melody's hands shook while her insides turned to stone. She had to swallow a couple times to overcome the desert that had suddenly taken up residence in her mouth. She'd come close to dying and wasn't quite sure how she felt about it. Happy that it didn't happen? Or cheated that it hadn't? "Because the man tried to kill me."

Gasping, Randi pulled her into a bear hug. Neither said anything for several long moments. When they pulled apart, she said, "I could use a drink."

She glanced at the clock on the mantel...not even nine o'clock. It was early, yet so much had happened in less than an hour. She felt as if she'd been run over by a tractor; every muscle in her body ached.

Randi blew out a harsh breath, misinterpreting her hesitation. "If you'd seen what I did, you'd be more than ready for a stiff drink."

After almost being shot at point blank range, a little alcohol did sound good. She didn't intend to get drunk, though. At least not before noon. "I think we both need something to calm our nerves."

Randi mixed and poured their drinks, then they settled on the couch. Melody took a small sip, letting the liquid warm her insides before she focused on her friend. "Want to tell me what happened? You aren't hurt, are you? I was afraid the plane had hit the house."

They told their respective stories from beginning to end, crying and holding each other's hands the entire time and mostly ignoring the alcohol. Once all the horror of the morning had been laid out in the open, they fell quiet, each lost in their own thoughts. Randi glanced out the window at the fog that continued to swirl. "Reminds me of pea soup."

Melody followed the direction of her gaze. "I never liked pea soup."

"Me neither."

****

A few hours later, the NTSB and FBI were on site. Jake gladly let them take charge of their respective areas. Unfortunately, the vultures, also known as the media, were there. So far, he'd been able to avoid them. The role they'd played in him losing his job in Chicago still stung and if he never spoke to another reporter, it'd be too soon. But being the sheriff meant dealing with the press, however much he disliked it. From his experience, they took the facts and twisted them to suit whatever agenda they had. At least that's the way it'd felt when they'd served him up on a silver platter the year before.

"Sheriff! Sheriff! Can we have a minute of your time?"

Grinding his teeth, he stopped in his tracks and slowly turned around. Holding a microphone, a female reporter rushed up to him. A cameraman stood behind her, the red dot blinking. They were On-Air. He did his best to not snarl at them and instead assumed a bland, professional demeanor. Waiting for her to ask her first question, he acted as if talking to her was no big deal.

The reporter turned toward the camera as if this had been a planned interview. "This is Shirley Young with KBLM Channel 43. We're at the site of a deadly plane crash outside of Rock Ledge, Arkansas, deep in the Ozark Mountains. Sheriff...?" She waited for him to supply his name.

"Bennett." He appeared bored as he watched her

scramble. He sensed her desperation to get the scoop on the story.

"Sheriff Bennett. What can you tell us about the crash? What caused it? Were there any survivors? How many people were on board?" The woman rapid fired questions at him.

"You need to ask the NTSB. They're in charge."

"They aren't talking to us."

He tilted his head to the side as if to say that wasn't his problem and started to turn away.

"What about the man you shot? Who was he? Did he have anything to do with the plane going down?"

The thought had occurred to him, but he hadn't had time to pursue it. His main concern had been to keep the citizens of this county safe. He stopped and looked at the woman, then into the camera. "This is an ongoing investigation. When we have information we can release, we'll contact you."

With that, he walked away.

In the background he could make out the reporter giving her own made-up facts, as if he had given her some information off the record. Yeah, they were all alike. He wondered where she'd gotten the data she spewed and decided it had to be one of the townspeople who had swarmed the site on the pretense of helping, only to get in the way and clog the road. Jake gave credit to the first responders of Rock Ledge, though. They knew their jobs. But someone didn't know how to keep their mouth shut about the shooting. He'd check with Larson later.

His stomach growled. The quiche he'd had this morning had been good. But he hadn't eaten enough of it and it didn't have enough staying power for his tastes.

However, eating came low on the agenda right now. He headed out to find the man now in charge of the cleanup, more than grateful the task hadn't fallen on his own shoulders.

****

Bored, I flipped through the TV channels until a story about a plane crash caught my eye. Aw, there you go. Nothing like a little destruction and mayhem to brighten the day. A bleached blonde reporter, who looked way too happy for the story she covered, faced the camera.

Stretched out on the leather sofa, I lit a cigarette, halfway paying attention to what the woman said. The crash occurred in some small backwoods town in the middle of nowhere Arkansas. "There isn't enough money in the world to entice me there."

Blowing a perfect ring of smoke, I almost choked when the camera brought the man into view. Dropping my feet to the floor, I stared at the screen.

"I don't believe it. After all these months without a trace of where you were, you finally show up." I threw my head back and laughed. I'd always been lucky in my games, and although it had taken a bit of a hiatus there for a while, it was back in full force.

The reporter fired questions at Jake Bennett nonstop, not giving him time to reply. He gave a non-committal answer, turned and walked away. I snuffed out the cigarette. "You didn't make your escape fast enough, old friend. Now I know where you are. I'll make sure our reunion will be extra special and we'll take care of our unfinished business."

Retrieving my ever-ready duffle bag, I laid it on the bed and added a few more things. Being meticulous and thorough paid off. Every detail was always preplanned or anticipated so the essentials were needed.

"This time, Bennett, you won't get away."

The rasp of the bag's zipper a forewarning of the upcoming deadly confrontation.

Chapter Three

Exhausted, but needing to check in with his office, Jake trudged back to his car, leaving behind the same men from the NTSB who'd been there since morning, still working. Everyone had been more than grateful when Melody and her friend had set up a food line on Ms. Johnson's porch in the middle of the afternoon and fed all of the workers. After the trauma the women had been through this morning, they'd still supplied food for the workers. Melody's doing he suspected. The woman had been full of surprises, especially since he continued to think of her as cool and aloof. At least where he was concerned.

Neither one of the women made an attempt to visit the crash site, probably because Ms. Johnson had already seen more than she cared to. Plus, Melody didn't seem the type to gawk, unlike a lot of people who tried their best to get through the security lines. Thank goodness the Arkansas National Guard did an excellent job of corralling the sightseers and media.

Late in the afternoon, Jake had asked the fire chief, Walt Streeter to take Melody home. He'd wanted to take her himself—to see if she was all right emotionally—but he was still tied up at the scene so was forced to delegate the task.

He'd spent hours with the FBI plus the Marshal's office, who had arrived to investigate the shooting plus their colleague's death. Jake shook his head. Of all the people to survive the crash, why did it have to be the one person society wouldn't miss? *Well, they won't miss him now.*

Jake hadn't had to shoot many people in his career, even though he knew when he strapped on the gun every morning, using it with deadly force could be a distinct possibility, and in Chicago, an eventual probability. In most cases, when he'd had to draw his weapon, he hadn't had to fire it. His job was to serve and protect and that's what he'd done today. Given the circumstances, he'd do it again without hesitation.

However, the interview with the feds had felt uncomfortably like the interrogations he'd gone through right before he'd lost his CPD badge. Thinking about it left a bad taste in his mouth. At least this time no one had accused him of a crime or dereliction of duty. FBI Special Agent Wade Malone had been cold, but he'd only been doing his job.

Jake's shoulders sagged. After hours of making sure all the minute details were taken care of, he just wanted to take a hot shower to get rid of the stench from the crash site, grab some food, preferably not anything he'd cooked, and collapse into bed. Not going to happen, though, he reminded himself. At least not the getting to bed part. As long as he might be needed, he'd be available. He'd wanted to show the powers that be of Rock Ledge he was a consummate professional. He had to prove they'd gotten their money's worth when they'd hired him.

But he'd think twice about wishing for more excitement again.

****

Jake dragged in well after midnight and collapsed into bed. His thoughts drifted to Melody and how she'd handled the situation that morning. He made a mental note to have her talk to a shrink to deal with the stress. He supposed he could've found out where she lived and gone by her house, but didn't think that such a good idea by the time he'd left the crash site for the day. Even Ms. Johnson's lights were out. She'd left the outside lights on. Although, he didn't know whether it was to help out the workers, or to discourage a reporter who slipped through the parameter, looking to get an interview. The media could be real hounds when they smelled a story. Luckily, they hadn't gotten wind of Melody's involvement in the shooting or they would've been camped out at her café.

Exhaustion ate at him, but he couldn't stop thinking about Melody…plagued by the image of the gun going off, of him not being able to do anything or getting there seconds too late. Of Melody dying in his arms. The scene from his last case swirled in his mind. Late in the night, he dropped into a deep, dreamless sleep.

When he woke, he felt like he'd been drugged. He knew the sensation was because he'd worked too hard the day before and then slept too hard. Yesterday had been endless and today didn't promise to be any better. The sun had already begun its climb over the mountain range, turning the sky pink. He'd slept in. The crash site workers didn't have that luxury as they'd worked through the night.

Brewing his high-octane coffee, he took a brisk shower to wake himself up. A glance outside showed no fog, thank goodness. He might not have known how to get to the Johnson place this time yesterday, but he could almost drive it blind-folded today. The difference a day makes.

He quickly made his normal rounds around town before heading to The Tangled Rose. Had Melody gone to work? Or had she stayed home—traumatized? Although, she'd seemed fine yesterday afternoon when they had served food to the workers. He beat the main breakfast crush at the café, barely. Holly greeted him and pointed him toward Melody, as if she knew he'd want to talk to her.

Melody came out of the back so he headed toward her. There weren't any customers seated in the area so he figured this would be as good as any place to talk in private.

He held his hat in his hands as he walked up to her. "Morning."

She didn't smile, but she didn't scowl like she'd done in the past, either. "Sheriff."

Why couldn't he get a read on the woman? "How are you doing this morning? You sure you want to be working?"

Initially she looked a little irritated, then she blew out a breath. "I'm shorthanded and don't have a choice. Mrs. King helped out yesterday, but has several doctors' appointments for her husband today in Fayetteville. There's too much traffic to ask anyone who's inexperienced. Besides, I'd rather stay busy."

Jake understood that. He didn't want to deal with what faced him today, but this was his town and it was his job. *His town.* That stopped him in his tracks. He'd never thought of here as "his" before. So what had changed? Then it dawned on him...the crash. Nothing like a disaster to bond people together. He hadn't expected it to happen to him, though.

"Listen, about yesterday morning. If you want to talk about it my doors always open. Or I can give you the number of a psychol—"

"Do you want breakfast? It's on the house." Melody looked at him expectantly, apparently not wanting to talk about the incident.

Not good in his experience. He'd bring it up again later. "No need. I'll pay for my food." He knew officers who routinely took handouts, but that had never been his policy.

Melody glanced down at her shoes, then back up at him, a somber expression on her face. "You saved my life yesterday. The least I can do is feed you." Her voice was pitched so low he almost didn't hear her.

He nodded, understanding how people didn't like to owe someone else anything, especially your life. "In that case, thank you. That'd be great."

She relaxed and the corners of her lips tilted upward. "Steak and eggs okay?"

His stomach rumbled. "Sounds good. Medium rare please."

She chuckled. "Medium rare it is. Take a seat and I'll see to your order."

After she'd disappeared into the kitchen, he took his usual place at the counter, noting several people had come in while they'd been talking. She hadn't been kidding about an increase in business. Some of them were locals, but the majority were out-of-towners. Great. More gawkers. He mentally dismissed them and turned his thoughts to the clean-up crews.

The NTSB had flood lights set up at the scene with

people working around the clock. The workers were used to this type of situation, but he still didn't envy them. He'd search out the agent in charge to see how else he could be of assistance…as soon as he had his steak, that is. His mouth was already watering.

Melody came out of the kitchen, a large tray loaded with food balanced in her arms. Jake swiveled on the stool, watching her deliver the order, interacting with the patrons. And not just the ones she was currently serving. Before she made her way back to the counter, she'd stopped to make sure the people at every table were happy. She retrieved the coffee pot and made another round, refilling cups, then took another order out to a couple.

Jake enjoyed the sway of her hips as she quickly but efficiently took care of her customers. Periodically he'd catch her glancing at him and he smiled to himself. Several minutes later she brought him his steak.

"It looks delicious." He didn't bother looking down at his meal. The high color on her cheeks captivated his attention.

"Do you want to make sure it's cooked all right before I go?" She looked almost bashful, uncertain of herself.

"It's fine." He still hadn't looked at it, much less cut into the huge slab of meat. Definitely wouldn't be getting hungry for a while, unlike after he had the quiche.

"Um, well. If everything looks okay I need to tend to my other customers." She didn't move.

An unspoken message passed between them. Her face, so expressive, conveyed her feelings. "Yeah. Uh, thanks again for the meal. It's a little much and unnecessary, but I sure appreciate it."

This time she did blush but continued to hold his gaze. "It isn't enough. Thank you again for yesterday, for…"

He wanted to squeeze her hand, letting her know he understood. Instead, he picked up the silverware, breaking the spell. "Anytime. Don't think any more about it."

Melody's face relaxed as she gave him a quick smile. "Do you need anything else?"

All sorts of things flashed through his mind. *Keep it professional, Bennett,* he reminded himself. "No. This is perfect. Thanks."

She nodded, then rushed to serve another table. Jake finished his breakfast without being able to make eye contact with her again. He had hung around here long enough. Time to get to work. Reluctantly, he claimed his hat and walked out the door.

****

Business was booming and the hours flew by. Mainly because of the extra people in town. That and all the locals must have decided this would be a good place to scope out the latest news. Small towns were renowned to be gossip central. In this case, it was true. She wished they'd go somewhere else and stop taking up her table space, though.

The bell over the door jangled and she heard Holly tell the newcomers to take a menu and find a seat, but be patient. The doc had told her to stay off her feet but she'd insisted on coming to work, stating she wouldn't leave Melody shorthanded if she could help it. Melody appreciated her loyalty, but worried even sitting there wasn't good for her or the baby. Normally, Melody's parents would pitch in. But they were on a well-deserved cruise to the Caribbean. Even if they wanted to, she doubted they could get off the ship and catch a flight back. They'd saved for years for this trip. No way would she ask them to come home.

An order was up. Roy shoved another plate onto the pass through, rushing as much as she. There wouldn't be a Wednesday special. There hadn't been time. Since they'd opened the doors, they'd had a steady stream of traffic. Even during the "slow" times, they were busy. She could sure use a break, but it wasn't going to happen. Her back and feet both hurt. And she needed to go to the bathroom something fierce.

"Excuse me. Do you mind if I help myself to the coffee? You seem short-handed."

Melody glanced up to see a woman in her thirties smiling apologetically. Reminding Melody of someone down on their luck, the woman's brown hair looked a little dull. She wore a brown and green oversized plaid men's shirt and baggy jeans.

"No, I don't mind if you don't." She'd take what little reprieve she could get and took the meatloaf dinner to table three. When she turned around, she found the stranger filling coffee mugs as she made her way back to her own table. Bless her heart.

Melody finally got around to taking the woman's order, surprised to see her sitting patiently. "Sorry. Didn't mean to take so long to get to you. I see you got your coffee."

"Yes, it's delicious. I bet your food is just as good," the woman said sweetly.

"Thank you. So what'll you have?"

"The easiest thing to fix. I know what it's like to be

snowed under like this." She glanced around. "Um, I don't mean to be forward, but would you happen to be looking for some help? I could sure use a job."

The woman bit her bottom lip as she dropped her gaze, then raised pleading eyes back up to look Melody in the face. Her heart leapt at the possibility of having help, but she reigned in her first impulse, which was to shout "Yes!" at the woman.

"I do need another waitress, but only temporarily."

"I don't care. I'll take whatever I can get." The woman's eyes lit up.

Melody hated to crush her hopes. "But I'm sorry, I don't have time to train anyone."

She jumped to her feet, a hopeful expression on her face. "You won't have to. I've worked in restaurants before. I can even start today if you'd like."

Melody glanced around the diner, which had thinned out marginally but she hadn't slowed once since she'd walked in at five o'clock. She didn't typically conduct interviews while standing next to a customer's table, but she was desperate.

"Do you live in the area? I don't think I've seen you before." She prayed the woman wasn't here simply because of the plane crash.

Pink tinged her cheeks. She sank back into her chair and Melody dropped into the chair across from her, grateful to be off her feet for even a minute or two. "I'm relocating from Tennessee."

"I don't understand. Are you passing through or what?"

"Yes. No." She let out a deep sigh. "Oh, shoot. I might as well tell you. I left my boyfriend. I got tired of being his personal punching bag so I grabbed what I could, got in my car and took off. I have family in Atlanta—not that they care one way or the other—so he'll probably look for me there. I'm trying to find a new place to live. I—I don't have any place else to go. If you'd give me a job, I'd really appreciate it." Hope shone in her eyes.

Melody had never been that down on her luck, with no one to help. Her heart went out to the other woman. It was an easy decision. "Then you're hired. Can you start now?"

"Um, can I eat first?"

The bell on the pass through rang. "Order up!" Roy yelled.

Nerves on edge, Melody glanced at him before returning her attention to her new employee. "Sure. What'll you have?"

"Cheeseburger and fries is fine."

Melody's shoulders sagged with relief. "You got it. By the way, what's your name?"

"Cora. Cora Conway."

She stuck out her hand and shook the other woman's. "Nice to meet you Cora Conway. I'm Melody Rose, the owner of The Tangled Rose." She turned and practically skipped to the kitchen, almost forgetting the order waiting to be served. Help. She had some help. Maybe now she'd get that bathroom break.

****

The rest of the day went much easier, even with the constant stream of customers. Roy had a steady rhythm going in the kitchen and didn't need anything…except for everyone to stay out of his way. Holly continued to man the register and hand out menus as people came in, while the new girl worked circles around Melody.

The woman definitely knew her way around, balancing multiple plates at a time. Cora took over Holly's station so now all Melody had to worry with was her normal tables. Whenever a new pot of coffee needed to be made, she found Cora attending to the chore. In fact, she would bus tables that weren't hers. As the day wore on, though, lines of fatigue appeared on her face. If she had looked in the mirror, Melody knew she'd find them on hers as well.

By late afternoon the crowds had thinned out so she sent Holly home. Mel was ready for the day to end and when the last customer stood to leave, she flipped on the CLOSED sign. She should probably stay open later, but just couldn't do it. Exhaustion ate at her and she knew Roy felt the same. She walked over to Cora as the woman cleaned the last of the tables in her section.

"Time to call it a night."

Cora stood, placed one hand on the small of her back and stretched. "Wow. You weren't kidding when you said you were busy. After tasting the cooking, I understand why."

"I'll tell Roy you said so, but I think the extra business has more to do with the crash than anything. It isn't normally this hectic."

"That's good to know." She looked around then back at Melody, a slight frown on her face. "I do have a problem, though."

She couldn't imagine what that would be. "Maybe I can help. What is it?"

"Is there a cheap motel around here? Sleeping in my car lost its appeal several nights ago."

Melody mentally kicked herself for not thinking of that earlier. "Yes, but I'm willing to bet all the rooms are already rented to either the rescue workers or the media."

"Oh. Okay." Cora chewed her bottom lip. "Well I've slept there before so I can do it again. Is there a park in town? I don't like being on city streets. Law enforcement frown on it, plus it isn't very private."

Her newest employee had been an exceptionally good worker and there was no way Melody would let her sleep in her car. The thought of taking her home crossed her mind, but she didn't know the woman and knew better than to invite a stranger into her own house, no matter how sweet she had been. Then she thought of the perfect solution and snapped her fingers. "I've got it! My folks have a small house on the lot behind the café. It isn't much, but you're welcome to stay there while you're here."

"Oh, I couldn't impose on them," Cora exclaimed.

"No, you misunderstand. They don't live there anymore. Besides, they're on a cruise right now."

She looked uncertain. "You sure it'll be okay with them? I'll pay whatever rent you ask, as long as my paycheck will cover it."

Cora's concern for her family made Melody like the woman more by the minute. "Yes. I'm sure and don't worry, the rent will be reasonable. I have to warn you, though. It isn't as clean as it should be and more than likely smells musty. It's fully furnished, sort of like a little vacation cottage. Compact but with all the amenities."

Cora smiled warmly. "It sounds wonderful. I won't even have to drive to work, saving gas."

Another weight fell away. "Let's finish up here, then I'll take you over and show you around. I think you'll be very comfortable."

"I'm sure it'll be perfect. Just perfect."

****

Melody took a hot shower the minute she got home, then dressed in yoga pants and an old, loose T-shirt. Man, her feet hurt! What a day. Not as eventful as the day before, thank goodness. Still…She shuddered as the unpleasant memory slid over her.

Finding someone to help out in the café was heaven sent, especially with Holly's pregnancy problems. Maybe her luck had turned around with Cora's arrival. She hoped so.

Her cell phone chirped, drawing her out of her musings. She checked the screen. Randi. "Hey. What's up?"

"Can I come over? I need to get out of this house for a while." Even over the phone Randi's voice sounded strained. Having a plane crash close to your home, killing all on-board, would be enough to stress anyone.

"Of course. You don't need to ask; you know you're always welcome."

"Thanks. I'll be there in a bit." Randi's heavy sigh echoed through the phone before she disconnected.

Melody stood there as sadness enveloped her. If there were any way to make her friend's pain go away, she'd do it. Not possible. If she couldn't help herself, how could she help Randi? By being there. By listening to what she had to say and by providing a shoulder to cry on if needed. To return the favor of what Randi had done for her.

She had held Melody's hand, helping her cope during Michael's funeral and afterward. It was as if

Randi knew what she was going through, even though she'd never been married. At least to Melody's knowledge. Odd that her best friend never talked about her past. But even with all her support, Melody hadn't opened up after Michael's death. No, she'd kept her darkest feelings as her own private hell. There was only so much she told others, even Randi.

Melody padded into the kitchen. The least she could do was fix them a snack and something to drink…a margarita, maybe. She didn't drink often so she needed to make sure she had all the ingredients. About the time she had almost everything gathered for the drinks the doorbell rang. That was a quick trip, she thought as she headed to the door. She peered out the side window, a habit she'd developed over the years of being alone. Instead of Randi, a large man stood with his back to the door, as if he were surveying the area. Her stomach clenched in trepidation; the events of the prior morning still fresh on her mind. Then he turned sideways and she got a profile view.

Jake.

Her heart skipped a beat as she took a step back from the door and frowned. What did he want? From the first day he'd stepped into her café she'd deliberately been aloof with him. Granted, at the time he hadn't shown any special attention to her, which she was more than grateful for. Despite the shrine to Michael in the café, with all the bullets and military paraphernalia the towns' people had left, she didn't want to be around weapons of any kind. And Jake Bennett wore his gun as if it was part of his body. And, in a way, she supposed it was.

Tempted to ignore him, she took a deep breath and

released the deadbolt before opening the door a crack. Whatever he wanted, he wouldn't go away until he'd accomplished what he'd come to do. Normally she'd think that was an admirable trait, but not when it was focused on her.

He turned at the sound of the door opening, and a light flared in his eyes for a brief moment. Melody wondered if it was her imagination. Still in uniform, he held his hat in his hands.

"Sheriff." She kept her tone cool.

Looking solemn, he twisted his hat before his hands stilled. "Mrs. Rose…Melody. Pardon the intrusion but I wanted to thank you again for the breakfast."

"Not a problem. It was my pleasure." And she meant it, she was startled to realize.

"I, uh, wanted to make sure you were all right, what with everything that happened yesterday. I know it was pretty traumatic."

Her heart warmed. When was the last time anyone had said they were concerned about her well-being? Not since right after Michael's death. The gesture touched her in places she didn't want to explore. Maybe there was more to this man than his badge and his gun. Her heart softened toward him.

"I also wanted to recommend a good therapist if you feel the need to talk to a professional."

Disappointment almost knocked the air out of her lungs. He only came to recommend a shrink? The hollow, empty feeling returned with a vengeance. Until just now, she hadn't known how much that bottomless pit had become a part of her…how that black void defined her. For a few brief seconds, Jake had shown a ray of light into her world, only to snuff it out before she had a chance to grasp it.

Before she could form a reply, gravel crunched in the driveway. He swiveled, hand on the butt of his gun, as Randi pulled in beside his SUV. When he recognized her, he turned back to Melody, his questioning gaze drilling into her.

Swallowing the sense of loss, she straightened her back and lifted her chin. She'd stood on her own for so long she didn't know how to lean on anyone else anymore. Except for a heartbeat or two…"I appreciate your concern, but I'm fine."

He raised his eyebrows. "I don't see how you could be. I sure wasn't."

That got her attention. "Seriously?"

"Been there, done that as the saying goes."

"Oh," was all she choked out before Randi's car door closed, drawing her focus. She waved at her friend. "Hi. Come on in."

"Well, I wanted to check on you. If you change your mind about my offer let me know." Jake exchanged pleasantries with Randi as she came up the walk, then nodded at them. "I'll leave you ladies to your evening. Consider what I said," he added, looking Melody in the eyes. Placing the hat on his head, he strode back to his vehicle without another word.

The intensity of his gaze had unsettled her. Part of her wanted him to stay, begrudging the fact Randi had gotten there faster than Melody had anticipated. The other part of her was more than grateful for the interruption. She didn't want to talk about the prior day's events—except maybe over a few drinks with her friend—but especially not with Jake Bennett.

The two women hugged. "What was the sheriff doing here?" Creases furrowed Randi's brow.

Melody pushed the door open. Glancing back toward the drive, she noticed Jake still looking her way as he pulled into the street. One more good thump of her heart, and she turned to go inside. "Nothing. Just making sure I was okay."

"That was nice of him. He did the same for me earlier in the day."

"He did?" Okay, so it wasn't personal for him…merely a routine run of the mill inquiry. For a moment, disappointment and yes, a little jealousy, hit her. Mentally shaking her head, she reminded herself this wasn't a competition. If it was, she'd give Randi the sheriff because she sure didn't want him. Right? Ignoring all those nagging voices, she headed toward the kitchen. "Come on. I've almost got everything ready for margaritas. Or would you rather have iced tea? I've got a fresh pitcher in the fridge."

"Something stronger than tea, if you don't mind."

"Gotcha. Alcohol it is."

As Melody fixed the drinks, Randi dropped into a chair at the table. Her haggard face spoke of the stress from the last couple of days.

"He's cute."

Melody didn't have to ask who she referred to since the man had just pulled out of her driveway.

"I hadn't seen him before yesterday. Why didn't you tell me he was so good looking? You've been holding out on me." Randi gave a weak grin.

Heat crawled up Melody's cheeks. Turning her back, she took her time getting the glasses down, hoping to get her emotions under control. But why bother? This was Randi, after all. Still holding the glasses, she blew out a breath and faced her friend. "It isn't like that."

"And why isn't it?" After an uncomfortable silence, Randi continued. "Mel, it's been two years, yet you continue to sit here in this house. Are you waiting for Michael to come back? This isn't a deployment, you know. It's time for you to move on."

Chapter Four

Shoot. Why did she have to go there? Randi had always made it clear she could confide in her, but Melody had never taken her up on the offer other than her initial reaction to Michael's death. How could she tell her best friend what a fraud she was? Even though she resented Michael for working with the vets, to say the words out loud would sound not only unpatriotic, but a betrayal to her husband. She had loved him, truly she had. But since that fateful day she'd hated him, too.

"Maybe," she eventually conceded. With raised eyebrows and an unwavering stare, Randi waited her out. "But not with him."

"Why in the world not? I mean, have you *looked* at him? I'm surprised every female within a hundred miles isn't beating down his door. And here he is knocking on yours."

She had a point. Unlike Michael's solid build, Jake had more height and muscles. She knew because he'd wrapped his arms around her when she'd sat in his lap. Crying on his shoulder had felt better than she would admit. But nothing would happen between her and the sheriff. She wouldn't let it. The thought of being in his arms again, though, sent ripples of longing throughout her body. His embrace had punched a tiny crack through her hardened veneer and it was the last thing she wanted.

Melody blinked to dispel the inappropriate images that came unbidden to mind and turned on the blender. When the noise died down, she poured the drinks and took them to her friend. "Did you see what he wears?"

Randi sipped her drink, sucked some juice off her upper lip, then grinned. "Oh, yeah. I always was a sucker for a good-looking man in a uniform."

Good grief. "Then you take him." As if they could decide who the man *belonged* to.

Something flashed in Randi's eyes a moment before it was gone. The corners of her lips turned up in a sad smile. "He's not my type. Besides, he doesn't look at me the way he does you."

"Don't be ridiculous." He wasn't interested in her. Was he? They barely knew each other. A tiny flame flickered before she snuffed it out with ruthless determination. "Even if I were attracted to him, which I'm not, I couldn't stand to be around him."

"Why?" Randi demanded, slamming her glass on the table and sloshing liquid. "Do you have any idea how hard it is to find love? Especially a second time around?"

Wow. Where did that come from? Instead of asking, she went back to the point she'd been trying to make. "Jake wears a *gun*."

"So?" Randi looked genuinely confused.

Melody cocked her head and raised her eyebrows, as if saying *duh*.

Randi squinted then leaned her forearms on the table, bringing her closer. "I don't get you. An awesome opportunity is pounding on your door and you're keeping it locked. If I had that chance…"

She waited for Randi to continue, but instead her

friend hung her head and refused to look her in the eye. Something else was going on here. Was this why she wanted to come over? First the outburst and now a defeatist attitude. Over the years they'd both learned to not push the other. At times like now, though, maybe she should. She didn't think this had to do with the plane crash.

She reached across the table and laid her hand on Randi's. "Hey. You can tell me anything. Whatever it is, I'm here for you."

When Randi lifted her head, her eyes glistened with unshed tears. "Thanks. I do have something to talk about…but not tonight. Okay?"

With one last squeeze, she withdrew her hand. "We're a pair, aren't we? Cheers." She raised her glass in a salute. Randi followed suit before they each took a drink.

Melody wondered what bothered Randi so much, but figured she'd open up when she was ready. Or not. They had that in common—both secretive. Maybe one day she'd spell out why she didn't like guns. It appeared as if Randi, like everyone else in town, assumed they didn't bother her.

They were wrong.

An hour later, they had discussed the issue of all the strangers in town, the weather changes, a new business going in down the block from the café, and all the minor gossip they could think of. Mundane stuff. Randi drained the last of the drink she'd been nursing all this time and stood.

"I need to head home. Thanks for the company."

When they reached the front door, they hugged. "You take care of yourself and be careful. I've seen a couple of people in the café who I wouldn't want to meet in daylight, much less in a dark ally. Not sure why they're hanging around town, but I'll be glad when all this is over."

Randi hesitated a second as sadness flickered across her face. "Yeah. It won't be the same when the out-of-towners leave."

Melody wondered what kind of problem Randi had but refused to share even with her best friend. At least she seemed more relaxed. "Why don't you spend the night? You know I've got an empty bedroom and I'd love to have the company."

For a minute, Melody thought she'd accept, but Randi shook her head. "Thanks, but I'll feel better at my own place."

"You sure? I'm worried about you."

Randi squeezed her hand. "I'll be fine."

They hugged again, then, shoulders slumped, Randi made her way to her car. Melody stood in the doorway as her friend pulled away. The car's taillights had just disappeared around the corner when a breeze kicked up. The hairs on her neck prickled, and she wrapped her arms around her waist. She had the overwhelming sensation of being watched. Eerie tentacles slid down her spine. With a shiver, she stepped back inside, closed and locked the door.

Their talk of unfriendly looking strangers had her spooked...that was all. No one was out there. Still, the feeling persisted and it was late into the night before she fell asleep.

Her dreams were plagued with images of gun toting men, hard chests, and smoke.

****

The bell above the café's door rang as usual, but once inside Jake didn't see Melody. Instead, a woman he didn't recognize waited on the mayor. She turned toward him and something flashed in her eyes before she acknowledged him with a slight nod. "Good morning, Officer."

"Morning. Is Melody around?"

She paused, then said, "Yes. She stepped out for a moment but she'll be right back. Can I get you a menu and some coffee?"

"Thanks. I appreciate it. Is Holly all right? I don't see her."

"Her doctor told her to stay off her feet for the duration of the pregnancy. Since Mrs. Rose hired me to fill in for a while, there wasn't a reason for Holly to come in." She turned in the mayor's order, then set a mug in front of Jake and poured his coffee, her eyes downcast.

Before he could thank her, Melody pushed through the swinging doors, arms loaded with bundles of napkins. She slowed when she saw him, then dropped the stack on the counter. "Sheriff."

"Mrs. Rose." Dark circles lined the bottom of her eyes and her shoulders drooped. Had she not slept well? She'd looked fine when he'd left her place last night. Instead of asking, he tipped his head toward the waitress. "I see you have new help."

Melody brightened. "Yes, I do believe she was heaven sent. I don't think I could've gotten through yesterday without her. Have you met?"

He shook his head.

"Sheriff Bennett, I'd like you to meet Cora Conway. Cora, this is our sheriff."

"Pleased to meet you, Sheriff."

Jake nodded his acknowledgement. "Nice to meet you, too, ma'am."

She tucked her chin, studying the floor, then scurried away to fill the napkin holders. He focused his attention on Melody. Lowering his voice, he said, "How are you holding up today? I know it can take a day or two for shock to sink in."

Her cheeks turned pink as she shot a quick glance around the café to see if anyone listened. "Like I said last night, I'm fine. What would you like for breakfast?"

She didn't want to talk. Okay. Some people were more private than others and he'd give her space. But in his experience, trying to deal with a traumatic event on your own didn't usually work out well. "More than a few bites of quiche."

She actually smiled. It was the first one she'd given him while in the café and he grinned back. "I appreciate you feeding me yesterday, but today it's my dime. I'll have scrambled eggs, hash browns, bacon and two slices of toast."

She didn't write any of it down and instead yelled through the window into the kitchen, "A number two for the sheriff, Roy."

She stared at him, then started to say something. The bell over the door jangled and she clamped her mouth closed, then hurried to take the new customers menus. Cora threw him a sideways grin before moving the newly filled napkin holders to various tables. A little later, Melody set his meal in front of him on her way to deliver someone else's food and he dug in. So far, everything he'd eaten was delicious, including the quiche from two days ago. It just needed a bit more substance to go with it. Like yesterday's twelve-ounce Ribeye.

More customers came in and neither woman paid him any more attention as they hustled about, taking care of the morning rush.

While Jake ate, he made note of the patrons...one of them the woman who'd tried her best to interview him. He'd hoped he wouldn't run into her again. Upon closer inspection, he noticed she had her eye on FBI Special Agent Malone. The woman was smart, biding her time and waiting for Malone to finish eating. Good luck with getting anything out of the man. The Fed was all business and wouldn't take any guff off of a pushy reporter.

Another man, with the hard look of someone who'd spent time behind bars, sat at a back table and kept glancing toward the front of the café. Or was it toward the FBI agent who faced the door? Warning bells went off. It might be nothing, but tragedy's like the crash brought out more than curious gawkers. Jake would keep an eye on the stranger, and if he felt warranted, would inform the agent. Malone already had his hands full.

With one last look toward Melody, he left enough money on the counter to cover the cost of the meal plus a good tip. With the restaurant being so busy, the women earned every penny. Gathering his hat, he walked out the door, climbed into his SUV and headed toward the previously empty warehouse where everything was being stored until all the parts and pieces of the downed plane were collected. If he had to, he'd go back out to the Johnson place. But visiting the crash site again, even partially cleaned up, was the last thing he wanted to do.

****

Out of the corner of her eye, Melody watched Jake's long strides as he left the café. The man could sure cover a lot of ground. Two days ago, she'd been more than grateful when he'd shown up when he had on the gravel road. Remembering the feel of the gun's cool metal in her hand still caused her stomach to churn...her hands to shake. For a terrifying minute she'd thought she and Michael would be together again, only this time in death.

Except she still hadn't forgiven him. And she might never do so. Even after all this time, it still stung he'd put the welfare of total strangers above hers. Perhaps that wasn't the way he had looked at it, but that was how she felt.

When she'd been at the crash site, she'd fallen apart after the fugitive had held a gun on her. Thankfully the sheriff had made sure her breakdown had been in private. No one in town would expect her to react the way she did. She was the wife—no, make that widow—of their hero. It was expected she'd be as brave as Michael had been despite the fact she'd had a gun pointed at her point blank. Melody was pretty sure if Michael'd had time to react before the vet with PTSD had pulled the trigger, he'd still be alive. Taking a bullet didn't make you a hero.

It made you dead.

"Earth to Melody." Fingers snapped in front of her face.

Disoriented, she blinked, then focused on Cora. "Sorry. What do you need?"

"I don't need anything. But you looked like you were in outer space there for a minute. You have an order up."

"Oh. Thanks." She turned back to the business at hand, embarrassed at being caught daydreaming, especially with a room full of customers. As she gathered the order she glanced around. No one stared at her. Giving herself a mental shake, she headed toward Taggert Reid and his daughter, setting their breakfast in front of them.

"Does everything look all right?" She smiled at the little girl, who grinned back but didn't say a word. Poor kid. From what Melody knew the child hadn't uttered a sound since her mom had died in a car wreck several months ago.

"It looks and smells great, doesn't it, sweetie?" He looked at Samantha, then continued as if she'd spoken. "Since I've been working so much the last couple of days, I decided we needed a special breakfast together."

"Well, I'm glad to see you. I hope you like your food and if there's anything you need, flag me down. We're a little short-handed right now so I'm not as observant as I'd like to be. Okay?"

"You got it." Taggert nodded, then began cutting up the child's pancakes for her.

Melody gave his shoulder a light squeeze then retrieved the coffee pot to refill cups as she made her way around the room.

For the next hour, she didn't have time to think. Trying to handle such large crowds with both Holly and her parents gone was difficult. She wished she hadn't told Holly to stay home. Even though all she'd done was sit at the register the prior day, it had helped.

Melody's reserve energy supply was running dangerously low, and all she wanted to do was take a three-day nap. Not that it would happen anytime soon, but she could always dream.

"Hey," Cora said later when there were only a couple of patrons left. "Do you need to take a break? I can cover the floor." When Melody hesitated, she added, "I'll let you know when these people are ready to check out."

Melody bobbed her head once. "Yeah, that'd be great. I'll be in the office."

Cora retrieved the tub then began busing tables. Melody watched her work. Where did the woman get all her energy? Whatever vitamins she took, Melody wanted some. Or, it could be desperation. Not knowing where your next meal came from would do that to you, she supposed. With a sigh, she headed into the kitchen.

"You doing okay in here, Roy?" She'd intended to sit for a few minutes, but this was still her business and she needed to make sure everything ran smoothly.

"We're getting low on eggs. See if Mr. Albertson can deliver a day early."

"I'm sure he can. If not, we can always go by the store."

"Our customers expect the best and I don't trust the store eggs to be fresh." He looked out the window to the dining room, then back at her, before jerking his head in that direction. "What's her story?"

"Cora?" Her heart went out to the woman. "She was in an abusive relationship and is trying to make a fresh start. I haven't had time to ask her many questions yet, but I'm hoping she stays at least until Mom and Dad get back from their cruise. She's been fantastic to help out. Why?"

"Just curious. She sure turned up at the right time."

"Lucky for us she did." She watched Cora as she worked. "I can't imagine what she's been through. She has a hard road ahead of her. But I suppose compared to the life she left behind it'll be easier than I would think."

"I can't abide a man who'd hit a woman. I'm still curious about her, though."

"You're a good man, Roy Maddox." She patted his back.

He huffed and went back to work.

Melody shot him a rueful smile, even though he didn't see it. Bless his heart. She wasn't sure what she'd do without him as her anchor. He and Michael had been best friends growing up, had served in the army together. Had stood by her side as they'd lowered Michael's body into the ground. She owed him a lot.

Melody continued on to her office and after a quick call for more eggs, she took a glass of water and headed back out front as the last of the breakfast crowd, two older gentlemen who came in every now and then, prepared to leave. She rang them up and encouraged them to return.

Cora finished busing the tables, then took a seat across from Melody. "Thank goodness. I didn't think they'd ever leave. I swear between the two of them, they drank two pots of coffee."

"They'll do that sometimes. They think if they hang around long enough, they'll hear more gossip. They should know by now they won't be getting any from me." She took another sip of water.

"That's a small town for you," Cora chimed in.

"So you've lived in small towns before?"

She gave a nervous laugh. "Oh, yeah. You can get stuck in small communities faster than you can blink. The people are usually kind but they can also be vicious, cruel and unforgiving."

Melody must have given her an odd look because she added, "But they're mostly nice...like you for instance. I don't know what I would've done if you hadn't given me this job. By the way, I wanted to let you know the house is perfect. Thanks for trusting me enough to stay there."

She shoved her curiosity—and speculation—to the back of her mind and focused on the conversation. "I doubt there's a spare bed in this town right now so it's my pleasure. It wasn't too dirty or anything?"

"No. I did a little light dusting before I went to bed but that was about it. Minor stuff. The house almost reminds me of a little New England cottage. I'm surprised you don't have it rented out all the time."

Melody laughed. "It hasn't been empty very long. I had intended to put an ad in the paper, but then this tragedy hit and I haven't had time. Lucky for you. If you think you might stick around for a while after things settle down, we'll discuss a long-term rental rate. In the meantime, think of it as an added bonus of bailing me out of a jam."

Cora squeezed her hand. "Thanks, Melody. You're so sweet."

Her heart warmed, yet again grateful for her good fortune to have stumbled across Cora. Or had Cora stumbled across her?

****

Jake sank into his office chair, glad to have a

reprieve. Clay Larson passed by his open door and he called out to him.

The young man stuck his head around the door. "Yeah, boss?"

Jake grinned to himself. He liked the sound of that. Detectives were constantly under scrutiny and being questioned about their activities. It felt good to have some respect for a change, especially after the way he'd left the CPD. "I wanted to let you know you did good work out there. Most people wouldn't have been able to stomach a crash scene and maintain a professional demeanor."

Larson hung his head a moment before meeting his gaze. "You didn't see me when I got there. I did lose it. Puked my guts out in the bushes. But I don't think I was the only one. It was pretty gruesome."

He nodded, no question about what the scene looked like. "You pulled it together, though, and did your job. I appreciate your work. You're a good deputy."

Clay straightened and drew his shoulders back even as his cheeks turned a soft shade of pink. He gave a brief nod and left. One day he'd make a fine sheriff.

Turning his attention back to his desk, there were more reports to be addressed than he'd anticipated. Must be because of so many people in the area, but there were complaints of traffic jams, a fender-bender right outside the city limits that Larson had taken care of without bothering Jake, complaints of out-of-towners parking on residents' lawns, shoplifting, and some vandalism at the Taylor place. Nothing major but enough to keep his staff hopping. Jake made a note to ask the council about giving them a raise, especially

Larson, who had been working eighteen-hour days.

Besides the one full-time deputy, his staff comprised of Roger Hunter, a man in his mid-fifties who had worked in law enforcement, but now served as a reserve deputy. And a couple of women worked as dispatchers. Brenda and Glenda Sullivan, twins, both unmarried and cousins to Councilman Bob Sullivan, liked to serve the town by manning the switchboard. The staff might be small, but they were efficient. Right now, though, Jake sure needed another deputy—preferably two—the council had authorized him to hire. Only he hadn't gotten around to it. His lack of foresight had bit him in the rear the last few days.

Despite being short-handed, everything was under control. The clean-up on the Johnson property had been completed late this afternoon. In the morning the NTSB would begin the process of transporting the remains of the plane back to their lab for analysis. They'd found the voice and data recorders intact so that should help in determining the cause of the crash.

The intercom buzzed. He was amazed the antiquated piece of equipment that still worked perfectly. "Yes, Glenda?"

"Do you need anything before Brenda comes in and I go home? She can bring you some cherry cobbler if you're going to be working late. You need to keep up your strength, you know."

His heart warmed at how readily the people of Rock Ledge had embraced him as one of their own. The twins weren't quite old enough to be his mother, but they sure mothered him all the same in equal measure. "Thanks, but I think I'll be able to call it an early night tonight. The NTSB will be clearing out the warehouse tomorrow so things should settle back to its normal pace."

"Oh, that's good." She tsked. "All those poor souls. I've been praying for them and their families. Maybe once they've been able to bury their dead, they can move forward."

It would be hard for some to get past this.

"Do they have any idea what might have caused the crash?" she asked.

"The assumption is mechanical error. Right now they don't know."

"They'll have a better idea once they go through the black box," she stated as if she knew how the process worked and had dealt with other crashes in the past.

Jake didn't want to start speculating beyond what he'd already said, even with his staff. That wasn't his job, and he didn't want any falsehoods surfacing because of guessing on his part. The media would have a field day with that.

"Is there anything else, Glenda?"

"No, sir. You get some rest now, you hear?" She might have put a question mark at the end of her sentence, but it came out more like a command.

"Have a nice night." With that, he hung up. He chuckled and shook his head. The twins weren't what you would classify as Aunt Bea…but darn close.

Chapter Five

Jake sat in his SUV outside Melody's home, reluctant to go knock on her door. She hadn't been too happy to see him the other night. This morning's visit would be worse. The sun had barely peeked over the horizon, and he wasn't sure he'd even gotten three hours of sleep.

Fatigue pulled at him. Ignoring his body, he climbed out of the vehicle and headed to the door. Not giving himself time to think, he rang the bell. There weren't any sounds from inside. After a full minute, he considered ringing the bell again when he heard footsteps and the door opened a few inches. Melody peeked around the corner. Her eyes widened at the sight of him.

"Sheriff?"

"I hate to bother you so early but I…" How could he finish that sentence? He scrubbed a hand through his hair. "May I come in?"

She took only half a beat to swing the door wide, allowing him entrance.

She wore a long red robe, cinched at the waist but revealing the swell of her breasts at the open throat. With no makeup and her hair hanging loose around her shoulders, she looked as if she'd just gotten out of bed. He'd like to take her hand and lead her back to that bed. The thought caught him off guard, and Jake swallowed hard. Why did he have the most inappropriate thoughts when he was around her?

Melody cleared her throat. "What are you doing here?" It took a couple of seconds for his sleep deprived brain to kick in. He didn't know where to begin without scaring her so he stalled. "Is that coffee I smell? It's been a long night and I could use some caffeine."

She frowned but turned toward the kitchen. Jake smiled when she re-cinched her belt. At least she'd let him inside. Following her, he slid into one of the chairs at the table. Neither spoke as she filled a mug, setting it in front of him. He took a sip, then looked up in surprise. It was almost as strong as what he made for himself. Melody took the seat across the table from him and waited, her brows drawn into a deep furrow.

Jake blew out a breath, meeting her gaze. There wasn't an easy way to tell her, but at least she was already seated if she took the news badly. However, from what he'd observed, she'd be all right.

"Let me assure you up front she's okay, but last night Randi Johnson was abducted."

She jumped up, panic written on her face. "What? Where is she?"

He held up a hand to stop her from barging out of the house in her robe. "An ex-con who had a grudge against Wade Malone kidnapped her from her home." The same man he'd seen eyeing Malone in the café.

"Who's Wade Malone, and why did that man take Randi?"

"Malone is the FBI agent investigating the marshal's death. Anyway, this guy used Ms. Johnson as bait to lure Agent Malone out to the old barn on her property. The guy blew it up, but they got away."

She lowered herself to her chair again, sitting on the edge of the seat, hanging on his every word. At least she hadn't fallen apart on him. Yet.

"Malone was injured with falling debris from the explosion."

"They were that close?" Her hand went to her chest, as if to hold in her pounding heart.

Jake kept his tone flat so as to not upset her more than he had to. "They tried running through the forest, but with Malone's injury slowing them down, the guy caught up with them."

Melody stared wide-eyed. Her breathing had become shallow. He'd considered sugar-coating the entire issue, or even giving the official cut-and-dried version. In the end, he'd decided to tell her all of the minute details.

"Don't worry, the perpetrator's dead. He fell into an abandoned well. However, Agent Malone lost a lot of blood and is in serious condition in the hospital. Ms. Johnson won't leave his side."

Confusion was written on her face. "I don't understand. She's staying there until he stabilizes or what?"

He blew out a heavy breath, still having a hard time believing this part. "Actually, they knew each other a long time ago and had a relationship. I don't know the particulars, but they lost touch somehow and now that they've reconnected, she refuses to leave his side. Looks like she isn't going to take any chances on losing him again."

"That's what she was upset about last night but wouldn't tell me," Melody said almost to herself. She slumped in her chair and sat quietly for several moments before looking at him expectantly. "Randi's okay, though? She wasn't hurt?"

He didn't know how to reassure her. So tired he was surprised he was still upright, he wanted nothing more than a few hours of uninterrupted sleep. He took another sip of the coffee, hoping it would help revive him, then set the mug down. "Some minor cuts and scrapes…a few bruises. I didn't want you hearing this from anyone else since you two are so close."

She raised her eyebrows. "Apparently not as close as I thought. She never said a word. Although I noticed she kept watching this one dark-haired guy in a suit the day of the crash. Was that him?"

"Yeah. Wade Malone."

Her lips flattened as she studied her clasped hands. "Guess we all have secrets we keep hidden from others."

She drew into herself. Despite his intention to stay detached from her, Jake wanted to know what was going through her mind…what secrets she had hidden. Besides her dislike for guns that no one seemed to be aware of except him.

His body still remembered how she felt against him after the fugitive tried to kill her, how she trembled in his arms and clung to his shirt as if he were a lifeline. He wanted to pull her into his arms now, but didn't see a reasonable explanation for his actions. So he continued to sit at the small table in her cozy kitchen, the aroma of strong coffee and her almond shampoo wafting in the air.

When the silence became unbearable, and he couldn't find any other reason to linger, he stood. "I should get going. Still need to make my rounds."

She took a deep breath, as if to compose herself, then rose. "You're very conscientious, aren't you?"

"That's why they hired me." He gave a half-hearted shrug.

"And to tick off Frank," she muttered.

Jake had been hired because of his experience and expertise. The fact it upset the mayor was a plus for some members of the council. "Yeah. There is that, too." He chuckled. The knowledge didn't sting like it had a few days ago.

On impulse, he took Melody's hand and squeezed. The feel of her soft skin against his calloused hands sent a jolt through him. He'd only meant to be comforting. Hadn't he?

"You let me know if you need anything. Or even to just talk, okay?" He could push her toward a counselor again, but didn't think it would do any good. Besides, he liked the idea of her coming to him, of using him for her sounding board. He held her gaze for a while before she slowly pulled her hand out of his and stepped back. Had he imagined desire in her eyes before she pulled away? Had she felt the same charge he had?

"Thank you, Sheriff. I—"

"It's Jake. Remember?"

She glanced down at this gun, then took a deep breath. "All right…Jake."

He walked to the front door, but paused before opening it. "Do you need to take the day off or something?"

"Why is it men think women need to be coddled? We're stronger than we look, you know." A smile played at the corners of her lips, softening her words.

He grinned back. "We like to pretend otherwise.

Makes us feel needed."

"That I believe." She gave a small laugh before she sobered. "I appreciate you telling me about Randi before I heard it through the grapevine. If I'd gotten bits and pieces from my customers, I would've gone crazy with worry."

"Knowing you, you would've stormed down to my office demanding to know the details." He held her gaze…watched as she moistened her lips. Heat pooled in his lower regions, taking him off guard. Again. What was wrong with him? She hadn't invited any advances from him. Just the opposite. He needed to get out of there, but his feet refused to move.

After a bit, she cleared her throat. "Well, at least I have all the facts and not half-truths or suppositions spouted by gossips. Thank you."

In an old-western style, he tipped his fingers to his forehead in a mock salute. "My pleasure." Instead of leaving, though, he continued to stand there, staring into her eyes. The temptation to lean into her, to brush his lips across hers, slammed into him. It was enough of a jolt that he regained his senses. He must be more tired than he realized.

After another minute, she said, "Well, uh, I need to get to work."

"Yes, ma'am. Me, too." He pulled the door open, stepped out and stuck his hat on his head. Giving Melody a short nod, he headed to his car. By the time he slid behind the wheel, she had already closed the door. The woman was definitely an enigma. When he thought she'd be strong, she fell apart, and when he would've sworn she'd fall apart, she pulled it together.

Twenty minutes later, Jake had finished his rounds

of the small community. He glanced at his watch; the café wasn't open yet. Rounding a corner, he spied Melody's car as she headed to work so he followed her. He pulled into the back parking lot behind her.

"Oh!" she said when she got out of her car and saw him.

"Sorry. Didn't mean to startle you. Thought I'd get a jump on the breakfast crowd, if you don't mind." Roy's Harley was already there so he assumed it wouldn't be too long of a wait to get some food.

"No problem. Come on inside." She didn't wait for a reply as she unlocked the door.

He didn't enjoy the view of her in the waitress uniform nearly as much as he had when she'd worn the robe. Still, the gentle sway of her hips held his attention until after she'd entered the building. Following her, she detoured to her office long enough to leave her purse and retrieve a clean apron, which she was in the process of tying when she walked out, pulling the material of her blouse tight across her chest. Jake averted his gaze. A man could only tolerate so much.

Cora came down the hallway from the dining area, stopping short. She glanced from one to the other of them. "Oh, dear. Is something wrong?"

"Jake came to tell me a friend of mine was abducted last night. She's fine, but I'm sure you'll be hearing all about it from the rumor mill this morning."

"How terrifying, but I'm glad she's okay." She paused and studied Jake, her brows drawn into a deep V. "Pardon me for saying so sheriff, but you look like you've been working too hard. Perhaps you need to delegate some of your work to others."

Her comment sounded a bit odd, and a little

familiar, but he couldn't recall where he might have heard it before. Not from Cora. He hadn't been around her enough to even carry on much of a conversation. He gave himself a mental shake. Exhaustion tended to play havoc with his cognitive skills.

She dipped her chin and took a step back. "I'm sorry. I overstepped my bounds."

The woman sure was shy. Jake wondered how she'd ended up in Rock Ledge. He'd ask Melody later. Right now, he wanted food. "Don't worry about it, but I do appreciate your concern."

Cora flashed a brief smile, then turned to Melody. "I've already got the coffee started plus most everything is ready to go for the day except for the cash register."

"Thanks. I appreciate it. I'll be right in." When Cora had disappeared into the dining room, Melody faced Jake. "Now, let's get you fed."

"You're very conscientious with your customers," he said, throwing her earlier words back at her in jest.

She followed suit and tapped two fingers against her forehead in a mock salute. "That's why I'm the most popular place in town."

She laughed, a sound he hadn't heard often enough. Somehow, some way, he'd have to find a way to make her laugh again. But not right now. His day had only begun and he already needed some of the high-octane coffee he'd brought from home to get through another round of red tape.

But starting the day off here, with Melody, made things bearable. Definitely a perk of the job…whether it had been intended as one or not. Yep. Small town life was growing on him.

Chapter Six

Melody sighed and flipped the CLOSED sign at the same time she locked the door of The Tangled Rose. With the prior day's events, the media had reappeared in droves, but had retreated to whatever cubbyholes they'd chosen for this trip. As long as she didn't have to see them, she'd be happy. Her experience with them after Michael's death was more than enough to last her a lifetime. Numb with shock at the time, she hadn't been able to avoid them, finding a camera in her face everywhere she'd gone.

She was smarter now.

This made two major incidents in the small town, and she wondered if, like deaths, they ran in threes. But that was silly. What else could possibly happen? She wasn't sure she'd be able to bear it if one more thing, even something relatively minor, occurred. Her nerves were on edge and she longed to have the peace that normally surrounded the area back.

She turned to find Cora sweeping up. Cora looked up, then frowned. "Are you all right? You look beat."

Melody let her shoulders droop.

When Jake had told her about Randi, she'd wanted to run to the hospital to be with her friend. But the café had held her hostage, like the madman had done to Randi the night before. Randi had called her earlier in the afternoon and assured her she was okay. She wouldn't leave Wade alone in the hospital, but had wanted to check in with her friend. It was too late to drive to Harrison tonight, so Melody intended to go home. She said as much to Cora.

"Why don't you come over to the house for a while? I have a pitcher of sweet tea, and you can unwind."

Girl time? She and Randi had girl time on a fairly regular basis, but this felt different. She studied her new employee. Here was someone who took her at face value. No preconceived notions of how she was supposed to act or who she was supposed to be, like everyone in town did. The idea appealed to her...it seemed like a lifeline in Melody's turbulent sea of emotions. Fear, worry, relief, and yes, a bit of disappointment that Randi hadn't confided about Wade, had all hit her during the day. Whether she went to Cora's or not, though wouldn't change her reality, so why bother?

"It's tempting, truly, but I can't."

Cora stood the broom in front of her and cocked her head. "Why not? Oh. Sorry. I...I don't mean to be pushy or anything, but do you have someplace you have to be tonight?"

"Well, no." Why couldn't she go? Just because she usually went straight home every night didn't mean she couldn't do something different. Like spend a little time with her new employee. A shadow of regret swept over her. Other than her life as a business owner, since Michael's death she had become a hermit. She'd never been a social butterfly, but there were times when she'd like to find out what it felt like.

"So come. You don't have to stay long, but you

look like you could use some company. To be honest, I could use some myself. What do you say?"

The idea was more than a little appealing. Besides, she hadn't considered Cora being lonely. "You talked me into it."

Roy came out of the kitchen, wiping his hands on a towel. "You need anything else before I leave?"

"No. I'm good. Looks like you're finished for the day." He'd already discarded his apron.

"Yeah. I'm headed over to the lodge for bingo night. Want to join me?"

Huh. She must look worse than she thought if both of her employees were inviting her out. She'd never asked Roy why he played bingo with the older citizens. They were a small town, but not so small that's all there was to do. Of course, he'd always been close to Perry Walker, and Perry showed up there almost every week. Perhaps he was the sole attraction.

"Thank you, but Cora already asked me to go over to her place for a bit. Being around a lot of people is a little more than I can bear right now. Maybe next week."

"Yeah, sure. Y'all have a good time, okay?" He gave her a quick hug, waved toward Cora, then headed toward the back. A moment later, the door banged closed. Fifteen minutes later, the two women had everything ready for the next morning. With a loud sigh, Melody yanked off her apron and dropped it in the hamper by her office.

"I'll second that," Cora said as she added her own soiled apron to the bin. "Man, it's been a long day. Too bad Roy didn't want to come over. I'd let him give me a foot rub."

Melody laughed. "Now *that* I'd like to see." She locked the door behind them and they crossed the parking lot to the small house.

"Make yourself at home," Cora said once they were inside.

She couldn't believe the changes Cora had made in the short time she'd been there. Melody turned in a slow circle as she took in the living room. Everything in the room had been rearranged, making the area inviting and intimate. The printed cotton curtains had been replaced with lined, dark drapes with a sheer fabric swag in a contrasting color. The couch and stuffed chair had slipcovers on them, making the furniture appear new. The old, battered coffee table was nowhere in sight. "You've been busy."

"I hope you don't mind. I've got a lot of nervous energy, so once I got started, I couldn't seem to stop making changes. I found a few things in the closets that I repurposed, plus picked up some other things at the resale shop. Do you like it?" She glanced around as if afraid she'd have to put everything back.

"Are you kidding? This is great. I love the colors." If she hadn't known this was her parents' house, she wouldn't have recognized it. All of the family photos that had been scattered throughout the room were now all in a nice arrangement on an end table in the corner, a reminder of who had lived there.

"Oh, good. I'm glad you like it. Come on in the kitchen and I'll get your tea. Or would you prefer something a little stronger?"

"Are you saying you have alcohol?" Hmm. There was another side to the shy and quiet woman Melody hadn't seen before.

"Um, yes. I don't drink much, but I've found it helps me unwind when I'm stressed. I had to hide it from my boyfriend. If he found out, he'd get ticked off I hadn't gotten his permission, then use it as an excuse to slap me around." She waved her hand dismissively. "Sorry. I don't want to talk about him. Don't know why I even brought him up."

"No problem." Melody dropped her purse on the couch and followed her into the kitchen. Again, heavy curtains were on the windows, but the room didn't seem gloomy. A cheery cookie jar with lady bugs, a vase of artificial flowers on the small table, as well as a blood red tea towel on the rack beside the sink brightened up the space. It was as if they were isolated from the world here.

"What do you have?"

"Well, I found this drink on the internet so wanted to check it out. If you're game, we can try it together. It's called a grapefruit martini."

"Never heard of it. What's in it?"

"It's pretty simple, actually. A little grapefruit juice, triple sec, and vodka. Shake and there you have it."

"O-kay. Let's give it a shot." Melody plopped into a chair at the table as Cora pulled out the ingredients for the drink. "How did I get so lucky in hiring you?"

Cora glanced over her shoulder and grinned before going back to the mixing. "I think I'm the lucky one. I'm not sure where I'd be right now if you hadn't given me a job…still living out of my car for one thing. You know, I think everything happens for a reason. Whether it's finding the job you've always wanted, running into an old friend or even meeting the perfect someone you're meant to spend your life with. If it's supposed to happen, then it will regardless of what obstacles get in the way. You gotta have faith."

Melody snorted. "Yeah, well, that doesn't always turn out the way you think it will."

Cora twisted around to look at her. "Are you talking about your husband?"

Melody stiffened, drawing into herself.

"Sorry. It's none of my business. I didn't mean to bring up bad memories." She turned back to fixing the drinks.

Melody didn't want to get into that subject. Still, she couldn't seem to stop the words from spilling out of her mouth. "How do you know they're bad?"

"I don't. I just assumed. How long were you together?"

"Together? Since high school. We were married for seven years before he died." She swallowed the lump in her throat. Being tired and emotionally upset like she had been today made it harder to keep the overwhelming hurt at bay. Thankfully, Cora concentrated on shaking the drinks, giving her time to compose herself.

Cora poured the liquid into glasses, then joined Melody at the table. "That's a long time."

She studied the glass. "Have you ever been married?"

Cora blew out a deep breath, then took a sip before answering. "No. Came close once, but it didn't work out. I've always regretted it, too." Pain etched her words.

Now it was her turn to comfort. "Want to talk about it?"

Tears glistened in Cora's eyes as she shook her head. Her chin trembled. She fiddled with her glass without taking another drink. The woman might believe things happened for a reason, but it wasn't always easy to accept. Melody took a tentative sip of her drink. "Hey, this is good! You have to give me the recipe."

Cora sniffed once, then quirked her lips upward. "You got it. I'm glad it turned out okay because I wasn't sure when I saw the recipe. Sometimes things look great online but turn out rotten in real life."

She held up her glass, then clinked it with Cora's. "Then here's to new friendships."

"Cheers."

For a while they simply giggled as they toasted first one silly thing then another. It felt good to just "be" for a change, the prior subject pushed to the recesses of her mind.

"Can I ask you a question?" Cora asked softly.

Melody's good mood slipped a little. She sounded a tad too serious all of a sudden. "Sure." She tried hard to keep her tone light.

"Why is there a shrine in the café?"

Yep. There it was. That heart rendering topic. Except it didn't sting quite as much as she'd thought it would. Taking a deep breath, she met Cora's gaze. "It's for my husband."

She cocked her head. "Uh, I don't understand. It's obviously painful. You never look at it. In fact, you work on the other side of the café, almost as if you can't put enough distance between you and it. Me? I'm not sure I could work every day with my dead husband watching me."

Melody sucked in a ragged breath. Cora was the

first person to suspect Melody's true feelings about Michael's shrine, the first person to actually sympathize with her. She felt like she'd been living in the shadows the last couple of years, keeping her true feelings where no one could see. No one except this stranger, who suddenly didn't seem like such an outsider.

"How do you do it?" Cora continued. "*Why* do you do it?"

Stalling, Melody stared into her drink, then took a slow sip.

"You know, you don't have to talk about this. I have a tendency to speak my mind without thinking. Which gets me in trouble more often than not." Cora gave a self-deprecating laugh and rubbed her arm. "I sure got enough bruises because of it, let me tell you."

"No one has asked me about the shrine. Ever. I guess they think talking about it, or what it represents is too painful, and in a way, it is. But not like they think." She looked up sharply. Why was she talking to this stranger?

Because it felt good to share what she'd held inside for so long.

So she opened up and told Cora the truth about the shrine and about Michael's service in the army. She let out the bitterness about his working with the vets and what it had done to their marriage. All the resentment, anger, loneliness, feelings of betrayal, then the guilt for feeling that way, exploded out of her. She held nothing back.

"Why do you think your husband worked with the vets instead of spending time on your marriage?"

That was what she'd wanted to know. After Michael had returned home, she had hoped they could at least get away for a week, to take the honeymoon they never had. Although, they had gone to Branson, Missouri for an extended weekend. She had wanted to restart their relationship, their marriage. To find the spark that had drawn them together to begin with. But she was disappointed when they'd run into a couple they knew. The other couple had problems in their marriage and Michael wanted to help, spending a great deal of time with them. Living in his own vacuum, Michael didn't see his own marriage faltering. It was hard to think of him discarding their love—discarding her—for the sake others. And it ripped her heart out to think she was no longer the center of his world; that she had slipped down on his priority list.

It hurt to think they'd wind up like the other couple, miserable.

Life was too short to be unhappy.

That stopped her cold. Life *was* short, yet she couldn't seem to move forward, hung in limbo. She took a big gulp of the martini.

"Melody?" Cora's voice broke her train of thought and downward spiral.

"I'm sorry. What did you say?"

"I asked why your husband spent so much time with the vets."

She blew out a deep breath. "Good question. I don't have an answer, though."

"So what did you do while he was gone?"

"What most women do, especially military wives," she replied, smiling ruefully.

"Yeah. You stood by your man, even when it might not have been in your best interest."

"You got it." Looking back, she questioned why

she'd so readily adapted to that role, why she hadn't been more vocal in her objection. When he joined the army, she knew and accepted the fact he'd be gone a lot. But once he'd been discharged, she had expected to be put first in his life. That hadn't happened. Soon after his return, he'd begun working with the vets, leaving her more and more.

Why hadn't she ever told Michael how she felt? Or asked why he'd been so focused on helping them? What had happened over there that he couldn't confide in her? Was it guilt that he'd come home when so many of his friends hadn't? Or gratitude to the men and women in uniform who had helped him survive? She knew it had been bad, but he never talked about his time in combat, especially as a sniper. At least not to her. Maybe it was easier for him to help others deal with their problems rather than face his own. A horrible thought hit her. Did Michael have PTSD and she hadn't had a clue? Were they so out of tune that neither felt they could confide in the other? It was too much to contemplate right now. Not here in someone else's kitchen.

Cora sat quietly, no sign of judgment. Embarrassed, Melody said, "Sorry I got all maudlin on you there."

"Don't you have anyone you can talk to about this?"

She blew out a heavy breath, and a sharp pang hit her at the thought of not being able to talk to even Randi. But then, both of them had their own secrets so maybe her friend would be there holding her hand in support if she knew how Melody felt. She preferred to think so, anyway. "Randi and I talk, but we've never gotten into this. Initially, she gave me space. Then, it slipped by the wayside and never came up."

"Well, people surprise you sometimes." Cora gave a small shrug.

"True." The reminder made her realize she'd prejudged, even her best friend. She needed to rectify that.

They sat in silence a bit longer. Melody took another sip of the drink, then met Cora's gaze. "Have you considered being a counselor? You're pretty good at it, you know."

"That's sweet of you, but all I did was listen."

Melody raised her eyebrows. "Exactly."

Cora started laughing. Before she knew it, Melody was laughing, too. She laughed so hard tears were coming out of her eyes, and she noticed Cora also had tears streaming down her face. Which made her laugh harder. She didn't know what was so funny. It didn't matter. The action was therapeutic. And healing.

When they finally stopped and had blown their noses, Cora said, "I don't like to brag, but I am a good listener. If you need to vent some more, you know where you can find me." She gestured around the kitchen.

"I'm so glad you happened to stop in the café the day of the plane crash. I feel like I've known you for ages."

Cora took a sip of her drink. "Ditto. You sure we didn't meet in another life or something?"

"You never know." Melody looked down to find she'd drained her glass.

With a giggle Cora refilled it for her, then sat.

"Can we talk about something else?" The buzz she

had from the martini was gone, and the familiar ache in the pit of her stomach was back.

"Sure." Cora cleared her throat. "So, you grew up here. Ever want to live someplace else?"

Melody shook her head, thankful for the change of topic. "Not really. I'd like to see other parts of the country, but I doubt I'll ever go very far."

"What's stopping you? All you have to do is load up the car or book a plane ticket, then head out. I mean, it's not like you've got someone here holding you back. Not like I did, anyway."

Shrugging, she glanced away before meeting Cora's steady gaze. "You make it sound so easy, but I have obligations that tie me down."

"Like what?"

"The café for one. People count on it to be open six days a week. Doesn't leave much time to go traipsing all over the place."

"And you're the only one who can run it?"

"Well, no, but—"

"Trust me. You can *always* find a way if you want it bad enough." Cora paused and looked away. "Or if you're motivated enough."

Oh, shoot. Lost in her own self-pity, she'd forgotten why Cora was here in the first place. Since she had unburdened herself, maybe Cora would like to do the same. "I suppose being beaten by the man who says he loves you is pretty good motivation."

Cora paled as a shudder racked her body. "You have no idea, and I hope you never have the same experience. He seemed like such a nice guy...until it was too late."

Melody reached over and took the other woman's

hand. "You're safe now."

Cora tilted up the corners of her lips, and the bleakness that had settled over her slid away. "Yes, I am. Now, tell me about the places you'd like to visit."

That easily, Cora shifted the subject. Okay. She wasn't ready to talk about herself yet. Melody didn't mind. Some hurts ran deeper than others. Cora would open up in her own good time.

"I'd like to see the Statue of Liberty. And Times Square. Maybe be there New Year's Eve and watch the ball drop."

"With those crushing crowds?"

She laughed. "Doesn't make sense, does it? Rock Ledge doesn't do much, and I always thought it'd be neat to experience the thrill of hundreds of people yelling Happy New Year all at the same time. What about you? Where have you been that you'd recommend?"

"I've been to Chicago. Tried to get into Oprah's show, but it was sold out. Then it ended. Man, would've loved to have been there for her last show. She gave away some awesome gifts." She sighed, a dreamy expression on her face.

"Seriously? Michael and I talked about going there one day but it…"

"Never happened. Sorry, sweetie." Cora patted her hand. "Okay. Where else?"

Gloomy thoughts dissipated, she continued. "Oh, I don't know. Maybe Alaska, Hawaii, Santa Fe, Seattle, San Francisco, Orlando, the Caribbean."

Cora threw her head back and hooted. "Girl, we have *got* to get you a travel agent."

For the next hour they talked about the pros and

cons of each place, laughing, each making suggestions on what to do and what to avoid in each city. By the time they'd finished, the effects of the martini were long gone. They both needed to be up early to open the café, so she said goodnight. Once she'd crossed the parking lot and gotten in her car, Cora turned off the porch light.

As she backed out of the lot, she noticed the dark curtains blocked the light from seeping out, giving the house an unlived-in look. Maybe she liked it that way in case her ex came looking for her. Made sense. At any rate, it had been the most relaxing and fun evening she'd had in quite a while. Cora knew how to get her to open up and take her mind off her personal troubles. Whether it was because of the cleansing discussion, or the delicious drinks, tonight she'd get a good night's sleep.

Tonight, she wouldn't relive her haunting nightmare.

****

I love the night and the concealing darkness.

Fading into the shadows, I stood behind a tree as Melody Rose pulled into her driveway. A laugh threatened to leak out. No. No noise. Might spook the prey. Can't have that. Not yet, anyway.

She got out of her car without looking around, juggled a bag of groceries, then unlocked the front door. The outside light wasn't even on. Who walked into a dark house with so many strangers in the area? And crime happened everywhere. I stifled a snicker. Especially with me around.

Once she was inside, I slipped around back and watch her through the partially open curtains on the sliding glass door. It didn't take her long to put the small bag of groceries away. The woman ate like a bird! How did she even survive? And she owned a café! Then she flipped through the mail before dumping most of it in the trash. She looked around the room as if she didn't know what to do. *Go to bed, you dumb twit,* I wanted to scream.

Finally, she got a drink of water, then headed to the back of the house. A few steps and I stood outside her bedroom. She hadn't pulled the drapes any closer together here, either, from the last time I'd paid her a visit. I snorted, not worrying about her hearing me now. She never did. Talk about walking around in a fog.

I couldn't get a clear view, but knew she undressed in the walk-in closet. What was she? Some kind of prude? The body should be celebrated, not hidden. She didn't even wear a sexy nightgown, just a cotton T-shirt and shorts. I shifted from foot to foot, waiting for her to finish stalling and hit the sack. Taking a deep breath, I reminded myself I had to keep my eye on the ultimate goal. And Melody Rose was an avenue to that prize.

Twenty minutes after she arrived home, all the lights went out. She was in bed. Good. Tamping down my impatience, I waited an additional hour to be safe, then picked the lock on the sliding glass door and slipped inside. Breaking and entering while she was home, watching her sleep, and knowing it would be so easy to kill her, added another layer of adrenaline. It was exhilarating! But it wouldn't happen yet. It was too much fun toying with her…too much fun watching her squirm.

I side-stepped the chair she'd left pulled out, and made my way to the open bedroom door. Curled on her side, her deep, even breaths indicated she was asleep. Not sure how soundly she slept, I kept my steps light. Closing the distance, I stood next to her bed, itching to watch her eyes bulge as I strangled her, laugh as she took her last breath.

Her brows puckered, as if she sensed someone there. Careful to remain undetected, I took a step back, putting space between us. She stirred. Holding my breath, I moved into the hall and pressed myself against the wall. Eventually, she rolled over and snuggled deeper into the covers.

Moving down the hallway, I glanced into the rooms where the doors stood open, not able to see much. One door, however, was closed. Judging by the rest of the house, it seemed rather uncharacteristic of her. I looked back toward her room, then turned the knob. Stepping inside, I closed the door behind me without even a soft thump. A musty smell assaulted my nose. What in the world? I retrieved the small flashlight from my jacket pocket and clicked it on.

Ah! Now I know your ultimate secret. Everywhere I looked, there were guns. I wonder if I took one...? She'd never know or miss it. Didn't look like she'd been in here in months, if not years. Temptation ate at me. Then the voice that always guided me when it mattered most, told me to leave everything as is. No sense in giving her a clue, no matter how unlikely she might find it, until the appropriate time. I turned the flashlight off and allowed my eyes to readjust to the dark. Should have brought the night-vision goggles. Too late now. Once I could see in the dark again, I left the room and returned to her bedroom. I wanted to see how stupidly peaceful she slept.

When the time is right, all will fall into place. Exactly as I have planned. Then Miss Melody Rose, you and Jake Bennett will get what's coming to you.

In spades.

Chapter Seven

Melody awoke refreshed. There hadn't been any nightmares, no dreams of any kind. In fact, she didn't think she had even rolled over during the night. For the first time since she'd opened the café, she hadn't dreaded getting out of bed and going to work.

Smiling, and an hour earlier than normal, she pulled into the employee parking lot, then jammed on the brakes, sending gravel flying as she skidded to a stop. Her heart stopped in her chest, and she stared at the building, trying to process what she saw. The back window of the diner had been shattered. Anger flashed. Why would someone do that? It didn't make sense. She had worked hard to make her and Michael's dream become a reality, albeit now her albatross.

Ready to jump from the car to confront whoever it was, she stopped, hand on the door handle. Indecision, then logic took over. Did she want to face off with them? Alone? She could be injured if they were still here. From where she sat, she couldn't tell if they had left or not. The thought of walking in on a thief was more than she wanted to face. Fumbling in her purse to find her cell phone, she dialed 9-1-1.

Once the operator came on the line, she was patched through to the sheriff's office "Do not go inside," Brenda told her. "Someone will be there as soon as possible."

Melody disconnected. Clutching the phone, she slowly lowered it to her lap. Sweat beaded on her forehead. The previous anger morphed into fear, holding her captive. Time stood still. She jumped when a rapping on her window broke her out of the stupor. Turning her head, she saw Jake leaning down, looking at her. Relief flooded her. She was safe. For a brief moment she wanted to collapse into his arms like she had before.

"You all right?" he asked.

Was she? No. Hadn't been for quite a while. For so long she'd held herself together and, except for the days and weeks after Michael's death, she'd sucked it up and done what needed to be done when it needed to be done. Tucking everything deep inside, she moved through life by rote. Now, the shattered window had put a crack in her armor and it disturbed her. A lot. But it didn't alter the facts. This was simply another issue she had to face alone. Snagging her purse handle, she pulled the keys from the ignition and opened her door. *Might as well get this over with.* People would still expect them to open on time.

"Thanks for coming so quickly." At least she thought it had been quickly. She didn't want to admit she'd been in a daze since she'd placed the phone call. If he hadn't knocked on her window, she'd still be sitting there staring without seeing anything or anyone. Not good. The vandals might still be inside and she'd be vulnerable if they came out and saw her there. Normally no one was here this early so they might feel safe to prowl around at their leisure.

"I was on my morning rounds so I was only a few blocks over. Stay here while I check this out." He didn't wait for her response and strode to the building. A few feet away, he squatted and studied the area, though it probably wouldn't do him any good since it was mostly gravel. Then he walked on up to the window and peered inside, studied the frame and once again checked under the window. He moved to the door, twisting the knob. It was still locked.

He walked back to where she stood. "Looks like someone threw a large rock, trying to cause as much damage as possible."

"But why?" Why choose her business? She didn't have any enemies she was aware of, and everyone practically worshiped Michael's shrine. This didn't make sense. Gripping her hands tightly together, her heart pounded against her chest. She glanced at the broken window, imagining the destruction inside. When she brought her attention back to Jake, his steady gaze unnerved her even more.

"You'll have to assess whether anything is missing or not."

She nodded and started toward the café...until he took hold of her arm, stopping her, his heated touch burning through her sweater.

"After I've cleared inside. Right now, I need you to stay in your car. If you'll give me the key..."

Of course. What was she thinking? But when she tried to find the correct key on the ring, her hands shook. She gave an exasperated sigh. Dang it! She needed to get control of her emotions.

"Here." Jake gently took the keys from her. Her hand tingled from where his fingers made contact. He paused, gazing deep into her eyes, before heading toward the building.

Melody noted he had his hand on the butt of his gun as he entered. She climbed inside the car as instructed, locking the door as soon as she slid behind the wheel. It took him forever. When he stepped out again, giving her the all clear, she followed him inside.

"It doesn't appear anyone entered the premises. The damage is to the one room." His no-nonsense demeanor helped calm her nerves.

They walked down the hallway and entered her office. Shattered glass lay strewn over a large portion of the area. A cantaloupe size rock had bounced off the old desk her grandfather had given her, leaving a large crack in the wood, and landed against the filing cabinet. Invoices and files she'd been working on littered the floor. The bevy of keepsakes and souvenirs she kept on the desk had also toppled onto the floor. Her fear morphed into anger. How dare someone do this to their dream? She'd worked hard to make a go of the business and this senseless destruction ticked her off.

Then she noticed the shards of a glass figurine Michael had sent her from Italy for their fifth wedding anniversary. It had been a delicately carved ballerina holding a long-stemmed rose high above her head. She had seen a picture of it on a jewelers' website and had fallen in love with the crystal. It had been wildly too expensive but he'd bought it anyway, saying she could have whatever she wanted. That and he wanted to make up for not being with her to celebrate in person.

Melody had kept the figurine at work instead of at home so she could see it any time she wanted throughout the day. The crystal had represented not only their last name, but the beauty of their life together. Its presence reminded her of what they'd had, the good, the purity of their love. White hot anger flashed through her as she rushed to pick it up. How dare someone take that from her? How dare they steal the last vestige of a time when she still had a hopeful future ahead of her? Still mad, she bit back tears while she stooped to collect and cradle the largest pieces.

Through blurred vision, she stared at the broken glass. All the fight went out of her. The destruction of the ballerina somehow seemed symbolic of the destruction of her marriage and Michael's life. There wasn't enough left to put it back together, for either the figurine or the marriage if Michael had lived. All that could be done now was to toss the glass remains in the trash. She didn't think it possible, but her heart cracked a little more.

Jake pulled her to her feet and wrapped his arms around her. Thoughts still on Michael, Melody slowly realized Jake might not be the ideal man for her—her ideal man hadn't been so ideal, either—but there was something special and new and promising about her feelings for the man holding her. The man who was never without a gun, reminding her again of how much Michael loved his firearms, warmed her and chased away the chill that had settled over her. He held her for several minutes. No judging. No running commentary about what she should or shouldn't do or feel. Simply quiet acceptance.

She was grateful beyond words.

Finally, she took a deep breath and stepped away. Her emotions were so raw, so tender, that she couldn't look him in the face, so instead concentrated on the room. "Why do people do stuff like this?"

"For the thrill of it, I suppose. There have been

several other break-ins the last few days. You're lucky nothing was stolen. Others can't say the same."

"I wonder who would do such a thing?" He stood too close, making it hard to think.

He scanned the room before his piercing gaze settled on her. "If I knew for certain who had done it, then we wouldn't be having continued vandalism in town because I'd have them locked up in jail."

Melody didn't doubt it for a minute. "Good point. The town hasn't had many problems in the past, though. I wonder what caused someone to start now."

"No clue. Yet. I'll check on the Freemont kid and his cousin. They went joyriding on their neighbor's tractor last week. Maybe they've decided to start breaking windows."

She set the remains of the figurine on top of the cabinet and reached for the rock, intent on cleaning up the mess.

"Don't touch that." He grasped her arm and pulled her away. "I'll try to get some prints off of it. I doubt it'll turn up anything, or if it does, they probably won't be in the system. Which will leave us at square one. So far, we haven't been able to retrieve any viable evidence at any of the scenes, which makes me doubt it was kids acting out. I'll still have Larson take pictures before anything else is moved, though. If you'll keep the door closed until after he has finished, I'd appreciate it."

"No problem." Looking around her ruined office, she said, "It's so senseless."

"True. This might be one of the out-of-towners here because of the plane crash looking to create more havoc. Or it might be someone who had too much to drink, or even a punk kid who's bored. It's hard to say." He glanced around again then turned to her. "I'd like you to check to make sure nothing else in the restaurant was disturbed. I didn't see anything out of place, but I need to be sure."

"Okay." She led the way out of her office and into the kitchen, then on to the dining room. They hadn't turned on many lights, not wanting to attract undue attention. "Everything looks all right. Guess my office window was an easy target."

Standing in the back hall once more, he met her gaze. Breath caught in her throat while she stood mesmerized, entranced. Recalling his scent as he'd held her against his chest flooded her and heat worked its way up her neck. "Thanks again for making sure everything's all right. I feel better."

"Just doing my job."

Oh. But if that's the case, does that mean you hold other women who have break-ins and calms them like you did me? Do you look at other citizens that way in the course of your job?

What was wrong with her for even thinking maybe there was some little something between them? She needed to get a grip.

Jake headed to the door, but stopped with one hand on the knob and turned back toward her. "Uh, since you helped me find my way the day of the crash, would you consider doing it again? I seem to get lost anytime I get off the main highway, and that isn't good. There have been a few times my GPS took me in the wrong direction so I wanted to learn my way around the old-fashioned way."

She stared in silence. Was he serious? Did he want

her to act as his tour guide?

Several heartbeats passed as he waited before resignation pulled at his features. "Never mind. I know you're busy. I just thought after you got off work and before it got dark..." Suddenly his boots were the most interesting thing in the hallway.

Despite not wanting to like him, Melody did feel sorry for the man. She'd never considered how hard it would be for an outsider to learn all the nooks, crannies and winding roads of the heavily wooded area. Growing up here, it came naturally to her to know the way to everyone's homes. But to him...Her first instinct was to tell him no. Then she reconsidered. The idea of a nice evening showing him all those nooks, crannies and winding roads sounded good. Enjoying the dusk, the cool temperatures, the wildlife and the peace of being out in the country would be relaxing.

"Sure. Why not? When?"

He jerked his head up, surprise flitted in his eyes. When he smiled, it sent little goose bumps down her arms.

"Tonight? There's still a good hour of light left after you close the café."

"Tonight it is." What was wrong with her? She'd be in the police car with the shotgun, plus he'd be wearing the pistol as if he were lost without it. Intending to tell him she couldn't go after all, the words died on her tongue. She could do this. Of course he'd have the shotgun and handgun; he was a cop. After witnessing his skills up close not once but twice, she was glad.

"I'll pick you up at your place." Jake gave her a final nod, then walked out the door.

She followed him and locked it behind him. She'd had enough unwanted surprises for one day. Then she grinned. The good mood she'd had earlier in the morning had returned. She didn't want it to return. At least not because she'd be seeing Jake Bennett again that evening. But there it was. Go figure.

Maybe this wouldn't be such a bad day after all.

****

The back door slammed closed as Roy stomped into the dining room, a deep scowl on his face. "What happened to the window?"

Melody had almost forgotten about it. Almost. "We were vandalized. Someone threw a rock through it."

"Did you call Bennett?"

"Of course. Clay came a little while ago, took pictures and dusted for prints. I think. Anyway, he said I can clean it up whenever I want."

That didn't seem to appease him. "Well? What did he say? Any idea who did it?"

She'd been putting money in the register but laid the cash aside and turned her full attention on Roy...anger rolling off of him in waves. "No. Ja— Sheriff Bennett couldn't find any tracks outside, and the only thing inside was the rock, which he didn't think he could get prints off of. There have been several cases of vandalism around town the last few days. Apparently it was our turn."

He headed down the hall and pushed open the door to the office. After a while, he came back and studied her. "You weren't here when it happened were you?"

"No, thank goodness. If I'd been sitting at my desk, I could've been hurt by flying glass."

"Or killed." Roy's tone was strangled, an odd

expression on his face. Was he thinking about the girl he'd been engaged to before he and Michael joined the Army? She'd died in a car wreck and Roy hadn't quite been the same since.

"I'm okay. It happened sometime during the night, so there wasn't any chance of me being injured."

Roy stood there a little longer before giving a brief nod and heading into the kitchen. A man of few words. That was his way of dealing with issues. He slammed a few doors and drawers shut, working off the head of steam he'd built up. More than likely he'd prefer to hit something—or somebody—but there was work to do. Roy Maddox never shirked his duties.

The backdoor closed again and a breathless Cora rushed into the room. "Oh, Melody. I'm so sorry I'm late. I overslept and got here as soon as I could. I promise I'll set the alarm tonight."

Melody smiled and pointed toward her head. "Yeah, you might want to pull your hair into a ponytail."

Cora's hand flew to her head, and she gave a tiny laugh. "At least I got my teeth brushed before running out the door."

"Don't worry about it. We all have our days." Melody gave her a one-armed hug before going back to work. Cora dug around in her purse for a scrunchy, tidied her hair and pulled on an apron. They were due to open in half an hour and even though Melody had been early, between the rock incident and Cora being so late, they were behind.

Forty-five minutes later the bell above the door dinged. Melody glanced up and met Jake's gaze. Her heart gave a small flutter as she kept her voice at the same tone she used for all her other patrons. "Sheriff."

"Mrs. Rose." Casually he dropped his hat on the peg he'd chosen the first time he'd walked in the café, then took his seat at the counter. "Everything all right here? No more problems?"

Melody caught the glint in his eye, but kept a straight face when she replied. "No problems that I'm aware of. Clay has already come and gone, giving the go-ahead to clean up the crime scene as you call it."

He nodded. "Good to hear I have such an efficient deputy."

Cora had been going back to the kitchen but stopped and gasped. "Did you say, crime scene? Holy cats, what happened here?"

Melody glanced at Jake, who didn't seem inclined to answer. "Someone threw a rock through my office window last night. You didn't see it when you came in?"

Cora's face paled, and her hands shook. "No, I—I had my head down. He—he couldn't have found me already. Please tell me…"

Jake turned and gave her his full attention. "Who couldn't have found you? Do you know something about this?"

"No. Um, maybe. I—I don't know for sure." She took a step back, then braced herself against the counter.

"Who are you talking about, Ms. Conway?" Jake kept his voice low and even, almost soothing.

"Um, my—my ex-boyfriend. He—he swore he'd hunt me down and kill me if I ever tried to leave him."

"Does he know where you are?"

She glanced out the window before she brought her

gaze back to his. "I didn't think so, but…"

"I'm sure it wasn't him. You don't need to be worried." Melody draped an arm around Cora.

Color returned to her face. "Are you sure? Do you think I should take any extra precautions over at the house?"

"Only businesses have been targeted. I'm sure there's no need to worry."

Cora glanced out the front window again. "You mean other places have been broken into?"

"Yes, but like I said, you should be fine." She patted the other woman's arm to calm her. Cora didn't look like she could deal with many more issues in her life. Melody knew the feeling all too well.

Jake furrowed his brows. "You live nearby?"

"Yes. Melody was kind enough to let me rent her house out back."

"You're new in town." It was more of a statement than a question. "So your ex doesn't know where you are?"

She explained her circumstances to him.

"Did you hear anything last night or see anyone hanging around the café after it closed Ms. Conway?" He waited for her response.

"Well, no I didn't." Hands gripped in front of her, she hung her head. "I was depressed and wound up drinking a little too much."

"You were at the Waltz Rite In? What time did you leave?"

She looked horrified. "Oh, no! You meet crazies in bars. I seldom have any alcohol, but when I do, I drink at home."

Jake frowned, studying Cora intently. Then he

seemed to shake himself out of his stupor. "If you think of anything unusual that happened last night, contact either myself or Deputy Larson." He swiveled toward the counter.

Cora glanced at Melody, then turned away when the bell rang again, announcing more customers. Time to get back to business. "So…what can I get you today, Jake?"

"The number two plus some coffee."

"In other words, your usual." Normally it took her months to remember what people ordered…a bad trait for a restaurant owner, she knew. So when had she started paying more attention to this particular customer?

"You got it." The corner of his lip tilted upward, giving him a boyish appearance. The man was sure good looking. Not that she'd admit it out loud. Especially to him.

She pulled a mug from the rack under the counter and glanced out the window, then lowered her head, speaking softly. "Mayor Davidson is on his way in and he doesn't look too happy."

Jake rolled his eyes before he schooled his features into total passiveness. How did he do that? She knew for a fact he disliked the mayor almost as much as the mayor disliked him. *The same way I pretend to be happy all the time.* Everyone had their own thing, their own way of dealing with life's unpleasantness. Being stone faced with the people he disliked appeared to be Jake's way of dealing.

Maybe she should take lessons, because lately her resolve had slipped. Badly.

****

Jake concentrated on his coffee, keeping his head down. It didn't work.

"There you are." The mayor climbed onto the stool next to him as if they had an appointment. At least he kept his voice low. Roy glaring at him through the pass-through to the kitchen might have had something to do with that, though. "I heard about the latest case of vandalism. This makes how many we've had in the past few days?"

Jake didn't bother answering. The mayor knew the numbers as well as he did.

"I'd like to know what you plan to do to keep the people in this town safe. We might be small potatoes to what you're used to, but we still deserve the best."

Grinding his teeth together, Jake counted to ten before opening his mouth. No sense in making things worse. "My department is doing everything it can to not only apprehend the perpetrator, but also gather enough evidence to convict them. And in case you haven't noticed, we've also been assisting the NTSB with the plane crash. No one in my department has gotten much sleep the last few days."

"It isn't enough." Davidson sat there, smiling like he was posing for a picture, but his low voice and menacing tone left nothing to the imagination.

Even though no one in the café paid them any mind, except perhaps Roy, Jake didn't appreciate being ambushed. This discussion should take place either in the mayor's office, or Jake's. Not in the middle of a public establishment.

"Mayor. Frank," he said quietly, knowing there was no way to totally appease the man. "Would you care to tell me how you found out about the latest incident?"

That threw Davidson off guard. "Well, I...I have my sources," he sputtered.

Jake raised his eyebrows in question. He'd thrown the question out there on impulse. So far his suspicions had been on one of the outsiders who'd come to town. But the mayor's reaction made Jake rethink his assumption. It was no secret Frank wanted him gone. What lengths would he go to achieve his goal?

"Where were you between midnight and five a.m. this morning?" He didn't want to embarrass the mayor, but the man shouldn't have chosen such a public forum to go on the attack against Jake and his department. They were doing the best they could with their limited resources, and right now he didn't care who heard them.

Frank's face turned beet red. "Are you accusing me of something?"

Jake took his time answering. He'd often found he could glean more information by remaining quiet and letting the other person try to fill an awkward silence. "At this point, *mayor*, I haven't ruled out anyone as a suspect."

As if to make sure the normal sounds of the café overrode his words, Frank darted his gaze around the room. He lifted his chin and attempted to regain his composure. Jake wanted to tell him he failed on a monumental scale.

"Yes, well. I'm sure you and your staff are doing fine. Carry on." Frank stiffly walked to his normal table, spread out the newspaper he'd had tucked under his arm and appeared engrossed in something on the inside of the page. The good mayor hadn't answered the question of his whereabouts, but Jake decided to let it slide. For the time being.

Without changing his expression, he turned around and took a sip of his coffee as if he hadn't had a very real but low volume heated argument with the town's most prominent citizen. Melody threw him a quick grin before going back to work. He noticed a few people closest to them had stopped talking and had taken in every word. Frank should be grateful there weren't more people in the café. But, knowing small town life, word would hit the streets with the force of a wildfire that Jake had accused the mayor of vandalism. Some would laugh, saying it served the mayor right for being so high and mighty. Others, though, would look down on Jake for even considering such a thing.

This was a no-win situation for everyone involved. For a brief second, he regretted posing the question. But once the thought had formed, he knew he had to ask, even if he hadn't gotten his answer yet. Being the consummate politician, Frank had skillfully evaded the question, but Jake wouldn't let it drop. Later, when they were behind closed doors, he'd get an answer. Who would benefit the most from the break-ins? If Jake were terminated for not doing his job well enough, then the mayor would get what he wanted—a family member as the sheriff. Poor Larson. You couldn't pick and choose your relatives.

As soon as he finished breakfast, he'd head back to the office to see if Larson had found anything connecting the different incidents. None of them appeared the same, so it could be multiple people committing the crimes. It could also be some of the out-of-towners or gawkers. Only, the majority of the people who were legitimately there due to the plane crash had already left. No, his instincts told him it was someone from here. Someone who knew their way around because they were good at hiding their tracks.

And that was what bothered him the most.

Chapter Eight

Jake pulled into Melody's driveway right on time. A pristine yard surrounded the single-story ranch-style house. The first time he'd come here, he'd expected to see flower beds, prepped and ready for the spring bulbs to bloom. Or at least find rose bushes everywhere since her café was named The Tangled Rose. Instead, there were a few evergreen shrubs next to the house but nothing that gave off any color. Despite the lack of flowers, the house and grounds were well kept.

Almost as soon as he knocked, she opened the door. He was struck again by how pretty and delicate she was. Simply looking at her was a joy. She gave him a small smile before she stepped outside, pulling the door closed behind her.

"Hi. Looks like you're ready." He stepped aside, giving her room to pass. Stifling a grin, he admired her butt, which looked so much better in tight denim than the shapeless dress she always wore at the café.

"Yes. I like being punctual." Melody slipped her arms in her jacket without looking at him and headed down the walk. When she looked up, she stopped. "Oh. You're not in the police car."

"No. This isn't official business, so I left the SUV at home. Hope you don't mind the Firebird." He'd washed it that afternoon, not that it needed much other than to rinse off the dust. He'd always been proud of the restored car. It had been in a chop shop when they'd raided the place. After the trial and all the vehicles had been released to the owners, no one had claimed it. Jake couldn't resist the low-slung look or ride. So far, he'd not regretted buying the vehicle.

He held the door for Melody, and she paused briefly before dropping into the bright red leather seat. Red interior, white exterior. Classic.

"This is nice," she said once he'd slid behind the wheel. "It's a standard?"

Jake turned the ignition over, loving the purr of the engine, and backed out of the drive. "Yep. Four on the floor. Wouldn't want it any other way. Can you drive a stick shift?" he asked as he glanced over at her.

She ran her hand over the dash, then a wistful expression came over her face. "My dad taught me to drive one when I was fifteen, but it was a three on the column."

"Yeah? Sounds like a good memory."

She leaned back against the seat before looking at him. "It was his first pickup and he has hung onto it all these years. Whenever I go with him in it, I always remember the times he spent with me out in the fields, patiently teaching me, telling me to slow down, or that I didn't let out on the clutch enough and I wound up killing the engine. He never scolded me, thank goodness. Makes it a lot easier to learn when you aren't stressed."

Jake could appreciate the sentiment. At the stop sign, he sat there, letting the engine idle. "Which way?"

"Hmm? Oh, how about we head north, then work our way around?"

"Sounds good." Shifting into first, he drove up the

street to the highway and took a right. The temperatures were cool enough that he'd left the windows down instead of running the AC and wondered if they should roll them up. One glance toward Melody told him no. The wind whipped her hair, her eyes were closed and a light smile graced her lips. The image punched him in the gut and he wanted nothing more than to kiss her luscious lips. He blinked and forced his attention back to the road before he wrapped the Bird around a tree.

An hour later, he had a better handle on who lived where and how the country roads all connected, one way or the other. Melody had supplied information about each family and who was kin to whom. He wasn't sure he'd remember all the relations or names, but at least he had a clue where to go if he got a call. Of course, Brenda or Glenda would provide him with all the data about the people in the area. Neither sister would admit to being gossipy, they simply knew everything about everybody. Not a bad thing really. Especially when dealing with family disputes or fights. In law enforcement it always paid to have your ear to the ground.

Dust kicked up behind the car as he drove down an unpaved road. He kept his speed down to keep from throwing gravel and dinging the paint job. He glanced over at Melody as they passed a small road that didn't look like it had been used in a long time. She turned her head, watching the road as they passed. "Who lives down there?"

She brought her gaze back to him but wore a wistful expression. "No one."

They were quite a ways out of town and hadn't seen any other traffic in a while. Jake slowed the car and, once it had stopped, put it in reverse.

When he pulled onto the path, he held his breath as the road dipped, then wound its way around one bend after another with hills stretching up on either side. Still-dormant grass and weeds lined the valley but was far enough away from the rutted lane where it wouldn't scratch the car's paint. Blackjack trees and low growing brush were scattered throughout the area. He inched over the rough road, if you could call it that. "I might be sorry I came down here. Maybe there's a place where we can turn around."

She gave a soft snort. "You'll be all right."

Eventually they came to a grassy clearing. With the windows down, he heard running water. She pointed to an area where the grass was flattened and tire treads were visible in the dirt.

"This is good," she said, reaching for the door handle when he stopped.

Once he'd cut the engine the quiet surrounded him. Nothing but the water and a light breeze. Melody was already out of the car, and he followed her toward the creek. The ground gently sloped down to the creek bed, littered with rocks large enough to create the gurgling he'd heard when he first drove into the area. Several larger rocks, small boulders really, were scattered about, both in the creek and on the bank. One on the bank was large enough to sit on, and he suspected Melody had done just that in the past.

Jake wasn't surprised when she perched on the boulder and gazed into the water. He stopped a few feet away. Here, like this, she looked like a different woman. The stress lines that seemed a permanent part of her face were gone. Her copper colored hair floated around her shoulders. A serene expression made her appear younger and carefree.

He'd never seen anyone look more enticing.

Sticking his hands in his back pockets, he stated the obvious. "You've been here before."

Nodding, she glanced around at the secluded area. "I like the solitude."

It was secluded, all right. There weren't many tire tracks, and the ones that were there looked like they were from one car. Hers, no doubt. The trail they'd been following wound through the woods even farther and he wondered if someone lived back there. If they did then there had to be another way in because they sure didn't come down this road. He briefly wondered if they were trespassing, but dismissed the concern. Melody had grown up here so would have made sure it was okay to be on the property.

"If you want quiet, then you've sure found it. Doesn't seem to be anyone around for miles." He crossed his arms and leaned against the boulder beside her.

"I don't think there is."

"So you've never gone farther down the road?"

She glanced behind her before returning her attention to the creek. "I walked it one time, but the road tapers off. There might've been a hunting cabin or an old homestead down there once, but I don't think anyone uses it if there is. The weeds are awfully overgrown. I'm not even sure who owns it."

Jake wandered over to the stream, squatted, and dipped the fingers of one hand into the crystal-clear liquid, then quickly pulled them out.

She laughed at him. "Cold, isn't it?"

"You could've warned me," he said as he wiped the moisture onto his jeans.

"And spoil your fun? Besides, from my experience men like to find out for themselves."

A haunted expression creased her features. Did it have something to do with her husband? If so, had the man been so hardheaded he needed to find out everything for himself, discounting everything she said? He wanted to ask, but it wasn't any of his business. He wiggled his eyebrows. "Yeah, we're kinda wired that way."

She lifted a corner of her mouth, the sad expression gone. "You can't fool me, sheriff. It isn't all that cold. Too late in the year."

"Cold enough. Now if we were in Chicago, it would be freezing." When was the last time he'd even gone out to the lake? He'd been so busy after he'd made detective he hadn't taken much time for recreation. When he was little, the entire family had gone to Lake Michigan all the time during the summer. They'd packed the car to the hilt with stuff Mom insisted they'd need, then still proclaim they had forgotten something once there. He grinned at the memories. His little brother always testing to see how far out in the water he could go before Dad went in after him. Seeing how many hot dogs he could eat before getting sick. Yep. Those were happy times.

"You miss it," she said.

Jake pulled in his thoughts. "It's where I grew up."

She gave him a sly grin as he evaded the question. "Do you still have family there?"

He picked up a flat stone and skipped it down the creek. Once the rock had sunk, he stood and dusted off his hands. Melody had leaned back against the boulder, braced by one arm, and watched him closely. "No. My parents moved to Arizona, and my brother's in California. They all wanted warmer climates."

"But you stayed because you loved the city and wanted to right some of the wrongs you saw." Her steady gaze drilled into him.

His heart did a little tug. He missed the city, not just the job. But he thought he'd hidden his emotions where no one could see, surprised Melody was so perceptive. Could the woman see into his soul?

A few heartbeats passed as she studied him. "If you loved it so much, why did you move to Arkansas?"

He'd been dreading when someone would ask him that question. It didn't feel right to give her the canned reply he'd rehearsed from the day he'd been hired. On the other hand, he wasn't ready to tell her how big of a failure he'd been on his last assignment. He'd let down his guard and an innocent man had paid for it. With his life.

He settled on a compromise of the canned version and the truth.

"I was good at my job but not at politics. Chicago is an extremely political city and that includes the police department."

She nodded her head knowingly. "That's true everywhere. Michael hated that about the army. He just wanted to do his job."

Because he wasn't sure he could keep his face impassive, Jake was tempted to gaze into the water so she wouldn't see the half-truth about to spill from his lips. Instead, he kept his focus on her face. "It became impossible to work for my captain any longer, and he'd made sure my transferring to another district would be equally unpleasant. I figured it was time to look elsewhere."

"Their loss, our gain, because you're an excellent officer. It's a shame you couldn't have gotten that captain removed. Sounds to me like the whole department would be better off without him."

The woman didn't even know the details of the case, yet she took his side. His ego expanded at the praise of his abilities. Yes, the woman was perceptive. Better than some of the people in the Chicago police department.

"Have you ever considered going into law enforcement?"

She choked out a laugh, stood and took a couple steps away. "You're joking."

"Nope." He moved to the spot she had vacated and leaned against the rock. "You're good at seeing things other people overlook."

Blowing out a deep breath, she averted her gaze and played with a loose button on her jacket. "I don't think I'm cut out to be a cop."

He hesitated. Should he mention it or not? Might as well and see where it led. "Because of the gun thing."

With a stunned look, she said, "H-how did you…"

"When I'm in uniform, you're skittish. When I don't have my weapon on, you're different…like tonight. Plus, you told me that day at the Johnson place." The image flashed through his mind and he had to suppress a shudder. If he'd been even a couple minutes later or if his aim had been off a fraction of an inch, she might have died. Another innocent on his watch. He tried to force the scene out of his mind. It didn't work.

"Oh, yeah." Averting her gaze, she watched a crow take flight, cawing as it disappeared into a tree on the other side of the creek.

Silence stretched between them as she withdrew into herself, pulling farther away from him. He wanted to take her hand in his. Shoot. Who was he kidding? He wanted to wrap his arms around her and hold her tight—like he did at the crash site—until her demons disappeared. Instead he settled for draping a wayward strand of hair behind her ear, letting his fingers linger in the silky strands. It wouldn't take much to lean down, to press his lips to the pulse on her neck.

To taste her.

With extreme effort, he refrained. "Want to talk about it?"

She cut him a quick glance, and the look of despair in her eyes tore at him. What had happened to her? He was certain there was more to her issues than just the scene at the crash site, though that would be more than enough for most people. This time he decided to keep his mouth shut. If she wanted to talk, fine. If not, he'd let the matter drop. For now.

****

Melody glanced at Jake, his devastatingly good looks and tousled hair making him appear more boyish than she knew him to be, and contemplated what she'd say. How did the man get under her defenses so easily? He reached out, took her hand, and pulled her to his side. He draped one arm around her and leaned her back against the rock with him, still not saying anything. Warmth spread throughout her body at the casual touch. She thought she'd be more nervous around him, but right now, here in this setting, she felt safe.

She stood quietly. When was the last time anyone had wanted to talk about her and not her hero-husband? Did Jake? Or was he simply being polite? She'd spare him the effort. "I don't want to bore you. Tell me about the big city. I've never been to Chicago."

"I'll take you sometime. Show you Wrigley Field, the Field Museum, Navy Pier, Lake Michigan." He turned and smiled at her. "You'll love the Miracle Mile. You can spend hours shopping for anything you want."

Her heart fluttered at his casual statement. Cora had urged her to take a vacation and had even mentioned Chicago. That sounded appealing, but only if she went with Jake. She almost snorted at the realization. What had gotten into her? Jake was making polite conversation. Nothing more. Although...

It had been a long time since anyone cared about what she had to say besides, "Order up." Or asked what was on her mind. Not since before Michael had joined the army. She and Michael used to talk for hours on end about what they'd wanted to do and had their lives all planned out. When they'd first started dating, he'd truly cared about her desires and ambitions. Over time, though, it had evolved into his dreams and goals, and she'd gone along. Being with him, sharing his hopes had been enough. At least that's what she told herself. *Had it been, though?*

After his death, his dreams had been all that was left; she had buried her childhood aspirations in a hole so deep she didn't think she would ever remember what they had been. Looking back, she regretted losing sight of what she had wanted and letting her life revolve solely around him.

Scooting back up onto the rock, with Jake doing the same, they sat side by side as the breeze fluttered the newly budded tree leaves. He'd let his arm drop and she moved a few inches away from him, still not totally comfortable with his touch. He didn't comment one way or the other and didn't press the issue. Silence and the beauty of the Ozark Mountains surrounded them.

After several peaceful moments, he cast her a sideways glance. "Your turn."

"I beg your pardon?"

"I told you a little about my background. I want to hear yours."

Melody didn't have any intention of telling him about her past. "You wouldn't be interested. I lead a pretty boring life."

"Aw, come on. Indulge me." When she didn't reply, he bumped her shoulder with his. "What's it like growing up in a small town? I've always been surrounded by the city so educate me."

At least he hadn't asked about Michael. "Fine. I'll give you a crash course." He didn't even try to hide the smug grin as he pulled one leg up and wrapped his arms around it. Melody rolled her eyes. The man oozed confidence, and instead of being irritating, she found it relaxing. And sexy.

"First, you should know everyone pretty well knows everyone else...*and* their business. I never got away with anything because some adult always told on me."

"Sounds like the neighborhood where I grew up. Everyone thought they were your parent."

"Yes, well, multiply that by the whole town. It was

frustrating. But, comforting to know others looked out for your well-being. Didn't appreciate it at the time, though."

He nodded, a far-off look on his face, as if he were remembering a particular incident. She let him drift down memory lane without a word. Finally, he brought his attention back to her.

"Sorry. Thinking about playing in the streets or at a friend's house until the streetlights came on. Then it was time to go home."

"At least you had decent streetlights."

"Mostly. But not all the time. Life wasn't perfect. Just different from here."

"There isn't a lot to do in the winter so the whole town turns out for all the sporting events. Doesn't matter if it's football, basketball. Whatever. We're all there to cheer the kids on." She glanced at him. "You'll be expected to be there, too, you know. And not always in an official capacity, either."

"Love sports. Doubt you could keep me away if you tried. Were you on any teams?"

She laughed. "No. I'm not what you'd call athletic. But I did help out with the school plays."

"Oh, so you enjoy being on stage."

"Me? I can't act worth a flip." She gave a half-hearted laugh, thinking of all her failed attempts to read a line and not sound as stilted as a telephone pole.

"Says who?"

This time she snorted. "Everyone! I was terrible so I volunteered to be part of the production crew. I was good at it, too. In fact, during one play my junior year I laid behind the couch on stage during the entire play so I could do scene changes without being seen from the audience."

"You're kidding. You laid back there the entire time?"

She held two fingers in the air. "Scouts honor."

Jake threw back his head and laughed. "You're dedicated. I'll give you that."

"I did what I could. In fact, during that particular play is when Michael first noticed me." She hadn't intended to talk about him, but when no sharp pains followed her announcement, she continued. "He was a year ahead of me and always landed the leading role. One afternoon he asked me to help him learn his lines. Before I knew what had happened, we had become an item and by the end of the year had fallen in love. *Much* to everyone's astonishment, I might add. We got married two months after I graduated."

"He waited for you. Smart man."

Heat crept up her neck at the compliment and she looked away. She forced her accelerated heart rate to slow before she continued. "Anyway, after he enlisted, he didn't want to move me away from my family then wind up leaving me alone on a military base somewhere. He was deployed more than he was stateside. We bought the house on the outskirts of Rock Ledge, expecting to expand it once we started a—a family."

Jake cleared his throat. "Which never happened."

Eyes downcast, she shook her head. Emptiness settled in the pit of her stomach. Their dream home had always been more hers than theirs, and she found that more than sad.

"That's where you live now?"

She nodded.

"Pardon me for asking, but why do you stay there?"

She didn't hear pity in his tone, simply curiosity.

Why *did* she stay? Because it was their home? The only place they'd lived together? Or because she really didn't care one way or the other?

A corner of her mouth quirked up, she blew out a soft breath, and gave the only answer she could come up with, feeble though it might be. "Why not?"

He didn't press her, and she was extremely grateful.

By now the setting sun cast a soft glow over the valley. When she shivered, Jake wrapped an arm around her and pulled her closer. For a time, the only sounds were the water beating against the rocks, the bullfrogs singing their tune and the slow, steady rhythm of their breathing.

Sitting there, in his embrace, felt like the most natural thing in the world. And good. She didn't have to carry the weight of the world on her shoulders, worry about the next day's menu, or face going home alone. Right now, all she had to do was enjoy being with Jake. He squeezed her arm, sending tingles of anticipation throughout her body.

He turned her head toward him, then leaned in close. His warm breath fanned her face before his lips lightly caressed hers. The intensity jolted her. She pulled back, staring into his eyes, desire burning in their depths. The corners of his lips lifted in a grin and she returned the gesture. This time, she made the first move.

He pulled her closer and deepened the kiss. His rapid heartbeat matched her own. The cool evening disappeared as she lost herself in the emotions he evoked. Tingles slid along her skin.

All too soon he broke contact, laying a hand on her cheek. "You're so beautiful."

Her first kiss in years and it had taken her breath away. The deep void in her soul cracked, a ray of sunshine replacing the emptiness. All because of a man she had avoided at all cost when he'd first come to town. Who would've thought it? Certainly not her. By the expression on his face, he was as much in awe as she was. He gave her a quick peck on the nose while he caressed her hair, letting each strand slowly slip through his fingers. He searched her face, as if memorizing each feature, then pressed his lips against hers for another deep kiss. Tasting, devouring. Conquering.

Oh, mercy she could get used to this, to him. This was more than nice, this was heaven. But is that what she wanted or needed right now?

Reluctantly, she pulled back and forced a lighter tone to her voice. It was harder than she'd thought. "You're kinda pretty yourself."

His eyes widened marginally at her change in behavior before he placed a hand over his heart, pretending to be wounded. "Pretty? Hey, that's not something a guy wants to hear."

Laughing, she said, "Oh, I think your ego will survive."

Planting another kiss on her nose, lingering a little longer than needed, he slid off the rock, pulling her with him. "More than likely. Are you about ready to head back? It's getting late and I don't want to be stuck down here after dark."

"Oh, afraid of the dark, are we? And here I thought you were a big, tough guy."

"Oh, I'm still big and tough. Don't ever doubt that. Besides, it depends on who I'm in the dark with." His voice became husky, shooting desire straight to her groin.

"Um, a friend?" she squeaked out.

"Friends with benefits?" He looked serious but had kept his voice light.

With a grin Melody stepped back. "We'd better get going."

Jake let her go. "Yeah, it is getting cooler. That rock sure did lose its heat fast." He rubbed his backside for emphasis before he snaked his arm around her waist and headed for the car.

"You are *such* a city boy." She hadn't teased and joked around with anyone in ages. She'd missed it.

His response was to laugh as he helped her into the Firebird. Melody didn't regret sharing her private refuge with him, only now she'd have entirely different thoughts about that boulder every time she came here in the future. And it warmed her heart.

Chapter Nine

The next morning Melody left her hair down instead of pulling it into a ponytail. Letting it flow around her shoulders, at least for a little while, as she thought of Jake running his fingers through it the night before. Her lips tingled at the memory of his intense kisses and it reminded her that she was still very much alive. The feeling put a bit more zest in her step.

She walked out her front door and stopped. Something was different about her car. Then it registered that it sat at an odd angle. "Don't tell me I have a flat."

But when she reached the passenger side, she discovered she had not one, but two flat tires. What in the world? She must've run over a bed of nails yesterday. It was the only explanation. At any rate, it looked like she would be walking to work. It would be nice if the town had a taxi service...but they didn't.

As she took off down the street, she dug in her purse for her cell phone and started to dial Taggert's Towing, then recalled the time. He wouldn't be there yet, and besides, he'd be busy getting Samantha fed and dressed. The child should've been in preschool by now, but Taggert kept her with him most of the time. Melody couldn't imagine the trauma the little girl had gone through, and understood his being overprotective. She'd call him from the café. Calling Roy and catching a ride on his motorcycle held little appeal, especially while wearing a dress. Straightening her back, she picked up her pace. It had been a while since she'd walked to work, but a little extra exercise never hurt anyone. It was a brisk morning, but not so cool to make it uncomfortable.

The town mostly slept, so she enjoyed the quiet. She still had a warm buzz from last night that even two flat tires couldn't dispel. She hadn't gone far when she heard an engine behind her. Then the vehicle slowed to a stop.

"Melody? What are you doing?" Jake asked through the open window of the SUV.

A glow started low in her belly and spread at seeing him. "Maybe people don't use this activity in Chicago too often, *Sheriff*. Here, it's called walking." She almost giggled at his goofy expression.

"I can see that. Why?"

"I've got a couple flat tires."

With furrowed eyebrows he glanced behind them as if he could see her house from here, all business now. "Two? At the same time?"

She shrugged. "I must have run over some nails on my way home last night. I'll have Taggert come and take care of it for me later today." She glanced at her watch. If she didn't hurry, she'd be late.

"Get in. I'll give you a ride."

Get in the SUV? With the guns? "Um, I can walk. It isn't much farther."

Jake put the vehicle in park and got out. His long strides carried him around the car in no time. He wore his uniform, including his sidearm. Naturally. Despite their time together the previous evening, she still didn't like to be this close to firearms.

"Come on. What kind of gentleman, or sheriff, would I be if I drove away and let you walk? You'd give me a bad reputation." His eyes pleaded with her as the corner of his lip tilted upward in a grin.

Relenting, she nodded but hesitated when he opened the door and she had to face the shotgun again. Taking a fortifying breath, she slid into the seat and sat as rigid as she had the first time she'd been in the vehicle. She wasn't with "Jake" now; she was with the "sheriff." A few minutes later, he pulled into the back lot of the café.

"Why didn't you drop me off out front?"

"Because then I couldn't do this." He leaned across the console as if he were going to kiss her.

Quickly she unsnapped her seat belt, leaning away from him...and that shotgun. She wanted to kiss him again—mercy the man had magic lips!—but those guns loomed larger than life.

"Thanks for the ride. I appreciate it but I need to get to work." She climbed from the car, standing with one hand on the open door, anxious to get away.

"Melody." His low voice, full of emotion, reminded her again of the night before.

"I'm sorry if the weapons make you uncomfortable, but I can't remove them. It's part of the standard issue."

"I know. It's just..."

"I get it." His shoulders drooped. "I'll go finish my rounds and see you in a bit."

She relaxed.

He put the SUV in reverse, then gave her a lopsided grin. "And for the record, I had a *hard* time sleeping last night."

Feigning innocence when they both knew she understood his meaning, she fluttered her eyelashes. "Pity. I had no problems what-so-ever."

He laughed and she closed the door. Waving, she walked to the café as he pulled out of the lot. The sun peaked above the trees and it promised to be a bright, cloudless day. It might be a good day after all. Perhaps the flat tires were heaven sent.

****

"Where's your car?" Cora asked when she walked in the back door, a perplexed expression on her face. "I didn't think you were even here since I didn't see it in the lot."

"Hmm? Oh, I walked." Melody had almost everything ready to open. Funny how a little happiness made your workload easier…and faster.

Cora moved farther into the room, tying on her apron as she went. "Whatever for? Don't you live pretty far out of town?"

"It isn't that far, about half a mile. Besides, I had a flat."

"Why didn't you call me? I'd have picked you up."

"I figured you were getting dressed and wouldn't have time," she lied. In fact, she hadn't even thought of Cora this morning, which was pretty weird since she considered Cora a good friend. Melody didn't want to hurt her feelings so kept the truth to herself.

After a while, with both women busy with the last-minute details before opening, Cora finally spoke up. "I don't blame you for not taking time to change the flat. I've had to do it a ton of times but always wind up greasy and dirty." She paused and her cheeks turned pink. "I'm sorry. I assumed you know how."

"Oh, I know how all right. But it's pretty useless to change one when two of the tires are flat."

"Two? Good grief. Where'd you go yesterday that you wound up with two flats?"

Melody turned her head to keep Cora from seeing her blush. She wanted to keep the events with Jake private, even from Cora. Sharing seemed...wrong, somehow. "I didn't drive anywhere last night"—which was the truth—"so I must have picked up nails on the way home."

"Well, I think you need to take a different route after you get the tires fixed. You don't want to go through this again tomorrow."

"Good idea." She went back to work and Melody soon forgot about their conversation. Right on time, she flipped on the OPEN sign and unlocked the door. Soon thereafter their first customer came in and business picked up.

At seven o'clock, Jake walked in and took his usual spot at the counter. For once, the mayor wasn't there yet and she wondered what kept him. When Jake glanced toward the empty table, she shrugged. "Haven't seen him. Don't worry. He'll be along. Probably about the time you start eating."

"I've got news about your car." He lowered his voice and leaned on the counter so only she could hear.

Surprised, she blinked. "What about it? I haven't had time to call Taggert yet so—"

"It wasn't nails. The tires were slashed."

"W-what? Who would do...?" Dumbfounded, she didn't know what else to say. "Are you sure?"

He nodded. "There's no mistaking the damage."

Melody glanced toward the office, thinking of the rock incident the day before, then back to Jake. "You don't think it's random, do you?"

He gave a slight shake of his head.

She tried to process the information that she might be the target of some deranged person, but for the life of her, couldn't figure out why. She glanced around the café, with more and more people coming in by the minute. Now wasn't the time to discuss it. Taking his order, she eased back into the routine and flow of the restaurant. He sat quietly, not throwing anymore issues at her. Just getting through the day, and keeping her mind on business, was all she wanted to do right now.

His meal finished, Jake stood and dropped some cash next to the register just as Mrs. Riddley, Melody's eighth grade English teacher, let out a loud gasp. Before Melody could check on the elderly customer, Jake moved to her table.

"Is there a problem, ma'am?" he asked.

"It was here a minute ago. I know it was." The older lady looked under her chair then back at him, tears swimming in her eyes.

"What did you lose?"

"My pocketbook. I can't find it." She turned pleading eyes on the sheriff. "How am I going to pay for my meal?"

Melody wanted to tell Jake this happened all the time. The older lady had the beginnings of dementia and everyone looked out for the retired teacher.

Jake made a show of looking under the table and in all the other chairs. "Your purse doesn't seem to be here. Do you want me to search the restaurant for you?"

Mrs. Riddley fluttered her hands, then stiffly

climbed to her feet. "That's sweet of you, young man. Your mother did a fine job of raising you. Were you one of my students? I don't recognize you."

"No, ma'am. I'm new in town but I'm sure I would've learned a lot from you." He took her elbow and guided her toward the door. "Let me take you home."

Mrs. Riddley stopped and pulled back. "But what about my bill? I can't leave poor Melody here in a lurch."

"It's fine. You can pay me next time. I know you're good for it."

"You won't forget to remind me, will you?" The elderly lady wrung her hands, a deep frown marring her forehead.

"No, ma'am. I won't forget." Melody stepped up and gave her former teacher a brief hug. When she pulled back, it warmed her heart to see Jake laying more bills next to the register. Hot kisses aside, there were more layers to the man than she'd originally thought. While he held the door for the teacher, Melody quickly told him where she lived and where to find the key to her house. The entire time they were walking outside the teacher talked nonstop. Knowing Mrs. Riddley, she was telling him how to diagram a sentence.

Melody turned in another order, waved at the three men now leaving who did as Jake had and left cash next to the register. One of the nice things about a small town. Everyone understood about her being short-handed and did their part to make things easier on her.

Except someone, perhaps one of those good citizens, might be the person terrorizing her.

Chapter Ten

Melody declined both Cora's and Roy's offer to drive her to the garage to pick up her car that afternoon. All day long they had watched over her as if she were a child who didn't have enough sense to come in out of the rain. Sheesh. After all, it was only five blocks down Main Street and there were people everywhere. Her independence had been too hard won to give it up so easily and accept she needed a keeper. Besides, the thought of someone doing her harm, for whatever reason, was incomprehensible.

Still, knowing someone had deliberately slashed the tires confused and concerned her. It was true there had been more vandalism in town, but it had mainly been directed toward businesses, including hers. But this was obviously more personal.

Despite the sunny day and a warm breeze, a shiver sent goose bumps down her arms. She pulled her jacket closer. She'd never been afraid for her safety before, just bone-deep lonely. Now, she wondered about her neighbors and friends.

At any rate, she wouldn't blow the threat off as nothing. After spending years alone, she realized she had become lax about her safety. *Time to rectify that issue.* She mentally went through the security at her home as well as the café. Roy had said he'd look into a security system for their business. Maybe she should do the same for the house. And get the window in the front bedroom fixed so it'd lock easier. A couple of sixteen penny nails through the frame should do for a while. The multitude of guns in the other bedroom flashed through her mind as a means of protection, and just as quickly, she dismissed them. No, she would not be picking up a gun. She'd find another way.

Watching her surroundings closely, she picked up her pace so it didn't take her long to walk to the garage. Her car was parked outside, new tires already on. It had cost her more, but she'd had Taggert put all new tires on instead of replacing only the two damaged ones. Not that she ever went very far or put many miles on her car, but she hadn't checked the wear or measured the tread on the old tires since…She took a deep, shuddering breath. Not since well before Michael's death. She swallowed the lump that had formed in her throat, then stepped inside the building.

The door swished closed behind her, shutting out the depressing thoughts. Samantha, Taggert's daughter, sat at a desk behind the counter, concentrating intently on a coloring book, but looked up when Melody approached. "Hi, Samantha. You look like the lady in charge today."

Of course, she didn't speak. Melody knew she wouldn't, but she didn't want to treat the child differently than she would any other five-year-old.

"Did Mrs. Gibson go home already?" Taggert's secretary had a few health issues so left early occasionally.

Samantha tucked her chin as she glanced at the empty desk on the other side of the room, then nodded.

"Well, I'm guessing your daddy is around here

somewhere, but told you to watch the front office and stay out of trouble. Right?"

A shy smile crept across the child's face as she gave another small nod.

"Yeah, I thought so," she teased. "Daddies do that. I bet he'll be back pretty soon, and when he gets here he'll expect you to have your picture all finished and ready to hang on the wall." She leaned on the counter and pointed toward the piece of paper on the desk as she spoke.

This time the little girl giggled, warming Melody's heart. The child didn't interact with others much, and Melody felt privileged she did so with her now. The back door to the shop opened and Taggert walked in, the sheriff right behind him. She straightened. Neither man noticed her at first, but when they did Taggert waved at her, then detoured to his daughter. He patted her head before turning to Melody.

"Looks like you're ready to pick up your car."

Jake glanced toward the front door then looked back at her. "Did Roy give you a ride?"

"No. He offered, but I declined. I do have two good feet, you know."

"That isn't the point." His pinched lips and drawn eyebrows radiated displeasure. "If you're a tar—"

"Hey, Sam. Why don't you go get your other coloring book out of Daddy's office?" Taggert turned to Jake once the little girl was out of earshot. "I'd rather you not have this discussion in front of my daughter."

Jake had the decency to look chagrinned. "Sorry. Wasn't thinking."

She wanted to tell him he was right, that she could be a target of some sick person and that she did need to take more precautions. But the scowl on his face kept her quiet. If there was one thing she detested, it was overbearing men, even if they did wear a badge.

Taggert nodded his acceptance and retrieved her paperwork from the secretary's desk.

"What do I owe you?" She pocketed the keys when he handed them over the counter. Taggert told her the amount and got her checked out.

"Well, since I don't have anything else pressing, I think I'll close up the shop early and take Sam to the park."

Samantha came out of the office in time to hear the word "park" and clapped her hands. Melody wished she could do something to help the child get over her trauma and start talking again. But the little girl would talk when she was ready.

"Thanks again for getting the tires on so fast, Tag. I sure do appreciate it. Bye, Samantha." She waved to the little girl, then turned and walked out the door, bothered that Jake was so ticked at her. Before she reached her car he was there, blocking her way.

"You need to be more cautious. In case you haven't realized it, you're a target. Exposing yourself by walking out in the open is idiotic."

Whirling on him, she jammed one hand on her hip. He was right, and if he hadn't been so condescending, she would have admitted as much. But being called idiotic had common sense and reason slipping right through her brain.

"I've lived here my entire life and walked these streets thousands of times. The worst that has ever happened is a dog chasing me out of his yard, which I shouldn't have been in to begin with. Why are you being so insulting?"

He pulled off his hat, raking his fingers through his hair before slapping the hat back on. "You're in someone's cross-hairs. You walking down the street is an open invitation for something worse than slashed tires happening to you."

It touched her heart he was so concerned about her, although he needed to work on his delivery. At this point, she'd welcome a cold, cut and dried statement as opposed to this heated proclamation. Melody started to lay her hand on his arm, but pulled back, tucking her hand in her jacket pocket instead. The memory of his touch—his caresses—last night flooded her senses.

"Thank you for your concern, but I'll be fine. This was probably kids acting up. I'm sure there's nothing to worry about." She prayed that was true.

He nodded toward her car. "Let me remind you this isn't the first time you've been vandalized."

Rolling her eyes, she faced him square on. "No, but let me remind *you* that I'm not the only one in town who has had problems." She wasn't sure why she was being so obstinate.

Jake stood and stared down at her. The intensity in his gaze captured her, holding her in place. Heat pooled in the pit of her stomach, and her breath quickened. He leaned toward her, as if he were going to kiss her. His gaze dropped to her mouth before coming back up to her eyes, searching.

The warmth of his lips on hers from the night before was still branded on her brain. If he did try to kiss her, would she let him? Here? In the middle of town? The thought snapped her back to her senses, and she straightened, pressing her lips together.

Jake blinked, then took a step back. Disappointment flashed across his face before he schooled his features. "My job is to keep the citizens of this town safe, and that includes you. Please let my office know if you have any more problems."

He didn't give her time to reply. He turned and walked to the side of the building, where she saw his parked SUV. Head swimming, she climbed into her car and, for once, immediately locked the doors. She'd never been afraid before in town or of being alone at home. Things had changed, though, making her feel vulnerable.

She hadn't told Jake, but she was glad he was there…glad he looked out for her.

****

Jake stomped to his SUV, mentally kicking himself with every step. What was the matter with him? Last night he'd held Melody in his arms, and longed to do so again, but this afternoon he'd treated her like she didn't have a brain in her head. Not only was she pretty, there was a quiet strength and self-confidence in the way she handled herself. No, the woman wasn't a fool.

So why was he treating her like one?

Because she wouldn't listen. Years in law enforcement had taught him to not take situations like this lightly. And that's what she was doing. The thought of her being injured, or worse, tore at him. He'd been too gruff with her because of his fear. All it had accomplished was hurt her feelings and make her even more stubborn. He swore under his breath.

He got into his car, but waited until she'd pulled away from the tire shop before starting the engine. When she drove past him, she kept her gaze averted.

She was ticked off, and he didn't blame her. He'd have to find a way to apologize for being so blunt, and yes, acting like an idiot. It dawned on him how he could do that. Smiling, he felt better already. He pulled into the street, going the opposite direction the lovely Mrs. Rose had gone.

Now if his plan would work.

He drove around the business district of town, then cruised down the residential streets. With the town being so small, it hadn't taken him long to learn the habits of the residents, recognizing them by looks if not by name. That would come in time...if he stuck around long enough. Waving and calling to several people as he drove past, he compared Rock Ledge to one of the many neighborhoods in Chicago. Each neighborhood had its own unique personality and ethnicity.

Jake had forgotten how much he'd loved growing up in one of those neighborhoods, playing in the streets, having his friends' parents treat him like one of their own, having a sense of belonging. Whether his parents lived there or not, Chicago was home. He turned onto another street, waving at a little boy playing in his yard, a sense of protectiveness slamming into him when the child recognized him and waved. Then it dawned on him. Within the short time he'd been in Rock Ledge he'd come to have the same feelings of contentment, of belonging, as he had in the old neighborhood.

When had that happened? He'd never expected it, never wanted it. Working here was supposed to be temporary. Nothing more. He wasn't supposed to get attached to anyone; not care whether a little girl ever talked again, not care if a retired teacher found her way home from the store. Not care if a little boy was excited to see him and call out his name. Yet he had.

A sick feeling hit his stomach at the realization.

No. He refused to feel that way. Working here was a steppingstone back to where he belonged—the big city. And constant crime. He loved everything about Chicago and hated that he'd left with a black mark on his name and reputation. His one and only goal was to rebuild his reputation and erase that mark.

He finished his rounds through town and made his way back to his office and the never-ending paperwork.

Glenda glanced up from her computer screen when he walked in the door. "I thought you'd be gone for the day. I left a couple of messages on your desk. And if you're hungry, there's carrot cake in the break room. I make it from scratch with cream cheese icing."

Yep. There were definitely perks to small town living. "With walnuts?"

"Of course."

"How do people keep from gaining weight around you and your fabulous cooking?" he teased.

A light blush warmed her cheeks. "Oh, it's nothing special. Besides, from the looks of you, you don't have to worry about a weight problem. If I were twenty years younger or a cougar…" She wiggled her eyebrows, then let the implied invitation drop.

Now it was his turn to be embarrassed, and he was grateful she didn't pursue the subject. With a wink, she waved him off and went back to work. Resisting the temptation of the cake, Jake went into his office to address the latest round of problems. However, half an hour later, he hadn't made much progress. He kept wondering if Melody had gotten home okay and whether or not she'd let him in her door when he showed up. He checked his watch, then dialed the local pizza joint, placing his order. It might not be Chicago deep pan pizza, but it was close.

He made one other phone call to set up an interview for another full-time deputy, then left. A quick shower, clean clothes, a swing past the pizza place and forty-five minutes later he pulled into Melody's drive.

After the way she'd responded to his advice earlier, Jake wasn't sure how he'd be received. Hoping the idea of not having to cook or eat alone would appeal to her, he rang her doorbell and waited. And waited. Had she gone out with friends, leaving her car here? He should've called beforehand. But then if he had, she might have told him to stay away. After several long moments, he heard movement from the inside. The window curtain next to the door fluttered a couple of seconds before the door opened a crack. With mussed hair, as if she had been taking a nap, Melody glared at him but made no attempt to open the door wider or invite him in. "What do you want?"

Jake had the good sense to look contrite. "To apologize." He stood there, holding the rapidly cooling pizza box.

Melody raised her eyebrows. "Okay. I'm waiting."

Huh? She wanted more? *Of course she does, you idiot.* "Listen, I'm sorry I acted like such a…"

"Horse's rear," she filled in when he didn't immediately supply an adjective.

"Um, yeah. I was worried about you, so my tone came out a little harsh."

"A little?" She crossed her arms over her chest, still standing ramrod straight.

Blowing out a deep breath, he said, "I'm sorry, Melody. Sometimes I get a bit pushy. Guess it comes with my job, but I'm worried about you."

"Yes, I got it. Loud and clear."

Finally, he had gotten through to her. He thought. At least she hadn't slammed the door in his face yet. Instead, she blew out a frustrated breath and turned her back to him. When she walked away, leaving the door open, he took the hint and followed her inside. Locking the door, he found her sitting at the kitchen table.

"So, Sheriff Bennett, is that a peace offering you have in your hands or do you always walk around with scrumptious smelling food?" Her face was deadpan, but her words held no heat.

Jake took his first full breath since he'd stepped on her porch and rung the bell. "Only when I've acted like a horse's rear, as you so politely stated."

"Hey, I call it like I see it." She met his gaze and gave him a lopsided grin.

"Touché. Now where can I set this?" He lifted the pizza box.

"How about the middle of the table? I'll get a couple of plates."

Watching her fluid movements around the kitchen as she set the table took his breath away. Leaning back against the counter, he rested his hands behind him. Partly to brace himself, but mostly to keep from reaching for her. Man, the woman was beautiful. Her hair down, no makeup and wearing those well-worn snug jeans and a light green sweater, she exuded sensuality.

"What do you want to drink? I have soda or water. Or how about a beer?" She licked her lips while she waited for his answer.

"A soda pop sounds good. Thanks."

Tucking her chin, she turned to the refrigerator and retrieved two cans, then placed them on the table. It didn't take long before they were seated and diving into the, thankfully, still warm pie.

While they ate, he took in her home. He'd been sleep deprived the other time he'd been here, and now did a more thorough perusal. He'd expected to see a multitude of frilly things scattered about, like doilies, lace curtains or pictures of flowers on the walls. Instead, the pictures were scenic shots of what looked like Arkansas, the brown leather furniture sturdy, warm earth tones of oranges and yellow throw pillows and the curtains a light green color that complimented the room. A patchwork quilt lay draped over the back of the sofa, adding a splash of bright colors. The entire room invited a person to make themselves at home. A total 180 from his place with the still unpacked boxes scattered everywhere. Maybe he should rectify that.

Jake wondered at her choice of décor. Or had it been her husband's choice and she couldn't bring herself to change any of it? Some people were like that, they hung onto the past. He could appreciate it since he hadn't given up hope of being able to return to his old position. Someday he'd like to be in charge of the department, kinda like he was here, only with a lot more people reporting to him. Calling him boss. He'd miss the people here when he left, none more so than the lovely woman across from him quietly scarfing down the pizza he'd brought.

"I don't know why, but I thought you'd be a delicate or finicky eater." A bit of cheese had stuck to her chin so he reached over and scooped it off with his finger, lingering a little longer than necessary. He appreciated the fact she didn't flinch when he touched her.

"Um, thanks." She swiped at her chin, removing the last remnants of the cheese, then met his gaze. "Why would you think I'm picky about my food?"

He shrugged. "I don't know. Maybe because your name is Rose and you named your café after a rose."

"What does my name have to do with the way I eat?"

"It makes me think you're delicate."

"Did you miss the part about 'tangled' in the name?" Her cheeks turned pink as she ducked her head. "This is great pizza. Did you get it from Fred's?"

He realized there was more to the name of her restaurant than he'd thought. And more to her, too. However, she apparently didn't want to talk about it so he let her change the subject. "Yeah. Being single, it didn't take me long to find the closest pizza joint in town. I'm glad there actually is one since the town's so small."

"You and me both." She took another bite.

Jake picked a piece of pepperoni off his pie. He figured if he ate too fast, she'd throw him out that much sooner.

After she finished off another piece, Melody leaned back in her chair, studying him. "You've been here a few weeks now. What do you think of Rock Ledge as opposed to Chicago?"

"There isn't much of a comparison. Sports, theatre, museums, the lake. So far I haven't seen anything in Arkansas that comes close to what the city offers."

Her face fell and he realized he'd summarily insulted not just the state, but Melody as well. "Although, I have to say Arkansas has its own unique attractions. I love the winding roads and the hills. The weather is a lot warmer, too. The cold in Chicago cuts right through you regardless of how many layers you have on."

He paused, watching as her face relaxed, losing some of the pinched expression. Grinning, he braced his forearms on the table, leaning closer to her.

"The people are friendlier and willing to accept me despite the fact I'm a born and bred Yankee."

This time she laughed.

A quiet settled over them as they finished the last of the pie. Jake had expected the evening to be awkward, but instead it had been good to sit with a pretty lady and enjoy a quiet dinner. He downed his remaining soda as she closed up the empty box.

"I should get going." But he didn't push his chair back. He wanted to make sure they were on solid ground again, especially after their rocky start when he'd first come to town. "I want to apologize again for being such a jerk this afternoon. Your safety was my main concern."

Melody worried her lower lip before meeting his gaze. "I have to be honest. You managed to spook me, and that's not easily done."

"I'm sorry."

"But you're right. I do need to be more aware and careful. There are still several strangers floating around town. Any one of them could be responsible."

"Or it could be a local using the extra activities as a smoke screen to get to you."

"You're sure this is personal? Especially since other businesses have been hit."

No, he wasn't. "It's a gut feeling, and I don't ignore those."

"No, I don't suppose you would."

Neither spoke for several minutes, only this time it had become uncomfortable. The longer they sat there, the more he thought of the kiss they'd shared the night before. And the more he thought of that, the more he wanted to do it again. Sitting here in her kitchen—in her home—made him want to kick off his boots and spend the rest of the evening with her in his arms. Before he did something stupid, he shoved back his chair and stood.

"Well, uh, I need to check in with Larson to make sure everything is quiet."

Nodding, she also stood. "Thank you for the pizza."

"No problem. Maybe you could show me some more of the countryside tomorrow. I know you aren't open on Sundays so that can't be an excuse."

Melody studied him skeptically. "That probably isn't a good idea."

"Why not?" He hadn't intended to ask her out when he'd come over, but now that the thought was in his head, he wanted more than anything to spend additional time with her. He leaned toward her, crowding her space. To her credit, she didn't back away. Jake watched the battle warring within her, and saw when she gave in.

"All right. I'll pack a picnic lunch. How does ten o'clock sound?"

Resisting the urge to take her in his arms, he leaned

Linda Trout

down, gave her a peck on the cheek, then headed to the front door. "Sounds good. See you in the morning."

With that, he walked out, pausing long enough to make sure she locked the door behind him. Once in his car, he reassessed his impulsive invite. Earlier in the day he'd reminded himself this job was temporary. He didn't intend to stay. Never had. According to Glenda, Melody had been through a lot with her husband and he didn't want to hurt her. And the more time they spent together, the more attached to him she'd become. And vice versa. He needed to throw a deadbolt on his heart because the very adorable Mrs. Rose was coming to mean more to him than he'd intended.

And it scared him to death.

Chapter Eleven

A picnic lunch? What had Melody been thinking when she'd agreed to go running around the countryside with Jake today? She'd opened her mouth to say no last night, and the next thing she knew, she'd offered to bring food. She shouldn't have let the man in the door to begin with. When someone had knocked, she'd thought it might have been Randi and was too stunned when she'd seen him standing there all sexy as sin to tell him to go away. After all, she was still mad at him. Wasn't she?

Even knowing she should have turned down his invitation, she couldn't deny she looked forward to spending time with him. It would be a nice change of pace for her, getting out of her cooped up world, yet showing it off to him at the same time. She wasn't sure why he had asked her, though. Up until a few days ago, she'd barely spoken to him except to take his order. Now here she stood, packing them a picnic lunch.

Whatever his reasons, it would be interesting to find out what made him tick. Besides his love of guns, vintage cars, and everything Chicago, was there something about her that intrigued him enough to ask her out? The thought caused little ripples of anticipation along her skin, but she shook off the sensation. No sense in reading more into this morning's outing than necessary. This was an opportunity for him to learn more about Rock Ledge and the surrounding area. That was all.

Placing the submarine sandwiches she'd gotten from the deli into the cold container, she slid it in next to the bag of chips in the old basket she'd dug out of the back closet the night before. She might own and run a café, but a cook she wasn't. She left that to Roy. Now planning a menu? That she could do. And for whatever reason, she'd chosen to feed the sheriff exactly what he'd probably be eating at home. Except for the chocolate cake. From the looks of him, she doubted the man ever indulged in sweets. She had wanted something so decadent, so sweet, he couldn't resist.

What else wouldn't the man resist? Her mind slid back to the sheriff himself. Her? Or was *she* the one who'd do the resisting? Except for the outing a couple of nights ago, it had been so long since she'd been out with a man, she had forgotten how to act. Mostly. Oh, she and Roy had hung out some, and she'd gone to the VFW and pizza parlor. But Roy was like her brother, and the other had been with groups. No one special. Not like today. Again, she shook off the implications.

Taking inventory of the basket's contents, she sat back and took a breath. With the addition of the quilt her grandmother had made for her when she was a child, she was ready. Her gaze slid to the quilt, now resting on the back of the couch, and remembered some of the fabric from her childhood dresses her grandmother had incorporated into what Melody classified as a work of art. If not art, then definitely a work of love. Melody didn't think the thing would ever wear out. With an army blanket as the backing and heavy corduroy blocks as the top, the blanket would hold together for decades to come. Her grandmother sure knew how to make them to stand up to wear and tear.

The last time Melody had used the quilt had been during Michael's leave, the one before he'd gotten off active duty. They'd spread it under a Blackjack tree at the 4th of July celebration at the park. Her insides warmed. That had been a good day. The twinkle in his eyes, his laugher as if he didn't have a care in the world, his warm arms wrapped around her. While waiting for the fireworks display to begin, they had made plans for the grand opening of the café.

Sadness overtook her. It had been a long time since she'd had any happy memories of her life with Michael. She'd shoved them to the far recesses of her mind. Yet here she was, getting ready to go on a date—date?— with another man, and warm fuzzy thoughts of Michael popped into her head. He had been a good man. Even though he'd been gone a lot, when he'd been home on leave, it had been magical. He had loved her. She knew that. It was only after he'd gotten off active duty that she'd realized their marriage was in trouble.

Melancholy tugged at her heart and a deep longing for what they'd had clogged her throat. Why couldn't their dreams have come true? Why did his life have to end so abruptly? And with a gun, no less? The one thing he loved above all else besides her and his family. She heaved a heavy breath. There was no way to turn back the clock and undo what was done.

Swallowing the lump in her throat, she refocused on the present. And Jake. Were they really dating? It hadn't felt that way last night when he'd asked for her help. He'd been all business. So why had she taken extra care when she'd dressed this morning? Not only had she applied makeup, but had spent extra time on her hair and even dabbed on a bit of perfume. She should've worn her old jeans and a flannel shirt. She would've been more comfortable.

The doorbell chimed. Glancing at the clock, she realized she'd been daydreaming for quite a while. When she swung the door open, she found Cora on the other side.

"Hi," Cora said with a cheerful lilt. "I hope I didn't catch you in the middle of anything, but it's too pretty of a day to stay at home. Want to go with me to Harrison? I found a thrift store where I can do a little shopping, plus there's a great new movie at a dollar theatre near there. I hate going alone so thought…"

Melody sighed. If it had been any other time, she would've taken Cora up on the offer. "Sounds like a lot of fun. I haven't been to the movies in years, but—"

"Great. Grab your purse and let's go." Cora looked eager and stepped back, beckoning her to follow.

Melody pulled a face. "I wish I could, but—"

"What's stopping you? You said the other night you hardly ever go anywhere. I thought this would be a good time for you to spread your wings and start flying a little. Come on."

She hesitated, not wanting to hurt her friend. "You're so thoughtful. Any other time I'd be glad to go."

Cora stilled as her hopeful expression faded. "But not today."

Melody stepped outside and touched Cora's arm. "No. Sorry. I…"

At the rumble of Jake's car as it came around the

corner, Cora turned. When she faced Melody again her entire demeanor had changed to concern. "Oh, no. Don't tell me something else has happened."

It took Melody a second to realize what Cora thought. "No, no. Nothing like that. I told Jake I'd help him learn his way around the area is all."

"Well, thank goodness there hasn't been any more vandalism. But I didn't realize you and the sheriff were seeing each other."

Heat flooded her cheeks. "We aren't. It isn't…"

Cora laughed and touched her shoulder. "Don't worry about it. We can do our thing some other time. You two have fun."

"Thanks, Cora." Before she could say more, the other woman quickly strode to her car and had closed her door as Jake pulled in beside her. She waved at Melody, then backed out and drove away. She felt bad that Cora had gone to the effort of planning a day out only to be turned down. She didn't have any other friends in town and had to be lonely. Regret stabbed at Melody as Jake came up the walk.

"Was that your waitress?" He narrowed his eyes and looked at her with suspicion. "Don't tell me she brought the food."

She shook her head, appalled. "No, of course not! I'd never ask her to do that. No, she dropped by on impulse to see if I wanted to go to a movie in Harrison."

"You could've gone."

"I know, but I'd already made plans with you. Cora and I will go another time. It's no big deal."

"You sure?"

"Yes. She's fine with it."

145

He looked down the street and watched as Cora's car went through the intersection and moved out of sight. "In that case, you ready?"

"Let me get my things." She turned back into the house, and he followed.

"What can I carry?"

About to lift the basket off the table, she dropped her hands to her side. "You carry this and I'll get the quilt."

Wide-eyed, he stared a moment before moving. "Huh. I thought you were kidding when you said we'd have a picnic. You sure it isn't too cool for you?"

Melody pulled on her jacket, retrieved the quilt and her purse, then waited by the door. "If we find the right spot, in the sun and out of the wind, we'll be fine. But thank you for asking."

The warmth emitting from his eyes sent a smoldering heat from the pit of her stomach throughout her body. Looked like she'd be the one doing all the resisting, *if* she chose to. Right now, she wasn't sure what she felt, or what to expect. She prayed her cheeks hadn't turned a bright pink. "Lead the way."

Jake helped her into the car, took the blanket from her, placing it and the basket in the backseat, then slid behind the wheel and started the Firebird. She loved the sound of the vintage car. He slowly drove out of town, following her directions. For once, Melody wished for a nice long straight-of-way so he could blow the cobwebs out of the engine. She'd love to roll the windows down and let the wind whip her hair, but didn't. Jake was right, it was a bit cool this morning. But by mid-afternoon, it might be a different story.

For some reason, being in this particular car gave

her a sense of freedom she hadn't felt in a long time. Memories from her past started to creep in, of her first date with Michael, of being with the most popular boy in school and how that had made her the center of attention of her classmates. Like being here now made her the center of attention as people turned and watched as they drove by. Glancing at Jake, she made a decision to push those memories away, and chose Jake over Michael and the past. Right now she just wanted to have a pleasant day.

"So, what do you want to see, Sheriff Bennett?"

He glanced over at her, probably ready to correct her—again—on how he wanted her to address him. After seeing her smile, he chuckled.

"I'd like to go back over where we went the other day to refresh my memory, plus see any roads we haven't already been down." His serious tone reminded her the outing wasn't for pleasure. He paused, then added, "Also, you told me there was a back way to get to the creek where we went before. I'd *really* like to find that road."

Renewed warmth spread throughout her body. "Oh?" What did he have in mind?

"We have to eat someplace and that sounds as good as any, don't you think?" He winked before turning his attention back to the road.

For the next hour or so they drove the county roads again, most of them gravel. Melody was sure Jake had to have been lost, or at least, turned around, but no. When they came up to one of the section line roads, he knew where they were.

"I go left here, and it takes me to the highway and back into town, correct?"

"Very impressive."

He grinned and turned right. "So, this is your back way to the creek."

"No keeping any secrets from you, is there?"

"Hey, I made CPD detective early for a reason."

Jake drove for several minutes, then slowed and pulled down the incline to the creek. The grass was a bit greener than it had been a few days ago. Spring would be here before she knew it, reminding her time marched onward while she'd been sitting and doing nothing. Glancing at her companion, she had to amend her thought. She *had* begun to take steps to move forward with her life. Finally. All it had taken was a plane crash, a crazed escapee and a couple acts of vandalism for her to see the man behind the badge. If he had a gun with him now, which she assumed he did, at least he'd hidden it so it wasn't in plain view. She didn't care.

Focusing on the surroundings and what she'd packed for their lunch, she wished she'd put more effort into the food. Granted, he hadn't given her much notice. Still, she could've at least *cooked* something besides the cake. Too late now, though.

Jake pulled the car to a stop in much the same spot he had the last time they'd been there. He came around the car and opened her door, taking her hand as he helped her out. An electrical current shot up her arm at his touch while she stood mesmerized by his gaze. Her pulse rate soared when his gaze lowered to her mouth. The fragrance of his aftershave wafted in the air. Would he kiss her? Did she want him to? Yes. No. Her emotions bounced all over the place and, reluctantly, she stepped away.

The corners of his lips tilted downward for an

instant, then, instead of getting the blanket and basket from the back, he nodded his head farther down the valley. "Want to go for a walk before we eat? I'd like to stretch my legs a bit."

"Is that the only reason?" She grinned up at him.

"Uh, no. I'd like to see what's around the bend." He met her gaze squarely, without a hint of anything other than curiosity.

She fell into step beside him. "Like I said before, more than likely there's an old homestead down there." He gave her a quizzical glance and she shrugged.

Walking side by side in companionable silence, they picked their way through the dormant weeds and grass. She halfway expected him to take her hand, but he didn't. He appeared to be scanning the area, probably in cop mode. Then again, he could be taking in the landscape of the Ozark Mountains.

Some of the grass was thigh-high but most was knee-deep or shorter, making their trek easier. She'd walked the path a long time ago. However, they'd now gone farther than she had before. Of course, it had been summer and she hadn't wanted to stumble across a rattlesnake. Glancing down at his right boot, she noticed a bulge near the top. Just as she'd thought, he had a gun on him. If a snake did happen to be out sunning itself, at least Jake could take care of it if need be.

Going around another bend, they found what she'd expected. The weathered house leaned to one side and had numerous broken windowpanes. The porch roof had caved in on one side, and she'd bet the local wildlife had made itself at home in the rundown structure. To the rear stood a barn that looked as bad as the house, and it appeared to still have a few bales of moldy hay stored inside.

Hands stuffed in his back pockets, Jake stopped and studied the farmstead. She tried to see it through his eyes. Would he think the place an eyesore, needing to be razed, making room for a new building? Or would he see what she did? A place where a family once lived with children playing out front, helping the parents with the farming and gardening and everyday chores. Where love and happiness was their reward for the hard work and sacrifice needed to eke out an existence.

He took a deep breath. "Sad, isn't it?"

She turned to study him, not expecting his assessment. "You don't think it's ugly?"

Tilting his head, he shifted his focus to her. "No. The place just hasn't been maintained—for quite a few years, by the looks of it. Want to go inside?"

"No way." She took a step back.

"Oh, come on. Where's your sense of adventure?" He grinned, the dimple in his cheek charming her.

She had to teach the city boy a lesson. "You do realize the place is probably home to a den of rattlers, don't you? Not to mention rats and who knows what else."

Glancing from her to the house and back, he shrugged. "I guess you're right. Maybe we should head back. I'm famished. Hope you brought one of the café's specialties."

Uh-oh. She swallowed, then forced a light tone to her voice. "I seriously doubt you'd care what I brought as long as you got fed."

He chuckled. "You got it. If I don't have to cook, I'm happy."

Which made her feel even worse.

They walked in silence for a ways before he spoke up. "Care to give me more information on small town life?"

"You go first. I did most of the talking last time." She wanted to know more about his past, about him.

He blew out a breath. "Okay. Chicago has always been my home. I attended public school with thousands of other kids, went to ballgames at Wrigley Field with my dad and brother, swam in Lake Michigan and took my dates to the Navy Pier. I attended Loyola for a few semesters, but never finished. I was a good kid, and never got into much trouble."

She shot him a skeptical look. "Oh? I find that hard to believe."

He scrunched up his mouth, then said, "Let me put it this way. I never got caught much."

"Ah-ha. So you weren't an angel?"

"Hardly." He snorted.

She thought about his admission, then a few things fell into place. "That's why you were such a good detective. You had a fairly good idea how the bad guys thought, what they might do next. Where they liked to hide out."

Jake shot her an appreciative look. "Not bad."

"So you're admitting it."

"I admit to outthinking them, nothing more."

"If you say so." She had to laugh at his incredulous look. "Don't worry sheriff. I promise I won't tell on you."

He relaxed. "You know, you're pretty sharp."

"Don't look so surprised. I haven't lived with my head totally in the sand all my life."

"Didn't say you had. Figured you'd be able to give me the lay of the land around here. So far, you haven't disappointed." He bumped her shoulder with his as they continued to walk.

She liked the casual banter between them. She and Roy had done the same thing, but this was oh, so different.

"Your turn."

"To what?" She knew what he wanted, but wasn't sure her small town life would stack up against the big city. Except she was proud of her hometown. Growing up here had given her roots, a moral compass, a sense of belonging. She didn't know what he'd come away with from his childhood, but hers had been happy, even if she had been shy and introverted.

"We have our moments. In the summer there was always a group of kids swimming in one of the creeks, guys worked in the hayfields, the girls babysat to earn money. There's Vacation Bible School at all the different churches, and we have a pretty good library. In the fall we'd have hayrides and weenie roasts, the kids run free in town during Halloween because everyone looked out for them, and at Christmas people from different churches went caroling.

"Once, my friend's dad was severely burned in an accident, and all the surrounding farmers left their own fields to go put up this man's crops so the family would have money to live on. That's what we do here."

"Sounds like a wonderful childhood. And admirable of how everyone looks out for one another."

"It wasn't all sunshine and roses, though. It can be hard to make a living in a small town. When I was younger, I thought I wanted to get away. Lots of my friends did leave as soon as we got out of high school and didn't look back."

He continued walking—more like strolling—and she fell into step beside him. "But you stayed because of your husband."

"Yes. Plus, my family and the business." Right now, she was extremely grateful she'd stayed. If she hadn't, she wouldn't have met the intriguing man beside her. "The timing has never been right for me to go anywhere."

They'd reached the car, and he retrieved the basket and blanket, letting the subject slip.

"Where do you want to sit?"

She thought about spreading the blanket next to the big boulder, but it reminded her of their kiss. "Let's go over to the clearing where there's a bed of grass to sit on. There's enough sun to keep us warm and we'll still be out of the wind."

When they found the perfect spot, she spread the quilt, grateful for the thickness to protect against any small stones that might be underneath. Jake set the basket in the middle of it, then took up a big portion of the space when he stretched out next to the basket. When she pulled out the sandwiches and chips, he didn't comment on the fare. "Sorry but I didn't have time to cook anything." It looked like such a pitiful amount of food. She should have at least brought an extra sandwich for him. Thank goodness she had cake.

"Not a problem. This is a bachelor's main food group, you know."

He winked and she wondered if he meant it, or if he was only being polite. Either way she was grateful he hadn't made a big deal out of her lack of planning.

She made a mental note to give him extra portions the next few times he came into the café.

****

Jake unwrapped the submarine sandwich. He knew exactly where she'd gotten it because he'd eaten the same thing a couple of days ago. But he didn't mind another one, as long as he got to share it with Melody. "Thanks. I love these."

"Seriously?"

"Seriously." He scooped a handful of chips out of the bag onto a large paper napkin, then popped a chip into his mouth. "I really do."

She took a small bite of her own sandwich. After she chewed and swallowed, she met his gaze. "I could've fixed something a little nicer, but this was much easier. Sorry."

"Not a problem. These are good sandwiches, and I can always eat a sandwich." Which was true.

She looked at him skeptically. "I'm not sure I believe you, but at least I brought dessert. I hope you like cake."

"Hmm. Don't know if I'll have room left"—she swatted him on the arm for his comment—"but depending on the kind, I think I'll be able to handle a small piece."

Melody squinted her eyes before the corners of her lips lifted upward. The entire valley lit up when she smiled like that. He wanted to reach over and kiss her with every fiber of his being. Instead, he took another bite. Sunlight bounced off her hair, giving it a coppery halo. Good sense told him to back off, to not get too involved with her, but he could sure get used to this…to her.

After a lengthy silence, that had become a little too uncomfortable, he watched Melody staring off toward the creek with a forlorn expression, her half-eaten sandwich still in her hands. He'd seen that look a few times in the diner when she didn't think anyone noticed.

He hated that look.

Finishing off his food, he balled up the wrapping paper and leaned back on his elbow, facing her, intent on making her feel better. "Okay, Miss Suzy Homemaker. What kind of cake?"

The sadness left her eyes as she studied him. She wrapped up the last of her food and tucked it in the basket. "I thought you said you wouldn't have room for dessert."

Jake glanced down at his out-stretched legs, not wanting to tell her how much it took to fill him up. "Yeah. Like one sub would stop me from eating cake."

"Oh. So, you have a sweet tooth, do you? I've never noticed."

She quirked her mouth, making him think of all kinds of other "sweets" he'd like to devour, and none of them could be found in the basket she'd brought. He didn't want to rush things, though. Granted, he'd kissed her when they'd been here before, but he wasn't sure how she'd react now if he leaned over and repeated the performance.

"You have no idea." Before he acted on his impulse to pull her to him, he reached for the picnic basket to see what else she had stashed inside. "Well, look here. There really is cake."

"I'll get it," she said as she gently smacked his hand and pulled out a square cake pan. Next came heavy duty paper plates plus real silverware.

She opened the container and his mouth started watering. "German Chocolate? You brought German Chocolate cake?"

About to cut a piece, she looked up at him. "Yes. I hope it's all right. It's my favorite."

"You're putting me on. Did you call Matt or something?" His old partner was one of the few people outside of his family who knew of his weakness for this particular dessert.

"Who's Matt?" She frowned.

He tried to not drool. "Never mind. This is my all-time favorite cake in the world."

She scoffed. "You're just saying that."

"No, I'm not. Now, if you want of any this, you'd better get it quick because I leave no prisoners—or leftovers—where German Chocolate cake is concerned."

Holding the knife in midair, she looked at him like he'd lost his mind. Maybe he had, but he hadn't had this in a while and knew he could eat the whole thing by himself. Granted, he'd make himself sick, but eat it he would.

Finally, she lowered the knife and cut off a good size piece—but not big enough. Except she kept the piece for herself then handed him the knife, surprising him.

"Will you want any more than that?" He pointed at her plate.

She laughed. "The rest is yours if you want it."

"That's what I wanted to hear." Not bothering to cut a piece, he picked up the fork and dug in, stuffing a large portion into his mouth. He'd died and gone to heaven. "It tastes too good to be store bought. You made it from scratch."

She still hadn't eaten any, and laughed at him. "You look like a little boy on Christmas morning who'd gotten everything on his wish list."

"Umm." It wasn't polite to talk with your mouth full.

"It's my great-grandmother's recipe that has been passed down through the generations."

He raised his fork in a salute. "My compliments to your ancestors for preserving the recipe."

She laughed again, then began eating her own piece.

He shoved another forkful into his mouth but chewed more slowly, savoring every morsel. When he had eaten about half of the cake, he decided to quit before he did make himself sick. "You know, I think I'll save some of this for later."

"I thought you were hungry. Looks to me like you're wimping out," she teased, wiggling her eyebrows.

Oh, man. Nothing like waving a red flag in front of a bull. And she didn't even know it. Or did she?

Placing the half empty cake pan back in the basket, he stretched out on the quilt. She finished cleaning up the remainder of the food but didn't lie down. A tiny smile tickled her lips. The woman was a goddess and Jake desperately wanted her in his arms.

Chapter Twelve

Jake's heart rate kicked up a notch as Melody drew her legs up and rested her chin on her knees. She didn't look at him, but stared toward the stream. Quiet settled around them, peaceful and comfortable. When the breeze blew his way, he caught a whiff of her soft floral fragrance. He rolled onto his side and propped his head in his hand. She looked so serene. Her facial features were relaxed, the normal tension in her shoulders gone.

Finally, she looked at him. "We can leave if you're ready."

"Why? Do you have someplace you need to be?" He wasn't ready for the day to end.

Turning her attention back to the creek, she shrugged. "No. I thought you'd…"

Melody sneaked a glance toward him, then the nearby rock, the one where they'd kissed. She turned her gaze back to him, studying him. Unable to resist any longer, he sat up and scooted close enough that only a breath separated them. Lowering his head, he brushed his lips across hers. They tasted as sweet as he remembered with a hint of the German Chocolate cake added on top.

She moaned softly, and he teased her lip with his tongue. When she opened her mouth, he slid inside, deepening the kiss. He lay back against the quilt, drawing her down with him. When was the last time he'd made out with a girl on a quilt, back when they were both young and carefree and the whole world was open to them? When they broke apart, he gazed into her eyes, getting lost in their depths. She had the most amazing eyes, desire radiating off her.

Melody placed a hand against his chest, putting a little distance between them. Had he imagined her desire? If he was the first man she'd dated since her husband died, perhaps he had moved too fast for her. He sat up, taking her with him.

Silence stretched between them as he searched for a topic they hadn't already discussed. He wasn't quite sure how to broach the subject, but decided the more direct, the better. "Why do you hate guns so much? Is it because your husband was in the military?"

She blanched and looked away. How many tours had the man served? Jake had never thought sending the same people back into combat time and time again was a good idea. The number of people suffering either physically, psychologically or a combination of both staggered the brain.

She gave a caustic laugh. "No. That's the ironic part. After serving six years, he'd gotten out of the army and come home. Our plan was to open the café. But he was consumed with helping others, especially vets suffering from PTSD."

His insides twisted. He had a bad feeling where this was headed.

"That last day was so dreary. Sort of like the day of the plane crash. Damp, foggy. We were going to celebrate after signing the loan papers for the café, but he wanted to stop at the gun range first to check on a man he'd been counseling. Even in bad weather, this guy was always there. Being around guns gave him comfort. Anyway, the guy had seen a lot of combat and hadn't handled it well."

"Sounds like Michael did okay, though."

She snorted softly. "That's the weird thing. Even though he'd seen more than his share of atrocities, once he came home, he left it all behind. I have no idea how he was able to compartmentalize everything, but he did."

Jake couldn't stop her from talking, but he gave her hand an extra squeeze for support during the telling. He knew from experience it didn't help to bury things inside. They festered and grew darker. Eventually, the darkness overtook you.

"The man's posture, the expression on his face, gave me the willies. I can't pinpoint what it was, just that something didn't feel right. His wife came up to me and almost collapsed in relief when she saw Michael talking to him. Have to tell you, that didn't make me feel any better, either. I asked Michael to leave, told him I was hungry. But he didn't listen."

She took a deep breath, her gaze unfocused as her story unfolded.

"They started arguing, with the guy getting louder and louder. His wife whimpered and said, 'Oh, no, no. Don't do it, baby, don't do it,' over and over." She turned and looked at Jake, her face ashen. "She knew. The woman knew what was about to happen and just stood there wringing her hands. Why would she do that? Why would she let him go out there with a gun and not warn anyone? Why would she let *Michael* go out there, unarmed, and face him? Why didn't she tell us? Did she think my husband was bulletproof?"

She gazed back at the creek. "Several other people were there practicing, but they stopped to watch this crazy man. A couple picked up their gear and left. I didn't blame them. He waved his gun in the air, pacing and shouting obscenities at Michael, but Michael kept trying to talk to him, to get through the rage. Nothing worked. Finally, the gun range owner headed in their direction, saying they needed to leave. Told the other man he wasn't welcome there anymore.

"That's when things got really bad. He pointed his gun at the owner, told him to back off, which he did. The wife cried out his name—John, I think she said—but he pointed the gun at her and asked if she wanted it, too."

Jake cursed under his breath.

"Michael put himself between the two, probably sure he would be able to calm him down. But that isn't what happened. The man looked him in the eye, then pulled the trigger," she choked out. "His wife screamed, but I—I couldn't move at first."

He cursed, then wrapped his arm around her, tugging her close. "You saw the whole thing."

"The weird thing is, as soon as he fired, he looked as stunned as Michael must have. He glanced up at his wife, regret written on his face, then he turned and ran into the woods, leaving Michael on the ground. He didn't even check to see if he was alive or dead. I rushed to Michael's side, but he was already gone."

He swore again. "I'm sorry you had to go through that. What happened to the other man? Did they catch him?"

She shook her head. "Shortly after he disappeared from sight, I heard another shot. He killed himself."

"Shot the wrong person first," he muttered. Tears streamed down her cheeks, and Jake drew her head down to his shoulder.

"I didn't even get to tell him bye. The last person he saw was his murderer. Wh—why wasn't it my face he saw before he died? Wh—why coul—couldn't he have told me he loved me?"

Leaning into him, she cried. Big, ugly, racking sobs as she clutched the front of his shirt. He gently rocked her, stroking her hair. He'd give anything to take away her pain, to take away the grief. The only thing he could do was lend his support while she dealt with the emotions assaulting her.

Eventually the sobs slacked off, but he gave her several more minutes to compose herself. "That's why you don't like guns."

She nodded her head against his chest.

He rubbed her back. "Can't say as I blame you. Hell, I'd hate guns too if I were in your shoes."

"No, you wouldn't," she mumbled.

"Are you calling me a liar, Mrs. Rose?" He chuckled and was rewarded with an answering vibration from her. At least he'd lightened the mood a little. They sat there for several long moments. It felt good to have her in his arms again, even if she was crying, but his back ached from being in an awkward position for so long and he shifted away from her. Mascara streaked her face, so he reached into his hip pocket and pulled out a handkerchief, handing it to her. She put a little space between them, wiped her face and blew her nose. He grinned to himself at how loud it was. At least she was comfortable enough with him to not worry about niceties.

"And that's why there's a shrine in the café."

She stiffened, and he wished he hadn't mentioned it. She'd done enough soul searching for one day. "Never mind. It isn't any of my business."

She didn't reply. Time passed, the only sound the babbling of the creek nearby and an occasional chirp of a bird.

"The whole thing pretty much happened on its own. More or less." She pulled her knees up again and rested her chin on them. She sighed. "After Michael was killed, I wanted to keep him close for a while so I put up a picture of him. Before I knew it, little mementoes started to appear. First it was a bullet—like I'd ever welcome that—but then someone put up the flag. One day some ribbons and a Purple Heart appeared."

Ah. Now he understood. "You keep the shrine not because it means something special to you, but because of the townspeople. Except you don't want it there."

She shot him a sharp glance. "No, I don't. But people keep adding to it all the time."

"And you don't want to hurt their feelings."

She inhaled a deep shuddering breath. "Seeing it every day…It—it keeps the wound open."

He couldn't imagine having the reminder thrown in her face every single day that her husband was gone. At some point she had to let go and start living again.

"I assume you've thought about taking it down."

She shook her head. "I told you before. Michael is—was—the town hero and favorite son. Having the shrine there makes them feel better, makes them feel closer to him."

"So you leave the shrine, enduring the pain. At the

same time, you're thinking about how they'll react and whether or not they'll be hurt if you take it down. But have you thought about how they really feel?"

She sat up straighter. "It's fairly obvious, hence the added items."

"You're missing the big picture. They leave the shrine there because they think *you* want and need it. Not the other way around."

She stood and walked to the edge of the creek. He followed, but stopped several feet away.

Turning back toward him, she held his gaze with steely determination. "You've been here just a few weeks, Jake. Do you think you know the people better than I do?"

How could he make her understand without hurting her feelings? "No, but I've got eyes, Melody. The people here love and respect you. They think by adding items to the shrine that's it paying a tribute to not only your husband, but to you. If they knew how much pain it caused you, they'd take it down in a heartbeat."

Jake felt sorry for her. She had no idea how much she meant to the town. Suddenly he envied her life. Granted, he'd been good at his last job. But other than his old partner and a few other people, no one had missed him when he'd left Chicago. In fact, there were quite a few who were glad to see him go because he was such a stickler for rules. Melody didn't know she sat on a gold mine.

And until now, he hadn't realized what she had was what he wanted.

She stared at him as if he'd lost his mind, slowly shaking her head the entire time. Eyes narrowed, she pointed a finger at him, self-doubt ringing in her voice.

"I don't believe you. You don't know what you're talking about, Jake Bennett. The shrine is for them, has always been for them."

Her eyes glistened with fresh, unshed tears. She blew out an aggravated breath and wrapped her arms around her waist...as if that would provide a shield between the two of them.

He shook his head. "I don't see it."

Shoulders slumped; she went back to the blanket, yanked it up and started folding it.

Jake couldn't stand it. He moved next to her and placed his hand over hers, stilling her jerky motions. Taking the blanket, he dropped it next to the basket.

"You don't have to hold it inside all the time, you know. Not with me. Not here. This is your sanctuary, Melody...your safe place. You can say and do whatever you want and it stays right here."

Her chin trembled as she searched his face for the truth of his words. When she accepted what he'd offered, she nodded once then walked back to the edge of the stream. If she'd gone any farther, her boots would've gotten wet. Jake didn't think she'd care. He allowed her the space she obviously needed. After several minutes he walked over to the large rock, the one where he'd kissed her before, and leaned on it.

She finally turned and gave him a wobbly smile. "Thank you."

"I didn't do anything special. I just didn't want our discussion to put a damper on what this place means to you." He held out his arms, and she joined him on the rock. At least he hadn't driven her away by his prying.

****

A dark cloud passed overhead, sending a shiver

down Melody's back.

"Hey, pretty lady." Jake kissed her cheek. She turned to see him grinning, at what she didn't have a clue. "Next time we have a picnic, mind if I bring the food?"

She blinked. *Next time?* He wanted to see her again? After she'd blubbered all over him and smeared mascara on the front of his nice, clean shirt? And practically called him a liar?

"I have it on good authority the cook at The Tangled Rose Café makes a great quiche, that I never got to finish, by the way, and I'm willing to bet he can also whip up some fried chicken, coleslaw, hot rolls and anything else I can think of." He winked, then grinned bigger.

She lost herself in the depths of his eyes, enjoying his sense of humor. An impulse to run her fingers through his hair flashed through her mind before she reined it in.

"Actually, when he decides to barbeque, he makes a mean pulled pork."

"Like in Texas barbeque?"

"Nooo. Like in down home Arkansas barbeque. Texas doesn't have a market on it, you know."

Jake rubbed his chin. "Hmm. I'm told those Texans know how to barbeque, so it'll take some convincing. I suppose I could give it a try."

"Oh, really? So you think Roy's isn't as good? I'd like to see you tell *him* that. Not sure you're quite that dumb, though." Was the man deliberately baiting her or teasing?

"Should I be afraid of him? He isn't that big."

"He was an army ranger and served alongside

Michael. He's tougher than he looks."

"Ah. Good to know. Of course, I liked him the minute he told the mayor to shut up."

She laughed, catching on to his sense of humor. "Yeah. The look on Frank's face was priceless. He knows not to mess with Roy."

Without warning, Jake leaned in and kissed her. The touch of his soft lips drove every other thought from her mind and she welcomed his familiar warmth. He didn't ask anything of her, simply gave. It was freeing, allowing her to enjoy the sensations rippling through her body.

When he broke contact, he cupped the side of her face in the palm of his hand, making her feel cherished. His eyes were dark with desire she knew was reflected in her own. "Woman, you take my breath away."

Her heart gave an extra thump. She needed to be careful around this man. Getting too involved would be so easy if she didn't watch herself. Better to keep things light. "Oh, that's the mountain air. You'll get used to it."

His brows creased before he said, "I'm willing to bet the country girl could teach the city boy a few things. After all, I need to know how to take care of myself here." He wiggled his eyebrows for emphasis and she laughed again.

"Another time. It looks like a front is rolling in so we'll probably be getting rain before too long. I don't think we want to be stuck down here once it gets wet. Not sure your car could make it up the incline and to the road."

"Oh, the car, like its owner, has a lot of power under the hood."

Melody swatted his arm and laughed at the double innuendo. "Come on. It's starting to cool off and my jacket isn't heavy enough."

He stood and offered his hand. She loved the fact that even though he'd always lived in the city, his hands still had calluses on them. Not like a farmer or anyone who made their living with their hands, but not baby soft, either. Once they collected the blanket and basket and were back at the car, he opened her door. Instead of letting her get in, he leaned in for another kiss, pressing her against the side of the vehicle. There was no doubt, with his body pressed against hers, he didn't want the day to end, that he'd like to take this to the next level. And she was on the verge of letting him.

All too soon, he pulled back, ran his thumb down her cheek and across her lips.

"You are so beautiful," he whispered as he studied her face. Blowing out a breath, he helped her into the car.

As she settled against the seat, Melody felt a contentment she hadn't had in a long time. And it was all due to the sweet talking, hard as nails, handsome as sin sheriff.

****

I'm going to be sick. It was pathetically easy to figure out you'd come here, but watching this little tête-a-tête unfold is disgusting. A couple of quick shots while you're sucking each other's lungs out. That's all it'll take to end my game. But why spoil the fun? I have so many more tricks to play before the grand finale.

Thank you, Jake for exposing your weakness. I suspected as much, but now I know for sure. Too bad for you. I never would've thought mousey Melody could capture your attention. Although, thinking back, you've always been a sucker for the stupid underdogs. It will be interesting to see how much she'll endure before she cracks and how far you'll go to rescue her. Then, and only then, will you learn who's in control.

An idea occurred to me as they drove away. This is where it began for them, and this is where it'll end. The final confrontation is always the sweetest, and this will be doubly so. Yes, the setting is perfect, plus, Bennett's blind when he's around her. I laughed so loud birds took flight. Fool.

He'll pay.

With her life.

Chapter Thirteen

Strange. A couple of weeks ago, Melody would have called anyone crazy if they'd told her she'd be dating a man who wore a gun. She sucked in a breath. Dating? Were they? They'd only gone out a couple of times, and that was on unofficial official business. Those kisses didn't feel like business, though. She touched a finger to her lips, recalling how Jake had held her; how the look in his eyes told her he wanted to take it farther. But he hadn't. When the time was right, and she was ready, she had no doubt they would make love.

While at the creek Sunday, she had shared her deepest, darkest secret with him and he hadn't run for the hills. Not yet, anyway. The thought of becoming involved with him hadn't sent *her* running for the hills, either. Major surprise. She couldn't help the joy surging through her. Looking in the mirror, she was surprised to see her cheeks were rosier. She was falling for the dark-haired devil who was the town's new sheriff.

And she liked the feeling.

She took a steaming cup of coffee out to her back porch and sat in the chaise lounge, then tucked her feet underneath her. The sun peeked over the horizon as she sipped the warm liquid. She loved living on the edge of town. With no houses behind hers, she had a clear view of the pasture next to her property. Mist rose from the pond down the hill. She wished she painted, or was a half-way decent photographer. She'd love to capture the image. Instead, she'd simply enjoy the view.

She took another sip of her coffee, pulling her afghan closer. Why was she holding back, though? The prospect of having sex again sent pinpricks of anticipation over her body, arousing her. What would it be like? She'd only slept with one man in her life so wasn't quite sure what to expect. Would she be able to relax? Was she good enough? Would he still want to talk to her the next morning?

Could she make love to another man and not think of Michael?

An image of the shrine in the café immediately came to mind. Hunching forward, she gripped the mug between her hands. That stupid shrine. She snorted. Jake was right about why she had left it there, for allowing the townspeople to keep adding to it. Yes, it was time to take it down. Time to let Michael go and move on with her life.

But first, she needed to tell Michael, to visit his grave. She tried to visualize the exact location in the cemetery, but nothing came to mind. When *was* the last time she'd gone out there? The day of the funeral? She racked her brain. Surely she'd gone on Memorial Day. Or Veteran's Day. Or at least on their anniversary.

No. She'd been in such a shell she'd avoided visiting his final resting place.

Ashamed of her selfish behavior, she hoped no one would be there this early and see her driving around, searching for a grave she should know the location of by heart. Standing, she downed the last of the hot liquid and went inside, determined to do this before she went to work.

****

Melody slowed to take the turn into the Citizens' Cemetery. Luckily, it was located down a tree-lined road on the outskirts of town. No one would see her unless they were coming to the cemetery. She had wanted to keep Michael close to home, so had buried him here instead of at the national cemetery in Fayetteville. Ironic, she thought. She'd wanted him close, but had never gone to the grave.

It took her ten minutes to find the spot. Like a lot of the plots, a wreath of artificial flowers sat on his grave. Who had brought them? His parents had left town within months of his death, unable to live here any longer because everywhere they turned they saw memories of their dead son. They said it hurt them too much. Perhaps they paid someone to keep flowers there. Or perhaps it was her parents. Heat flooded her cheeks. If so, then they knew she hadn't come out here, yet they never said anything.

Guilt ridden, she climbed from the car and made her way across the dew damp grass. The headstone was much the same as others, gray granite. The one difference was the inscription. *He gave his all, yet left the best of him behind.* What did it mean? More importantly, who had ordered it? She hadn't been able to do anything for so long after his death, leaving details for others to handle. She hadn't cared who or what, as long as she didn't have to deal with the minute issues. It embarrassed her that, for two long years, this stone had been here, and she hadn't known.

Worse, she hadn't cared.

Squatting, she gingerly touched the stone, studying the dates, reliving the final day of his life. Tears leaked from the corners of her eyes. "I don't understand why you did it. Why you were so insistent on counseling those men. Most of them didn't know how to go on living, yet you're the one who died."

Hot anger bubbled to the surface. She'd wanted their love for each other to be the foremost thing in his life. When he was with her, she'd felt like a queen. But too often he'd postponed their plans to go help a fellow vet, leaving her at home. Alone. And that was the way she'd remained.

Until Jake Bennett came along.

"I'm still mad at you, Michael," she said to the stone. "You kept leaving until one day it became permanent. I know you didn't plan it that way, I know you didn't want it, but it happened just the same."

She sucked in some air. "I've sat and waited all this time. For what, I don't know. All I know is you left me. Just like when you were in the army, you left. Only this time you can't come back. I'm not sure I can ever forgive you for not loving me more than them. For not ensuring your own safety. I feel as if you cheated on me as surely as if you were with another woman."

Hanging her head, she fisted her hand and slowly started beating the headstone...to beat Michael. Tears continued to stream down her cheeks. "Why, Michael? Why wasn't I enough for you?"

She wasn't sure how long she stayed there like that, beating on the cold stone, so when a sharp pain in her hand penetrated her brain, she realized she'd bruised her hand and tucked it against her body. Wiping her nose, she took another deep breath. "I'm done, Michael. I've walked around for two years pretending to live. But you and I both know I haven't been. Well, no more. I'm moving on. I'm leaving you behind with your war buddies, where I think you really wanted to be, and I'm getting on with my life. I hate you for leaving me, but I'll always love you. I've tried to stop, but I can't. At least I can stop living in the past."

She stood, the muscles in her legs cramped for squatting so long, and took a step back, still staring at his grave. "I'm sorry I've never visited you before, and I can't guarantee I'll come again. But I needed to say my piece."

She hesitated, as if he would reprimand her or lightning would strike. When nothing happened, she ended her conversation. "So. There it is."

Lifting her chin, she swiped at her eyes with the back of her uninjured hand and walked to her car. She sat there for several minutes as her eyes dried, and she blew her nose. Once she had herself under control, she started the car.

Why hadn't she done this before? Michael's grave had always been here. All she needed to do was come talk to him. Now, it was as if a burden had been lifted from her shoulders. Not all of it—some would always be there—but at least it wasn't as oppressive as before. When she drove out of the cemetery, her thoughts turned to Jake, and she smiled.

Time to start living again.

****

Melody pulled into the back parking lot of The Tangled Rose, confused to see Cora standing there, staring at the building, as if she were in a trance. Melody parked the car, then ran to her friend.

"What's wrong? Are you okay?" She clutched Cora's arm.

Tears swimming in her eyes, Cora pointed a shaky finger at the café.

Melody had been so focused on Cora, she hadn't noticed anything else. She finally looked up. Huge red letters had been painted on the building.

LIARS BURN IN H

A cold chill swept down her back. It had been a few days since anything had happened and she'd become lax. All the little incidents hadn't bothered her, had never swayed her much from feeling safe. But this? This was personal, and it scared her spitless. Like Cora, she stood and stared until the rumble of a motorcycle caught her attention. Roy. Unlike her, it didn't take him long to assess the situation, and as soon as he stopped, he pulled his cell phone out of his pocket.

"Get the sheriff down to The Tangled Rose back lot. Now." Without looking at them, he said, "Go inside."

Neither woman moved.

Melody's newfound freedom from Michael's ghost deflated. Before she could say or do anything, Jake's car came skidding into the lot. He was out the door almost before the car had stopped moving.

"What…?" He glanced up, scowled, then stormed over to Roy. "Did you see who did this?"

"No. Just got here. Don't know who found it first." He inclined his head toward the women.

Roy remained where he was while Jake searched the ground around the building, then studied the blood red paint, touching it with his finger. The paint was still wet. The two men exchanged looks, then Jake came toward them. When he looked at her, the hardness in his eyes softened before he went back into "cop" mode.

"Who found this?"

"I—I did."

Jake focused all his attention on Cora, making her squirm. "How long has it been since you discovered the graffiti?"

Wide-eyed, she licked her lips and took a deep breath. "I saw it right before Melody arrived. At first, I didn't notice anything, but when I looked up…"

"What did you do then?"

She glanced toward Melody, then back at Jake. "Nothing. I just stood here. Like I said, I saw it right before she got here."

He narrowed his eyes. "Did you see anyone hanging around or hear anything?"

Cora shook her head.

Melody could envision the wheels in Jake's mind turning. She'd seen it enough times to recognize it.

"You must have scared them off when you came out your door. It looks like they were going to write something else." Jake looked from the rental house, with a few bushes in the small front yard partially blocking the view, to the café and back.

Cora followed his gaze, then shivered.

"Why don't you ladies go inside?"

Grateful to not have to look at the wall anymore, she retrieved her purse and keys from her car, then escorted Cora to the café. As they walked inside, Melody looked back at Jake, who now wore a frown. Or was it a puzzled look? She couldn't tell. Maybe it was frustration that these things kept happening and he couldn't solve them. She didn't want to let on how scared she was.

Roy stayed to talk to Jake, so Melody closed the

door and headed to her office, Cora close behind. With the window still boarded up, the room was dark. She couldn't wait until the glass was repaired. She stuffed her purse into the desk drawer and looked up.

Cora stood in the doorway, nervously twisting the handle of her purse. "Are you sure I'll be all right? If someone's out to get you, then they might decide to attack me to get to you."

That thought had never crossed her mind. "I doubt they'd care about you. After all, you're just my waitress—"

"Who happens to live in *your* house right next door!" Panic made her eyes wild.

Melody rubbed her temple. A headache formed when it dawned on her what she'd said. "Oh, Cora, I'm sorry. I didn't mean to sound so insensitive. You know you're more to me than that, don't you?"

Her chin trembled, and it looked as if she might cry.

Shoot. The last thing she'd wanted was to hurt her friend's feelings. "Don't you see? Whoever is doing this is trying to scare you off, leaving me shorthanded and in a bind."

"But those words on the wall…"

"Yeah. I know. They're trying to scare me. And honestly, it's working."

Cora's eyes got even bigger. "So you're scared, too?"

She didn't want to tell Cora how terrified she was. Just when she thought her world had righted itself, it seemed as if someone wanted to ruin what little happiness she'd gained over the last couple of weeks. It wasn't fair. She'd thought she could start living again, but now she was being pulled back into a shell.

A shiver ran down her back and she had to force saliva to swallow. To hide her trembling hands, she leaned against the desk for support. "Actually, I'm terrified."

"But you don't look it."

She wanted to laugh. "Looks can be deceiving. Besides, I don't want to give the person who's doing this the satisfaction of knowing they've knocked me to my knees. This time it seems pretty personal, and for the life of me, I can't imagine who it is or why they're doing it. I just want them to go away." She slumped into her chair and rested her head in her hands until she heard the back door open and close, men's voices drifting down the hall. Cora looked out, then moved deeper into the office.

"There you are. You okay?" Jake's rich voice soothed her nerves as he stepped into the room.

"Yes, I'm fine," Cora responded before Melody had a chance to say anything. More tears swam in the woman's eyes.

Jake nodded his head toward her. "Glad to know you aren't too traumatized. Let my office know if you need anything."

Cora tucked her chin, scooted around Jake, and walked into the hallway, headed toward the front. Roy followed her without a word.

Jake stepped around the desk and pulled Melody into his arms, holding her close. Her frantic heartbeat slowed with the steady rhythm of his heart. Inhaling deeply, she relished his scent, his cologne. From the time she'd made her peace with Michael, she'd wanted to be in Jake's arms. She hadn't anticipated how soon that would be, though.

His hold tightened marginally before he set her at arm's length. "You shouldn't—"

"Don't you dare tell me to not go anywhere by myself. Someone is trying to frighten me—"

"Doing a good job of it, too."

Lowering her gaze, she had to nod. "True. I can't pretend this didn't get my attention more than anything else. They're only trying to scare me, right? You don't think they'll hurt me, do you?"

He squinted. "I don't know, but I'm not going to take any chances. I'm putting you under surveillance."

Her temper flared. "Is that what you two were talking about out there? I can take care of myself." Even with her bluster, she was frustrated this situation was beyond her control or capabilities. She'd been on her own for so long, it was hard to accept she couldn't handle this by herself, and it had her running scared almost to the point of being irrational.

"It isn't like that. We—"

"Stop. Just stop. I don't want to hear anymore. Changing my lifestyle gives them power and I refuse to be manipulated by them."

Jake looked like he was about to protest, but she didn't give him time. Pushing around him—and past her own fears and self-doubt—she headed to the door. "I have work to do, Sheriff. I'm sure you do, too, so if you'll excuse me. Oh, and if you find out who did this, let me know. The not-so meek and mild Melody will make them wish they'd never picked on me."

****

Jake watched Melody walk down the hall into the main part of the café. He admired her spunk and sass,

179

but couldn't help worrying about her. The perpetrator had gotten more personal with his activities. When that happened, the ending was never good. If they carried through with the implied threat on the wall…

Wearing a white apron, Roy came out of the kitchen. "Will she follow your advice?"

"Not a chance."

"Didn't think so. She's nothing if not stubborn. I'll keep an eye on her, getting here early, staying late. I'll even follow her home at night."

"She'll know you're doing it. No way to miss the sound of your bike."

"Don't care."

"She won't like it."

"Again, don't care." An iron resolve reflected in the man's eyes.

"She could fire you over this, you know."

Roy grinned. "Doubt it. I'm her business partner. Besides, she can't cook worth a damn. She needs me."

Jake clapped him on the shoulder. "Good. Keep me posted if anything suspicious happens."

"You got it." He turned and headed back to the kitchen.

Jake went outside, taking pictures of the writing on the wall and the ground underneath. Why had Melody and The Tangled Rose been targeted? Nothing made sense. The crimes were similar to others in town over the last couple of weeks. Except this had a different vibe and feel.

He went back to his office to compare notes of all the other acts, to see if anything jumped out at him that he'd previously overlooked. An hour later, he rubbed his eyes. He hadn't found anything except petty acts of vandalism and theft. So why was Melody's case different? His gut told him there was more than met the eye here. But had he allowed his libido to cloud his judgment where she was concerned?

Before he could delve into his thoughts further, his phone buzzed.

"Sheriff, the mayor is on line one requesting to speak to you as soon as possible. Says it's urgent," Glenda stated matter-of-factly.

Great. Just what he needed. "Put him through." He knew his dispatchers didn't particularly care for the mayor, either. How the man kept getting elected, he didn't know. Wait. Like Chicago, politics was politics and money talked. Why couldn't Jake simply do his job, and not have to play all the petty games some people got off on?

He punched the button on the phone. "Mr. Mayor. What can I do for you this morning?"

"You can catch the vandals who used the side of my barn for graffiti, is what. I thought you would've had those thugs locked up by now, not letting them run loose in my town! I swear, if you—"

"Don't touch anything. I'll be right there." He hung up before the other man could say anything else. His thoughts instantly went to The Tangled Rose. Were they the same? If not, then he had two perpetrators to chase down. It sure seemed like a big coincidence to have two graffiti vandals on the same morning. Yeah, like he believed they weren't related.

If they were the same, then what was the connection between Melody and Davidson? Anger flared at what they'd written on her wall. Did someone also have a bone to pick with the contrary mayor?

Couldn't blame them if they did. He was the most exasperating man in town. Heaving a deep sigh, Jake stood and dropped his hat on his head. The day wasn't getting any better.

A few minutes later, Jake pulled into the mayor's driveway. The man stood on his porch, arms crossed, glaring. Like it was Jake's fault the vandals had hit his place. Jake wasn't in the mood for a tongue lashing, so when he got out of the SUV, he slammed the door and stomped up to the house.

"This better be worth my time," he all but growled. Two could play this game. Time to let the mayor know Jake Bennett wasn't the push-over the man thought he was.

Frank reared back, and shock registered on his face. He quickly regained his composure. "Now watch your mouth."

"Care to show me the damage?" Jake set his feet and glared right back at the mayor, who stuttered and stammered before clamping his lips closed, and left the porch. Jake followed him to the other side of the barn. He stopped short when he saw the spray-painted wall.

LIAR LIAR PANTS ON FIRE

"What are you doing about this?" Frank demanded. "The next thing you know they'll be painting graffiti on the side of the courthouse." Jake barely registered the complaint; the painted words glaring in the early morning sun taunted him, teased him with his inability to find the culprit. The putrid greenish/yellow color and the shape of the letters were different from what had been on The Tangled Rose, as if the person writing it was deliberately trying to make it look different. But the fact both used the word liar and the reference to fire had him more than concerned, especially since both had happened on the same day.

He tore his gaze away from the barn and focused on Frank, who had turned his head away. Was that a smirk on his face? Suspicion crawled up Jake's spine. If this was some stupid game the mayor was playing…

"When was the last time you were back here?"

Facing Jake, Frank screwed up his face like a child who always got his way, annoyed anyone would question him. He puffed up before answering. "It's been a few days."

"So, this could have been here for a while and you wouldn't have known. What made you come back here this morning?"

"I know what's going on at my place. I'm not an idiot!" When Jake remained quiet, still leveling a steady gaze at him, the mayor continued, albeit in a more conciliatory tone. "I heard something during the night, and thought it was a wild animal."

"You didn't get up to check?"

He huffed. "It was the middle of the night. You can't see much in the dark. Besides, it'd be gone by the time I got out here."

"So this morning you decided to see if it really was an animal that made the racket."

Frank narrowed his eyes at his implication. "That's what I said, isn't it?"

Jake didn't respond. Instead, he stepped over to the barn and touched the paint with one finger. Still a little tacky, but not as wet as the paint on the café. It also hadn't been the middle of the night when it had happened like Frank had stated. Interesting.

Another thought occurred to him. Whoever had

written this would've had time to get from here into town and paint The Tangled Rose before anyone arrived at work. That included the mayor. Right now, he wouldn't put anything past the man who was determined to regain his position of power in the community and make Jake look bad.

He took pictures of the barn, plus the ground below the graffiti. Who knew? He might get lucky and find some physical evidence this time. He stifled a sigh. Then again, maybe not. Like all the other times, there were no discernible traces of evidence to be found. The guy was good. A few minutes later, he packed up and headed back to town, the mayor having grumbled the entire time.

By the end of the day, he wasn't any closer to having an answer than when the vandalism started. And it irritated the hell out of him.

Chapter Fourteen

The day had lasted forever. A few more minutes and she could leave. She simply wanted to go home, prop up her feet, have a nice quiet evening and try to forget the horrible graffiti on the café's wall.

"Ready to go?" Roy asked when he stepped in her path as she headed toward the door.

Let's see: apron off, purse in hand, lights out. What do *you* think? she wanted to bark at him. Biting back the retort, she said, "Yes, I am. Goodnight."

Outside, Cora gave her a quick squeeze and an encouraging smile. "Be safe. If you need anything, call me."

Why were they treating her like her entire world had ended because of some stupid graffiti written on the wall, even though it still sent chills down her spine? At least Roy hadn't said anything to her. Yet. His grim expression told her it was only a matter of time, though. But not if she made her escape quickly enough. With a wave, she climbed into her car, started the engine, and pulled out of the lot. A relaxing bath and a good book were just the things she needed. Maybe then she'd be able to forget the entire day.

About halfway home she glanced in her rearview mirror and saw Roy on his Harley a block behind her. She must be out of it because she hadn't even heard the loud engine. Determined to be more observant in the future, she pulled over and waited for him catch up. When he was alongside her, she rolled down her window.

"What are you doing?"

He didn't even blink. "Following you."

"Why?" she demanded. Having him watching her like a hawk at work was one thing. This was entirely different.

Wearing his black leather jacket, Roy sat astride the rumbling bike. His hard expression gave the image of a man she didn't want to cross.

"You're like my family, Mel, and family takes care of family. I want to make sure you get home okay."

She glared at him. He glared back. Several seconds ticked off. Finally, she blew out a frustrated breath. "Fine. Be that way. I can't stop you from driving down the street, anyway."

Roy's hard expression melted into a wicked grin. "That's right."

Then he winked, the rat. How did he always manage to get his way around her so easily? She hoped one day a woman would come along who would twist him in so many knots he'd never get straightened out again. It would serve him right for being so overbearing with her. Shifting into Drive, she spun out, wishing she were on a gravel road so she could throw dirt on him for being so cocky. Not that she would've actually followed through with it. But she was tempted. When she pulled into her driveway, he stopped beside her, put the kickstand down, turned off the engine, and got off the bike.

"*Now* what do you think you are doing?" she asked when she exited the car.

"Making sure it's safe inside."

"Oh, for Pete's sake!"

He took a few steps down the sidewalk, then waited for her to catch up. She wanted to smack him, but didn't. He was taking care of his best friend's wife, pure and simple. Which reminder her…"Will you answer a question for me?"

"Depends on the question." He threw her another wicked grin.

"Did you put flowers on the grave?" She didn't have to explain which grave.

He seemed to turn into a statue; not breathing, not blinking, not moving. His gaze was so intense, so penetrating, she had to look away. "How long have you been doing that?"

"Since the beginning."

"Oh." She barely breathed the word. Then, a little stronger, "Why didn't you tell me?"

Roy stepped closer and took her hand in his. "Initially, you didn't know which way was up. When I realized you weren't going to go out there, I kept taking them. I knew you'd eventually go see him, would put your own flowers there."

Heat crawled up her neck. "You never told me."

"I never told anyone. I didn't want people thinking you didn't care, when I knew you did."

Melody threw her arms around his neck, then kissed him on the cheek. "Thank you."

He gave her a quick hug, then pulled away. "You can cough up the cost of the next bunch, okay?"

Fighting tears, she said, "Deal. I have one other question. Who ordered the inscription on the headstone, and what does it mean?"

Shaking his head, he blew out a soft breath. "I think you can figure it out for yourself. Just think about it a little while."

"Roy—"

"Ah. The cavalry has arrived." He cocked his head and looked back down the street.

"What?" Melody turned to see Jake drive up in the SUV. If he'd been in his Firebird, she would've heard him before now. At least she'd like to think she would have. But after the crazy day she'd had, maybe not.

Still in uniform, Jake climbed from the vehicle in a fluid, easy motion and came up the walk. "Any problems?" he asked Roy.

"No. Didn't see anything out of the ordinary on the way. We got here a couple minutes ago so haven't had a chance to look around or check inside yet."

She didn't like this. Not one little bit. Common sense told her they were only trying to protect her, but she wanted her nice quiet life back. No plane crashes. No crazed killers. No threatening vandals. No escorts home. Although…Having them make sure her house was safe would make it easier to enjoy a soothing soak in the tub without worrying.

"I'll secure the perimeter. You check inside." Roy sounded like he was back in the military and in charge, not talking to the town's sheriff. He strode off around the house without giving Jake a chance to respond, who apparently didn't need to say anything. He simply took her keys from her and entered her home.

He wouldn't find anything. At least she hoped not. If he did, that would mean she wasn't safe anywhere. Suppressing a shudder, she followed close behind him as he moved from room to room, checking out the small laundry room off the kitchen before moving down the hallway. When he stopped outside the door to the spare bedroom, she sucked in a quick breath.

"Is there a problem?" he asked in a low voice.

She did her best to stay out of that room—too many memories buried in there. "No. Sorry. Go ahead." Jake furrowed his brows before he slowly pushed the door open. Melody stayed in the hallway.

He paused inside the door and scanned the room that had been Michael's study. A case with the flag from his coffin sat on the dresser. An old desk with an antiquated computer took up one corner. Makeshift shelves, overflowing with books, three-ring binders, and file folders ran along both walls next to it. The rest of the walls were covered with plaques and framed citations of Michael's awards and medals. His trophy room, he jokingly called it. On the wall next to the door hung a multi-layered gun rack with a couple of shotguns, a muzzle loader and a Marlin Saddle rifle. Jake raised his eyebrows at her, but she refused to comment. If he'd asked, she would've told him they were loaded.

Every. Single. One. Extra shells on the closet shelf.

Michael had always been prepared for whatever might come his way. Except that last morning. That had taken everyone by surprise. Roy had removed the files of vets suffering from PTSD and the information on various organizations' that could help them, saying Michael wouldn't want the people to fall through the cracks because he wasn't here anymore. She hadn't cared as long as she didn't have to deal with it.

Moving through the dust covered room, Jake cautiously opened the closet. All of Michael's clothes, his uniforms, boots, and boxes with his childhood mementoes took up the space. Even if someone had wanted to use it as a hiding place, there wasn't room.

She stepped away as he came back into the hall, closing the door behind him. At least he kept a professional demeanor and didn't look at her with pity or scorn for leaving the contents of the room to collect dust, especially the guns. It had to bug the heck out of him, though.

When he reached her bedroom, he hesitated before stepping inside. Thankfully, it was neat. No dirty underwear or bra on the floor. No clothes strewn about. No unmade bed. Seeing Jake in her bedroom caused little butterflies in her stomach, and heat rose in her cheeks when he looked in her closet. He glanced at the bed, then gazed at her. His eyes turned dark, causing her breath to quicken. The air between them sizzled, and she swore the hairs on her arms stood up.

Before either of them could say or do anything, Roy called out from the living room, breaking the spell. Neither moved for a second, then, with a look of regret, Jake turned and left the room. She followed a few paces behind, still trying to get her racing pulse under control.

"It's all clear," Roy said to Jake. "Although, someone has stood outside of her bedroom window. The footprints were smudged, as if they were trying to obscure them, or so the size couldn't be identified."

"How do you know it was Melody's bedroom?" Suspicion etched Jake's words and he gave him a hard stare.

Roy looked at him as if he'd lost his mind. "Michael was my best friend. I've been in the house a time or two over the years."

Running a hand through his hair, Jake relaxed. "Sorry. A little too keyed up, I suppose."

Shifting his gaze between the sheriff and her, Roy shrugged. "Don't worry about it. Now if you don't need me for anything else, I promised Perry I'd help him out on his farm this evening."

"Sure, go ahead. Thanks for your help."

"You two keep talking like I'm not even in the room. I do live here, you know."

Roy snorted. "Oh, darling. You're so bossy no one could ever forget you're around."

Melody swatted him for being mouthy, but at least it lightened the mood in the room. She gave him a quick hug. "Admit it. You love me just the way I am."

"Weelll."

She swatted his arm again. "Go away, Maddox. I'll see you in the morning."

Roy winked at her, then gave Jake a nod before walking out the door. Melody waited for Jake to follow suit. But when she turned, he was still standing where he had been. "Uh, thank you for making sure no one is in my home. I'll see you at the café in the morning." She took a step toward the door, ready for her solitude.

"I'm not leaving."

A sinking feeling hit the pit of her stomach. "What do you mean you're not leaving?"

"Exactly what I said." His jaw was set and he had a hard glint in his eyes.

"Well, I've got news for you, Jake Bennett. You are *not* staying here tonight." It didn't matter she'd been dreaming about him when she got up this morning, more than ready to be wrapped in his embrace again, or that the hairs on her arms had been standing on end

191

only moments ago. This was too presumptive on his part. Who did he think he was, anyway? She jammed her fisted hands on her hips, ready to do battle.

****

Jake almost smiled, but held himself in check. He didn't think Melody was in the mood. He loved it when she went all feisty on him. She had more grit than she gave herself credit for.

"Stop and think about it. Someone has been watching you. In your bedroom. Probably while you slept. You received several acts of vandalism and a very public threat today. Whoever is after you isn't going to stop." Her shoulders slumped and some of the fire went out of her eyes. He hated taking it away, but he had to make her understand. "Their activities will escalate. I'm not leaving you alone."

"But—"

"It won't do you any good."

She blinked. "What?"

"Trying to change my mind. You can't." He thought of the last person he had protected dying on his watch. He could not, would not, allow that to happen here. "From now on you'll have 24/7 protection until we catch the person responsible."

Melody set her jaw and glanced around the house as if searching for something, maybe a nice heavy object to hit him over the head with. He couldn't blame her. If the tables were reversed, he wouldn't want to be babysat, either. That still wouldn't make him change his mind, though.

She brought her gaze back to his, the fire back. "Now look here, Jake Bennett! I will not have you staying in my home overnight. I don't need my neighbors talking."

"And saying you're finally starting to have a life?" he teased. At her crestfallen expression, he amended his comment. "Look. I'm sorry if this upsets you, but right now, your safety comes first. Tomorrow I'll interview the people living nearby. Maybe one of them saw or heard something in the last few days that'll give us a lead."

She whirled and paced to the kitchen, then back again. Fear flashed across her face. "But what if you don't find them? The vandalism in town has been going on for a while now, and you said yourself that you didn't have any evidence. You—you can't stay here with me indefinitely."

What could he say? That it was precisely what he wanted to do? He hadn't been looking for a long-term relationship, but getting to know Melody better sure sounded appealing. If that meant spending nights at her place, all the better. Except for the fact someone was out to get her, his staying here was a win-win.

"Melody." He sighed, his voice pleading

"Jake," she said flatly, and nodded toward the front door.

"You have to listen to reason."

"Do I? I think I'm perfectly safe here."

"Someone has been prowling around."

"But they weren't inside."

"What if they break in?"

She raised her arms up in the air, then let them fall to her side. "Did you *see* all the guns in this house? It's like a small arsenal in there."

In three quick strides, he stood directly in front of her. Taking her hand in his, he said, "Yes, it is. In

193

there." He inclined his head to the room in question. "None of those weapons are within easy reach. From the looks of them, they haven't been cleaned in years. Even if you fired one, there's the possibility of a backfire."

She flinched and tried to pull away, but he wouldn't let go. "Besides, you haven't touched any of them. Tell me, *would* you pick up one? Even to save your own life?"

"I…" Dropping her gaze, she studied the floor.

"That's what I thought. I don't blame you, and that's why I'm here." He pulled her into a hug, tempted to kiss her. Finally, he set her at arm's length, refusing to give in to his distraction. "Now, why don't you go get comfortable or whatever you had planned for the evening? I'll double check all the locks in the house. I don't want any unwanted surprises. Then I'll make you dinner. Might not be anything fancy, or as good as Roy's cooking, but it'll be filling."

She blew out a weary sigh. "Since I can't seem to run you off with a stick, I'm going to go take a long, hot bath. Maybe I can steam away some of the day's unpleasantness."

Stepping away from him, she turned and headed to her room. When the door clicked shut, he let out a groan. Why did she have to tell him that? Now all he would think about was her lying naked in a tub of warm water. Probably filled with bubbles. Getting all soapy and slick and…

Oh, man. He was in trouble. He was here in an official capacity only, not to mess around with the woman he guarded. When the sound of running water floated down the hall, he headed to the back of the house and began meticulously checking the locks. He tried planning what to fix for dinner, wondering what ingredients she had in the house. He tried thinking about the case, about motives, about who could be the culprit. He tried thinking about sports.

Nothing helped.

****

Melody scooted lower into the tub, water up to her chin. This was supposed to be relaxing. *Not working.* Not with the sexy sheriff in her house. She tried to focus on anything but Jake down the hall, moving about as if he belonged there, belonged in her life. But what? Maybe specials for the next week? All thought of food faded as his face rose before her. Clamping her jaw so tight her teeth hurt, she forced her mind back to lunch specials. Monday, mac and cheese, Tuesday, smothered steak. The last time she'd had smothered steak, Jake had eaten two full servings, and would have eaten a third if they hadn't run out. How did the man eat like a high schooler and still look so good? Finally, she gave up, climbed out of the tub, and dried off. How in the world was she going to get through tonight? Their attraction to each other grew stronger by the minute.

Could she take the next step? Was she ready? Her analytical brain said no, but her heart said otherwise. Pin pricks of anticipation slid down her spine. She fanaticized about what it would be like to explore every inch of his body, to have him explore hers. Then reality set in.

Nothing would happen she didn't want to happen. He had made it clear his job was to protect her, not make love to her. Wrapping the towel around herself, she walked back into the bedroom. She thought of putting on her new cute jeans, but she was dead tired and just wanted to spend the night in comfort, not skintight clothes. Instead of trying to look "pretty" for the sheriff, she slipped into a faded blue T-shirt and a pair of yoga pants. She unclipped her hair, finger combed it and slid her feet into a pair of slippers.

A glance in the mirror confirmed there wasn't anything special about her looks, especially with no makeup. If Jake Bennett was determined to be part of her world, then he could take the no-frills version of what she looked like at home.

Before she'd climbed in the tub, she had made sure there were no cracks in the curtain, no way for anyone to see inside her room. How could she have been so careless before? But this was small town America. They didn't have things like peeping-toms. Did they? Since Roy had found footprints outside her window, apparently so. She checked the curtains one more time to be sure. Satisfied, she opened her door and the aroma of food wafted down the hall. The good sheriff really could cook. Go figure.

She made her way down the hall, but stopped at the kitchen door. Jake stood at the stove, his back to her. She resisted the urge to drool. It had been a long time since a man occupied her kitchen, taking care of her. Standing in his stocking feet, his muscles rippled underneath the uniform shirt and his tight butt wiggled a little as he stirred whatever was in the pot. Mmm-mmm. Now *that* was a view she could get used to seeing every day. Surprisingly, it took her a heartbeat or two to realize his gun belt, with all the paraphernalia, had been hung on the back of a kitchen chair.

"There you are." He had twisted around to face her.

Lost deep in appreciation of the man's backside, a thrill shot through her at the sound of his voice. She had to work to keep from blushing.

"Hope you don't mind me digging through your cabinets and refrigerator. You weren't kidding when you said the selection was limited. I did find enough to make ham and cheese omelets, if it's okay with you."

She took a step into the room. "That's fine. I'm not picky. And I warned you I don't keep a lot in the house. I'm surprised you even found what you did." A lot of times she brought leftovers home from the café so she wouldn't have to cook. Or even think about what to prepare. Tonight, it hadn't even crossed her mind. Too bad. Now poor Jake was reduced to being her personal chef if he wanted anything at all to eat.

"Good thing I can improvise." He refocused on the stove and continued stirring, then threw over his shoulder, "Dinner's about ready."

Ignoring his cute backside, she focused on the meal. "Want some coffee to go with dinner or would you prefer water?"

"Coffee's fine."

She filled a couple of mugs, then gathered the utensils and condiments. Silence stretched between them as he concentrated on dishing up the food and, for some unknown reason, she tried to be as quiet as possible. When the silence became too much for her—she swore she heard his every breath—she went into the living room and turned on the radio to her favorite 70's and 80's soft rock station. She glanced up in time to see him watching her.

"Here you go." He slid two plates onto the table.

****

Jake waited for Melody to take her seat, then sat in the chair across from her—the same chair he'd sat in the first time he'd been in her house. When she had walked into the kitchen, all fresh and clean, her hair floating loose like a halo, it took everything he had to keep his mind on the food and not pull her into his arms. To resist the temptation, he'd turned his back on her, willing his pounding pulse under control.

The woman had no idea of how sexy she was with no makeup and wearing the soft-as-butter looking clothes. But he was here to keep her safe, nothing more. Not that he wouldn't love the chance to wrap his hands in the fabric of her shirt, then pull it over her head…

He coughed. Man, he needed to get his mind somewhere else, and fast, before he made a fool of himself. "I like the station you chose."

She dumped some ketchup on the omelet—what was wrong with her?—and took a small bite, while he stuffed a good portion of his into his mouth. He should've added more cheese, he decided.

"I don't like to watch much TV, so I listen to the radio. I get the majority of the news there and get to hear some good songs."

"Hmm. For some reason, I thought you'd be a country and western fan."

She laughed and mugged a face. "And why is that, Jake Bennett?"

"I don't know. I thought that was the preferred music of people in the area. I know Clay listens to a lot of it."

"Well, I'm not Clay." She speared another piece of the omelet.

Taking his time, he let his gaze slide over her, then

he twitched his eyebrows. "No, ma'am. You definitely are not."

Blushing a deep crimson, she took a moment, then grinned. "I like the music from that timeframe. There's a lot of new artists creating new sounds, but I seem to gravitate to the soft rock. Guess I was born in the wrong era."

"Or have good taste in music." He lifted the corner of his lips before taking a drink of coffee. "I like listening to Lynyrd Skynyrd, ZZ Top, The Eagles, even some Pink Floyd from time to time."

"Seriously?" She didn't look like she believed him. "You're not putting me on?"

He raised two fingers in a mock salute. "Scout's honor."

"Huh." She went back to eating.

Jake took the last bite of his omelet, wishing he'd made more. He scraped the plate, and when there wasn't another morsel left, laid down his fork. "Any chance you have some kind of dessert stashed somewhere?"

She gave him a sly grin. "Do you like ice cream?"

"Let's see. Cone or cup?"

"Neither. Bowl."

"Aw, now you're talking." He leaned back in the chair and rubbed his stomach in anticipation.

Standing, she picked up their plates and carried them to the sink. "So, what's your poison, big guy? Chocolate, vanilla, strawberry, or rocky road?"

"You've got all those? Where? I didn't see them when I went through the fridge."

"Ah. You didn't look deep enough in the freezer."

He snorted. "I must be losing it. Although, in my

defense, I didn't look too hard because I didn't want to defrost anything."

"I keep them buried in the back. It's my out of sight, out of mind kind of logic. If I don't see it, then I'll forget it's there."

"Don't see why. You sure don't need to watch your weight, or anything." She blushed again, not that she had anything to be embarrassed about.

"So, what flavor do you like?"

"It doesn't matter. Whatever is the easiest to get to."

She chuckled as she turned away.

Melody might not have any culinary skills, but she sure looked good moving around the cozy kitchen, pulling out bowls and digging through the freezer. She retrieved the chocolate and strawberry cartons and proceeded to scoop a good portion into each of the bowls, then set the chocolate in front of him.

"How'd you know this was my favorite?"

"Oh, maybe because of your reaction to the chocolate cake I brought to the picnic." She didn't wait for a reply and took a bite of the strawberry, licking the spoon, then her lips afterward.

Jake couldn't take his eyes off her mouth, off the way her tongue caressed the spoon, licking the cream off the bottom. Would she let him do some caressing later? He savored the rich chocolate cream as he savored the possibility of Melody in his arms. If not tonight, then soon.

Chapter Fifteen

Melody tried her best to ignore Jake's stare. It was disconcerting, and way too intimate. He finally picked up his spoon and took a bite of the ice cream. After asking for dessert, she had begun to wonder if he would actually eat any. She ducked her head, letting her hair fall across her face to hide what surely must be a deep blush.

Before long, both bowls were empty. "Want some more? There's plenty."

He scooted his bowl to the middle of the table. "Not right now. But you go ahead. Don't let me stop you."

"One bowl is my limit. Any more and I'll have to start exercising."

Jake leaned back and crossed his arms over his chest. "Too bad."

She frowned. "I beg your pardon? Do you want me fat, or something?"

"Not that. I enjoy watching you eat."

"Oh." Now she was positive she blushed. Not sure how to respond, she picked up the bowls and carried them to the sink. She turned to see him in the same position, watching her. "So, what now?"

"What do you normally do in the evenings?"

She shrugged. "Read. Quilt. A little TV. There are a couple of shows I enjoy during the week."

"That's it?"

Grabbing a tea towel, she wiped down the table to hide her embarrassment. "I know I don't live an exciting life."

Without commenting, he stood and wandered into the living room. "Did you make this?" Picking up the corner of the quilt on the back of the sofa, he fingered the fabric.

"Yes, that one's called a Log Cabin pattern, and it's one of my favorites."

"Looks hard to do."

"Not if you know what you're doing, but it is a little tricky."

"I bet my mom would love to have one. Do you sell them?"

"You'd want to buy one?"

He looked at her in surprise. "Why not? I don't know much about sewing or anything, but this looks like good quality. I bet you could get a pretty good price for anything you make."

It warmed her heart that he'd complimented her work. "I give them away as wedding or anniversary gifts. I never considered selling them."

He lightly ran his hand over the quilt, then went to the front window and peered out before turning back to her. "Since I'm not into sewing, what books do you have?"

"Basically romance and women's fiction."

"Oh. Well, that's okay. I don't need to be entertained, anyway." This time he went to the back door and looked out.

"I've got some board games if you'd be interested."

The boyish grin was back. "That's more my style. I haven't played any games since I was a kid, though. Might be a bit rusty."

"Don't worry about it. I'll have to get them out of the closet and dust them off. Not sure how good I am anymore, either."

A few minutes later, there were a stack of boxes on the table. They tried Monopoly for a while, then Scrabble, then Clue, never spending too much time on any one particular game. Sometimes she won, sometimes he did. Neither of them made any effort to keep much of a score. They laughed and joked, and periodically one of them sang along with a song on the radio.

She didn't know how long they'd played, but the warm bath earlier and the long day she'd had caught up with her as she stifled a yawn.

He looked up in time to see. "You need to get some rest."

"No, I can keep—" She looked at the clock. "It's almost eleven? I didn't realize it was so late." She stood and started to pick up the pieces.

He placed his hand over the board. "Don't worry about this. I'll take care of it."

"You sure?" She didn't want to be rude, but the alarm blaring at five a.m. would roll around way too soon.

"Yeah. I got it."

He smiled and Melody wanted to melt right into him. She jerked her mind away. No. None of that. From the way he'd acted earlier in the evening, he wouldn't have been adverse to some cuddling. Except he'd thrown himself into the games. She had to admit, she liked the easy banter between them. Still, the thought of a goodnight kiss sounded awfully appealing. Following through on the thought, not such a good idea.

"What about you? You've been up all day the same as me. You need your rest, too."

He flashed her another boyish grin. "Are you kidding? I used to do this sort of thing all the time. I've got your high-octane coffee to help keep me awake. Besides, I don't need much sleep."

Exhaustion clung to her. "You're the expert."

Steel determination glinted in his eyes. "Don't worry, I'll keep you safe."

She hesitated before she turned and walked down the hall. Gathering an extra pillow from the closet, she carried it back and laid it on the couch. "You can use the quilt, too."

Frowning, he said, "It's too nice."

"I made it to use. You won't be the first, if that's what you're worried about."

"All right then. Thanks. I appreciate it."

He continued to study her until she headed back to her bedroom. If he'd didn't look so delectable, his being here wouldn't be so bad. Despite being tired, she had a feeling sleep would be a long time coming.

Normally, she left the door open, but with the hotter than sin sheriff only feet away, she closed it. For a fraction of a second, she thought about locking it but decided not to. If someone did try to get in through her window, she didn't want Jake breaking down the door. But nothing would happen. Jake and Roy were overreacting to the situation. That was all.

After brushing her teeth, she turned out all the lights except the small lamp on the nightstand. Not bothering to change except to discard her bra, she climbed between the sheets. Once she clicked off the lamp, the room was darker than normal. All this time she'd inadvertently been using the illumination from the streetlight coming through the crack in the curtains as a nightlight. No wonder someone could see in—she had given them the perfect opportunity. She shivered at the thought. Well, she certainly knew better now.

Melody turned her back to the window and snuggled deeper in the covers. She squeezed her eyes closed, willing the image of the threat on the wall to go away. After what felt like an eternity, she drifted to sleep.

Faint light from a dirty, tiny window failed to penetrate much of the darkness. Where was she? Focusing, she took in her surroundings. A well-used cot sat on one side of a small room. She couldn't see any other furniture. Slowly, she circled the area. She found a door, but it was locked. The window was too small to crawl through. There was no other way out of the room. All she knew was it was imperative she get out. Then, as if her thoughts alone had conjured it, a few trickles of flame appeared and began working their way up the far wall. Smoke wafted upward.

The words on the wall of the café came back to her. LIARS BURN IN HELL. *Frantic, she twisted the doorknob, and pounded on the door.*

"Let me out! Someone help me!" She glanced back. The flames were getting higher.

Panic gripped her. She screamed and kicked on the door, pounding with her fists. "Don't do this. Please. Let me out. Please!" She heard a sound on the other side of the door, but no one answered her pleas.

Heat from the fire grew stronger. She'd be burned alive. "No!"

****

A little after midnight, Jake lay down on the sofa, grateful for the pillow and blanket. He'd taken off his shirt but had left on his pants. His service weapon was in easy reach on the coffee table next to him, and the small light over the stove provided enough light to see his way around.

He'd done stakeouts where he spent most of the night sitting in a car, so having a place to rest helped a lot. For a long while he lay there, listening. Eventually, his eyelids grew heavy.

A piercing scream from Melody's room had him fully awake and moving within seconds. He grabbed the gun and rushed into her room, expecting to see an intruder. The room was so dark he couldn't be sure where they were. He flipped on the lights, quickly scanning every corner.

"Let me out. Please!"

Alone on the bed, Melody thrashed about as if her life were at stake. A quick check of the bathroom and closet verified no one was there. He went to the bed and sank down next to her, setting the gun on the nightstand.

"No!"

The covers were twisted around her, yet she continued to fight them, as if they were holding her down. He leaned close, then pulled back to avoid her fist. She missed his jaw, but the blow landed on his arm. The woman packed a punch.

"Melody. It's me, Jake."

Not opening her eyes, she flailed her arms and

kicked at the sheets. She screamed again, this one blood curdling. Jake grabbed both of her arms, trying to not squeeze too tight, leaned into her and shook her. Hard. "Melody! Wake up!"

Her breath coming in quick pants, her body slowly relaxed. He loosened his hold. "It's okay. I got you. You're safe now."

A couple beats later, she opened her eyes, terror etched on her face. She blinked, as if she had been in a haze, then jerked, looking around the room. When her gaze came back to him, she threw her arms around him, a keening cry emitting from deep within her. *What the hell?*

Her entire body shook and he let her cling for as long as she wanted. Finally, she released her stranglehold on him and lay back against the pillow. Her breathing was almost back to normal, and the pupils of her eyes weren't quite so dilated. Her skin was still wet and clammy, though.

"What—?"

"Bad dream. You were screaming."

"Oh." She looked around again, as if to verify no one else was in the room. Then she coughed, the sound raw and raspy.

"I'll get some water." He jumped from the bed and headed to the kitchen. When he came back, she had scooted against the headboard.

After she'd taken a long drink, she set the glass on the nightstand, her hand trembling. "Thank you."

"Feeling better?"

She nodded.

"Want to tell me what that was about?" Maybe it would help to calm her down. Plus, he had to know what had her so terrified. Had someone tried to break in, causing a bad dream, and he hadn't heard? She chewed on her bottom lip and turned her head away. "Have you had it before?"

"No. Tha—that was the first time." Her voice quivered.

He wanted to know the details, but he wouldn't push. "You don't have to tell me if you don't want, but sometimes it helps to talk about it."

Taking a few deep breaths, she said, "It was because of the graffiti at the café." She paused and shuddered.

Her hands were twined together in a tight knot. Reaching over, he placed his hands on hers giving a reassuring squeeze. "Take your time."

"I—I was locked in a small room. Then it burst into flames. I knew someone was on the other side of the door, but they wouldn't let me out. Th-the smoke became unbearable, and the heat…"

Jake pulled her into a tight hug. The thought of someone doing that to her, even in a dream, ate a hole in his gut. If he could, he'd take the nightmare away from her, take away the terror. But until he caught the culprit, her life was in danger. He had to admire her, though. Through all of the things that had happened, she'd held up well. Except it had caught up with her, sending her subconscious into a state of horror.

He held her tighter, the only thing separating them from being skin to skin was the cotton T-shirt she wore. Winding her arms around his neck, she leaned into his chest, her breath fanning his skin. A man could only stand so much. He took hold of her wrists, intent on pushing her away.

Then she kissed him and all reason evaporated into thin air.

****

Jake took control of the kiss. And Melody let him, joy surging through her. His kiss slowly drove the darkness away. In his arms, she was safe. Needing more, she deepened the kiss. When she thought he was on the verge of making love to her, he pulled back, breaking their contact.

"Melody, I want you more than you know, but not like this." He searched her face, as if memorizing it. Tucking a strand of hair behind her ear, he said, "This isn't the right time. You're too vulnerable. When we do make love, I don't want it to be an excuse to get rid of a bad dream. I want you to be focused on me and nothing else."

She sighed, knowing he was right. "I know. Would you do me a favor, though?"

He kissed the tip of her nose. "If I can."

"Don't leave me tonight."

"Melody. I just—"

"I'm afraid, and don't want to be alone."

Conflict and desire flitted across his face. Finally, he nodded. "I can bring one of the kitchen chairs in here, and—"

"Would you hold me? Nothing sexual, I promise. I—I just need to know you're close."

He searched her face before nodding. "But I'm staying on top of the covers. I only have so much self-restraint. Okay?"

Planting a quick kiss on his lips, she said, "Thank you."

Jake blew out a deep breath, then mumbled, "I

hadn't planned on getting much sleep tonight, anyway. Now I know I won't."

Snuggling under the covers, she lay on her side. Jake turned out the light, then lay down behind her, spooning her backside. He draped an arm over her, holding her close. Even if they weren't making love, she felt safe and protected.

"Good night, Jake."

"Night, Melody. Now hush and get some rest."

She knew the nightmare wouldn't return. But if it did, Jake would be there to rescue her.

Chapter Sixteen

Jake's cell phone buzzed, jerking him awake. Melody, still tucked under the covers, barely stirred. He slipped from bed and tiptoed out of the room, closing the door behind him.

"What is it, Larson?"

"Sorry to disturb you so early, Sheriff, but we have a break in the vandalism case."

Adrenaline surged through his system as he walked down the hall. "Give it to me."

"Got an anonymous tip about Tony Freemont's cousin, Richard, the one from Little Rock. He had a run-in at the café not long ago and wasn't too happy when Mel asked him to leave."

Why hadn't she mentioned that before? Jake wondered.

"When I went out to Freemont's farm, Henry gave me permission to look around. Found a couple cans of paint in the barn that match the colors used on the café as well as at Franks'."

"Have any trouble bringing him in?"

"Not much. Henry told me to haul his sorry hide away, saying he was a bad influence on Tony. He'd let the kid stay there as a favor to his brother, thinking if they got Richard away from the gang he ran with, he'd straighten up. Didn't work out that way.

"Richard claims he was set up. I've got his rap

211

sheet from Little Rock and I'm waiting now to see if his fingerprints match what's on the cans. If they do…"

Jake blew out a deep sigh of relief. "Good job, Clay. Looks like this nightmare is about over."

"What's about over?"

He turned to see Melody standing in the hallway, listening. The beauty of her wearing nothing more than a thin cotton top and yoga pants, plus having sleep-tousled hair, just about sucked the air from his lungs. He had to force himself to concentrate on the phone conversation. "Keep me posted. I'll be there shortly."

She took a couple steps into the room. "Jake? What's going on?"

He wanted this to be over so she could stop worrying. But at the same time, he loved the evening they'd spent together. With the case wrapping up, the next time he spent the night, he'd be under the covers, not on top. Anticipation kicked up his heart rate again.

"Clay has a suspect in custody."

Hope flared in her eyes. "Really? Who?"

"I can't say at this time. Nothing is official or confirmed yet—"

"Don't give me that! I have a right to know. Even if it turns out it isn't true, I need to know." A heartbeat passed, then another. "Please."

He couldn't stand the pleading in her voice, the desolate look in her eyes, and knew he'd relent. "Remember, this could be a false lead. Richard Freemont."

She drew her brows down, concentrating, then shook her head. "Sorry. I don't think I know him. Any relation to Henry?"

"His nephew. Clay said you had an altercation with

him at the café not too long ago."

Still looking confused, she walked to the sofa and sat, tucking her legs underneath her. "I can't place him. I did have a little trouble with some boys during spring break, but they were just acting like normal, obnoxious teenagers. After I asked them to leave, I didn't think any more about it. I suppose he could've been one of them."

Jake sat in the chair opposite her, afraid to sit next to her. She was too darn sexy for her own good. "Apparently *he* thought more about it. Guess the chaos after the plane crash gave him enough of a smoke screen to start acting out, and once he started, kept escalating his activities."

She sat quietly for a couple of minutes, staring at the floor. He let her absorb the information. Finally, she looked up at him. "It's over?"

Over? He knew she meant the case, but that word slid over him like the fog the day of the crash. Cold. Silent. He swallowed hard, forcing his voice to remain normal. "If everything checks out, then yes, it's over. You'll have your life back."

She looked both hopeful and disappointed. "The case is over, Melody. Not us."

A sly smile played at her lips. "I was hoping you'd say that."

He crossed to the couch, taking her hands in his. "I won't have an official reason to spend the nights here anymore."

"But *un*-officially?"

"Why don't I drop by this evening to demonstrate what I'm capable of when I'm off the clock?" Her cheeks turned the prettiest shade of pink while her eyes sparkled.

"I don't know how long it'll take today, so it might be late. I'll give you a call when I'm free. Okay?"

"I'd like that."

He leaned in for a kiss, wishing for the day off. Wishing he could stay right here with her wrapped in his arms. They both had obligations, though. Ending the kiss, he finished dressing, collected his gear, then stopped at the door for one more embrace, one more taste of her sweet lips.

"Be careful today," she whispered in his ear when he broke contact.

"Always." Settling his hat on his head, he had a lighter step as he headed to his car. The thought of having someone waiting on him at the end of the day, someone who cared, made him feel as if he could conquer the world. The sun wasn't even up, yet the day held a promise he had never expected.

****

Exhausted, Jake got home around eight that night. They had yet to crack Richard Freemont, the kids answers were a little too quick, a little too canned. Jake would bet the troublemaker was guilty, though. It would just take more time to get all the evidence against him lined out. At least it hadn't been the mayor. That would have been a fight he didn't want to be involved in if it had been true. Jake still didn't like the man, and vice versa. He could live with it, though. At least Melody was safe.

He showered, then pulled on an old pair of jeans and a T-shirt. He needed to unwind a bit before calling Melody. Grabbing a beer, he headed out back, sat in the porch chair, and propped his feet on the railing.

He took a swig from the bottle and surveyed the yard. A few flowers had already poked through the ground with the promise spring would soon follow. How hot would it get this far south in the summer? He hoped being in the mountains would keep it cooler than he expected, but he still longed for the Chicago spring. Breeze off the lake kept the temperatures down most of the time, but it could still be sweltering by August. Would he be back there by then?

Did he *want* to go back?

A couple of weeks ago the answer would have been a definite yes, but now...Melody's image floated across his mind and he found himself smiling. It'd been a long time since a woman had captured his attention so completely. In Chicago, he had the tendency to attract two kinds of women—the ones who loved the badge more than him, and the ones who didn't want to compete with the badge and job. The realization depressed him. What a sad testament to his life.

Small town America was different than the big city. Even though he was the sheriff, most nights he could kick back and relax. It dawned on him that he rather liked it, then he frowned. This wasn't in his game plan. He had intended to stay only as long as he had to, then go back to doing what he did best, solving major crimes in Chicago. Although, the last couple of weeks had been hectic enough to give any crime unit a run for its money.

The world of Rock Ledge had settled back into its normal routine after the plane crash. Or as normal as any small town could be, Jake thought. Especially since they'd caught the guy causing all the trouble at the café plus the other businesses. Now it would probably become even more dull. The prospect didn't bother him as much as he'd once thought it would.

He took another draw on his beer as dusk settled. The temperature had dipped some, but he could already tell the difference since he'd moved here. It was warming up. He checked his watch, hoping Melody had also had some time to unwind. He was anxious to see her again.

Before he even moved, his phone chimed, the personalized ring tone a sound he hadn't heard in quite a while. Digging the phone out of his pocket, he checked caller ID to make sure, then smiled. Matt Ackerman, his old partner. They had talked a few times after he'd left the CPD, and Jake had sent him an email telling him about his job here.

"Yeah?" he said when he answered the call.

"Hello to you, too," Matt responded.

"What's up?" He'd missed talking to his friend...to his last connection to Chicago.

"Thought I'd check in, see how the gig is going."

Jake surveyed the view from the backyard. The neighbors' lights had come on, the town settling in for the night. Definitely a one-eighty from the city. "Can't complain. Had some excitement recently."

"Yeah, saw you on national news. You looked good. That got your blood to pumping, huh?"

"You could say that." The memory of the fugitive holding a gun point-blank on Melody sent a cold chill down Jake's spine. The warmth she'd brought into his life had surprised him. Simply thinking about her had his chest tightening.

"Still interested in coming back?" Matt's question brought him back to reality so fast he felt like he'd been

Tazered.

He dropped his feet to the porch with a loud thump and leaned forward. "What are you talking about?" All the years of being a good cop hadn't meant a thing when the witness died. Then to have the entire department turn on him…

Matt cleared his throat. "It took a while, but Captain Bingham slipped up and got caught in a sting. Not only has he been canned, looks like he'll be brought up on corruption plus murder charges."

"Murder?"

"Turns out he was on the take from the mob and he's the one who ordered the hit on the witness you were guarding."

His lungs deflated, and he had to force his mouth closed. Bingham was responsible for the death of an innocent? A murder witness who was just trying to do the right thing? Bingham had made Jake's life a living hell, and had been instrumental in his having no option but to resign. But to be directly involved in killing a witness? A part of Jake felt vindicated the man who had cost him his job had not only lost his, but would also spend time behind bars.

Running his hand through his hair, he remembered how powerless he'd been those last weeks. Of course, it was Bingham who had spoon fed the department, as well as the media, false info.

Finding his voice, he said, "Whaddaya know? There is justice, after all."

"Tell me about it. Several others have also been let go and are looking at charges. It's a different place around here, that's for sure."

His mind reeled with the news. "And this helps me

how?" He held his breath.

"Internal Affairs is looking at Bingham's dealings over the last few years. Your name came up."

"And?"

"They'd like to talk to you. There's a good possibility you can get your job back."

Jake leaned into the chair, unable to draw a deep breath for fear that what he'd heard wasn't real. "You mean they aren't lumping me in with his dealings? I'm not being brought up on charges?"

"No. I made sure of that." His partner had always had his back.

Forcing air into his lungs, Jake stood and paced the small porch before bracing one arm on the doorjamb. "You're a good partner."

"Yeah, well, don't go getting all mushy. You'd do the same for me."

That he would. Without any hesitation. "Over the phone or in person?"

"In person would be better if you want a real shot at it."

"When?"

"Monday morning. Come in over the weekend and you can crash at my place."

Monday?

He hesitated. Excitement but discomfort at the idea of getting his job back crawled over him. If Matt asked him why he wasn't more excited, he wouldn't be able to explain. He wasn't sure he actually understood himself. This was what he'd wanted from the minute he walked out of the Chicago Police department the last time, without his gun and badge. Getting his name cleared and his old job back, to be able to throw it in the faces of those who had doubted him, was what he'd always wanted. So why didn't it feel right?

Shoving down the sensations, he refocused on the conversation.

"Why don't I fly up Saturday evening? I appreciate the offer of a place to stay. It'll be great to catch up. Plus, you can bring me up to speed on what's happening around there. I want to walk into the meeting and let them know I can hit the ground running. Give them a reason to rehire me."

"Sounds like a plan, bro. Text me when you know your flight info and I'll pick you up at the airport."

"You got it. And, Matt? Thanks. I owe you."

"No problem. I hated it when you got railroaded, and this'll be a good way to shove it in IA's face for taking Bingham's word about you in the first place. Hell, they should've known by looking at your service record. But we'll get it all straightened out."

They said goodbye and disconnected, then he stared into the night. Chicago. Reinstatement. What he'd always wanted. Scrubbing a hand over his face, he knew he had to tell Melody before anyone else. The thought of leaving her stabbed him in the gut. He'd become accustomed to being around her, to seeing her face every morning at the café. To having her in his arms. The thought of not having her close by almost brought him to his knees.

Maybe they could still have a long-distance relationship, although it wouldn't be the same. Better yet, she could relocate and move to Chicago. Hadn't she said she wanted to see more of the world? One way or the other he'd convince her to give up small town life for the excitement of the big city—after he found out whether or not he got the job.

He downed the last of the beer for some liquid courage. This wouldn't be easy.

****

A light knock sounded at Melody's door. Climbing out of the comfortable recliner, she peeked out the side window. Jake. Her heart fluttered, and she yanked open the door. She had hoped it would be him.

"Hi. Thought you were going to call first, not that I'm complaining." She stepped aside to let him in.

He came inside, but didn't quite meet her gaze. "Listen, I need to talk to you about something."

Melody's guard immediately went up. Anytime someone started off a conversation with that tone, it wasn't good. She ushered him into the living room. He waited until she'd sunk onto the couch and he took the other end. Dread spiked through her. What had happened now? A lump formed in her throat. She didn't say anything, letting him take the lead and tell her whatever was on his mind.

Jake stared at the floor a minute before turning to her. "I've got a chance to go back to Chicago."

O-kay. That didn't sound so bad. "How long will you be gone?"

Holding her gaze, he said, "If things work out, I'll be reinstated with the CPD."

Her heart stuttered as the air rushed from her lungs. Her head swam, and she gripped the arm of the couch. A sinking sensation threatened to suck her into its abyss.

Leaving? Permanently? She thought things had been going so well with them. For the first time in years, she'd felt alive. Jake had shown her the sun still shone, had given her hope of new possibilities.

She had told herself she would never open her heart again, but deep-down Melody knew she had already fallen for the new sheriff. Jake had been her salvation. She'd never told him…didn't think she had to. After the way he'd tenderly held her, it had been her assumption they were on the same page, and that he cared for her as much as she cared for him.

Obviously not.

Forcing a lightness to her voice she didn't feel, and hoping it didn't come out as a croak, she said, "What brought this about?"

"Listen, Melody—"

"Just tell me, please." Every ounce of her being didn't want to hear another word. Yet she had to know. Somehow, she had to understand why he wanted to leave Rock Ledge.

Why he wanted to leave her.

"You have to understand, this has nothing to do with you…with us. It had always been my intention to get my foot back in the door of the CPD when I took this job." He swallowed hard before he continued. "This is sooner than I thought, though."

She'd keep it civil if it killed her. "Have you told anyone else yet?"

"No. I had to talk to you first."

How considerate, she thought uncharitably.

"I'll have to go through an interview process in Chicago, so it all depends on how that goes."

She gripped her hands in her lap, trying her best to absorb everything he said instead of about every third word. She didn't want to ask him to repeat himself. She'd fall apart if she had to listen to it a second time. It took every ounce of her energy to keep from screaming at him, from pounding her fists against his chest...

...from begging him to stay.

"When will you leave?" She hated that her voice shook.

"I'll fly up tomorrow night; the meeting is Monday." He paused, his hands hanging between his knees as he searched her face. "Nothing's guaranteed. Some of the people conducting the interview were instrumental in me leaving in the first place."

Was that supposed to give her hope? Or encouragement? "You were fired?"

"I was given the option of leaving on my own instead of being fired. Someone died on my watch. I thought it was a setup, even though I couldn't prove it at the time. In the end, I took the fall and made an example of." He paused, looked around the room, before he brought his gaze back to her. "Melody, it *was* a set up. They dragged my name through the mud, made it look like I was incompetent. That I wasn't worthy of wearing the badge."

He fell silent, watching her intently before looking over her shoulder at a picture on the wall, apparently unable to meet her gaze any longer. "I've got to clear my name."

The clock on the mantel ticked away the minutes as neither spoke. In a state of shock, she didn't know what to say...what to feel. It was as if her entire world had come to a screeching halt.

He cleared his throat. "This is what I've always wanted."

What he *wanted?* She snapped. "Is it? Seems to me you wanted to learn all about the county, where people lived, what they were like, what you could do to get them to trust you. Not once did you give any indication you intended to turn your back on them." Her voice rose on the last sentence. Her breathing became shallow, and she gripped her hands tighter to keep them from shaking.

All the years she and Michael had been married, it had been a given he'd leave on deployment, but that he'd come home. And he did. Until that last day long after his service to the government had ended. When she began falling for Jake, she had thought he'd be there for her…that he wouldn't leave her alone.

That she'd have the normal life she had craved.

Her heart cracked.

So much for dreams. Jake would go back to his exciting world in Chicago, walking away from small town life…and her. She, on the other hand, would remain stuck in the café.

Stuck with no hope of being happy again.

"I thought you knew…" His voice trailed off. He reached for her, but when she stiffened, he let his hand drop. "Melody, you have to believe me when I say I never meant for things to get so serious between us."

Her eyes widened in disbelief. "So, I'm simply a diversion? Something to occupy your time?"

"No, I—"

"Was your staying here last night simply a way to get into my bed?"

His eyes flashed fire. "You know it wasn't."

Deep down she knew the truth. If that had been the only reason, why hadn't he taken advantage of her vulnerability and actually slept with her? It galled her, but she would've let him. How pathetic was she? The first time a man paid any attention to her in years, and she fell for him as if she were some inexperienced schoolgirl. Except she *was* inexperienced.

"What do you want from me, Jake?" Her heart cracked a little more, and she fought tears, but she had to know what he thought of her. Was she so flawed, so pathetic, that even the new man in town could walk away so easily?

His lips flattened as his gaze searched her face. "I didn't want to hurt you. I figured we could have a good time, enjoy each other's company."

"It was all just a game?" How much deeper could he drive the dagger?

"No. That's not what I'm saying. We're both adults, Melody. I thought you knew the score."

He was wrong. On so many levels. Opening her heart had cost her, and she wasn't sure how much more she could handle. Standing, she moved to the door, holding it open. "Have a safe trip."

Jake hung his head, blew out a deep breath, then stood and followed her. Once again, he raised his hand as if to comfort her.

She'd crumble into a thousand pieces if he touched her. If he kissed her when she knew there was no hope for them, she'd disintegrate. All the times those hands had touched her, first in friendship, then later in sweet caresses, sent a shiver of regret down her spine.

Jake hadn't asked her to go with him; and she would have gone. If he'd only asked. So here she was. Alone. Again. She'd had enough of men to last her a lifetime. Her heart was broken beyond repair. From now on, living for herself would be her main priority.

After she had a good cry.

"I'm more sorry than you know," he whispered as he paused close to her.

She turned her head to the side, unable to hold his gaze. He blew out another weary sigh, then stepped over the threshold. If he looked back, she didn't notice. Hot tears blurred her vision as she swung the door closed with a resounding thump.

The finality of the sound echoed through the house, and to the very core of her being.

****

Jake raked a hand through his hair, unable to believe how badly the entire conversation had gone. He turned back toward the house, hoping to see Melody at the window…letting him know she wasn't as upset as he thought. The house had already gone dark, as dark as he felt. Going back to Chicago with his head held high had always been his goal…his dream. So why did it feel wrong?

Sliding behind the wheel, he fired up the Firebird and pulled into the street, then drove aimlessly out of town and down country roads. Was he doing the right thing? Clearing his name with the CPD and getting his reputation back? Definitely. Leaving Rock Ledge, leaving Melody…?

The ache that had begun while watching the light go out of her smile, out of her eyes, spread. He hadn't realized how much he'd come to care for her. The first time he'd held her while she fell to pieces after almost being shot; the first time she'd laughed at one of his corny jokes; the easy banter they'd developed during their time together; the first time she'd melted in his arms while he kissed her.

The image of her bedroom blasted through his

brain, and how he held her after the nightmare.

Rolling down the windows, he let the cool air wash over him, to no avail. His gut still told him it was wrong to leave. But if he didn't, he'd always have the stigma of his failure hanging over his head, even if no one knew or cared except him. If a man didn't have his pride, what did he have?

But what good is my pride if I lose Melody?

He pulled over to the side of the road, then scrubbed his hands over his face. Surprised to find moisture on his cheeks, he studied his palms, as if they could tell him what all this meant. Finally, he wiped the wet against his jeans, then took note of where he was...Melody's personal hideaway. It had become their special place...where he'd kissed her the first time.

Letting the car roll down the incline, he slowly drove around all the bends, then came to a stop next to the creek and climbed out. Leaning against the front fender, ankles and arms crossed, he visualized the handmade quilt she'd insisted wasn't special that they'd spread for the picnic lunch. Sunlight bounced off her hair as she looked at him with complete trust...and desire. The memory ate at him.

Damn. Had he just screwed up the best thing to ever happen to him? He'd never been this close to a woman, never cared what someone else thought. Melody was different. She was special. Regret ate at him for what he'd tossed away.

Jake stood there wallowing in his misery long enough for the engine to cool. When damp from the dew seeped through his clothes, and it registered in his foggy brain, he shoved off, got in the car and headed back to town. Regardless of what happened between them, he had to see this thing in Chicago through. Otherwise, he wouldn't be any good to anyone.

Including himself.

Linda Trout

Chapter Seventeen

Melody hadn't expected to sleep at all the night before, but to her surprise, had fallen asleep quickly. Now, as she went about preparing the café for the Saturday business, she thought about her life. She'd lived in limbo all this time, hanging on to one man's image and not knowing how to move forward. She was still angry with Michael but had found the depth of that anger had faded as she'd spent time with Jake.

Jake. What did she mean to him? Apparently, he was simply passing through the area, touching her life, her heart, without much effort. But being with him had opened up her soul to new possibilities, new opportunities. Did she dare take hold of the dreams that had begun to gather in her subconscious, to explore new horizons? His leaving hurt, no doubt about it, but for the first time in years, Melody could see herself moving forward again.

She'd lived through Michael's death and she would live through Jake's leaving, even if it did sting to think he'd walk away from her so easily. The way he'd held her—kissed her—spoke of deeper feelings. But she must have read more into their embraces than she should have. At least he took the effort to tell her in person instead of hearing it through the gossip mill.

"Hey, you," Cora said as she bumped Melody's shoulder. "Have you taken up residence on Pluto?"

Melody mentally shook herself. Time to stop wool gathering and pay attention to the present. "Sorry. Just a lot on my mind this morning."

"What's going on? And don't say it's nothing." Cora cocked her head, a slight frown on her face as she placed her hand on Melody's arm.

She hesitated, not sure if she was ready to confide in anyone yet.

"Mel, I can tell something's bothering you. You know you can tell me anything." Cora squeezed her arm, waiting.

First Jake and now Cora. Two people who believed in her enough to encourage her to move on with her life. Despite the fact he always had a gun strapped to his hip, Melody understood the attraction to Jake. But it still surprised her how fast she'd bonded with Cora. The woman was the sister of her heart—if not blood.

"It's Jake," she said in a low voice. No sense in broadcasting her troubles, even if Roy was the only other person in the café.

The concern on Cora's face deepened. "Has something happened?"

"No. Well, yes. I thought we'd become close, you know. Like we had something special going on." She fiddled with the napkin holders at the end of the counter, thinking she needed to get them out on the tables.

"But he doesn't feel the same way?"

"I don't know." She paused and thought a minute. "No, I'm sure he doesn't."

Cora clucked her tongue. "What happened?"

"He told me last night he's going back to Chicago."

229

Cora jerked to attention, her eyes wide. "Chicago? Why?"

"There's a chance he can get his old job back." Saying it out loud hit her between the eyes. Here she'd been congratulating herself for being so strong, but now the finality of it slammed into her and she sagged onto one of the bar stools.

"Oh, Melody. I'm so sorry. But why would he leave here to go back to that awful city?"

"He mentioned a case and said he needed to clear his name. At any rate, I don't care." *Yeah, and pigs fly.*

"Oh, you poor thing. When is he going?" Cora gave her a brief hug.

Thinking about him leaving sent another sharp pang through her. "Tonight. The interview is Monday."

A long moment passed, then Cora said, "Don't worry. It'll be okay. I bet he doesn't take the job even if they offer it to him. I mean, he seems to like it here plus he has you. No, I don't think you have anything to worry about."

Melody could always count on Cora being kind, supportive, and understanding. "Maybe you're right. He did seem torn up about it when he left my house last night. But I can't be sure because I was sort of in a state of shock. I managed to get him out the door before I completely fell apart."

"Well, that's something. We have to keep our dignity intact, don't we?"

She needed to concentrate on something else before her emotions got the better of her. Blowing out a deep breath, she stood. "We'd better get busy or we'll have customers banging on the door before we're ready."

Laughing, Cora agreed and went to work. Like clockwork the two women had everything ready with time to spare. Melody said another prayer of thanks for the woman who had helped center and ground her, a feat no one else had been able to accomplish.

Except Jake. She hitched a breath. It hurt to know he was walking away, but now she could stand on her own. For that, she'd always be grateful.

Ten minutes after she flipped on the OPEN sign, Jake walked in, He paused as he watched her, twisting his hat between his hands a while before he placed it on a peg. Despite her good feelings a short time earlier, a chill settled over her. She still felt as if he were abandoning her.

"Sheriff." She intentionally kept her voice cool. If he thought she'd make this easy on him, he needed to think again. Although, the dark circles under his eyes indicated he hadn't slept a wink last night. He looked as bad as she felt.

He slowly moved to his usual spot at the counter and took a seat. She followed his glance toward Cora, who appeared to be watching them intently despite the fact she was taking Perry Walker's order. Warmth settled in the pit of Melody's stomach. Cora continued to look out for her like a mother hen, bless her heart.

"If I order breakfast, do you promise not to poison me?"

She would've laughed, but she had the distinct impression it wasn't a joke. "Regardless of what you think, I'd never do anything to ruin business." Her voice broke on the last two words, and she hated that. She didn't say anything about not hurting him and knew he'd caught that, too. Good. Let him squirm.

"I'm sorry, Mel—"

"Sorry is not on the menu." No way would she allow him to apologize, and in public no less. Other patrons had started to arrive and she didn't want this encounter to continue. "What will you have?"

His shoulders slumped, more than they already had been, and he gave a slight shake of his head. His gaze had locked with hers and he held it, regret radiated from him. She didn't want his pity. She might not have been doing so well before he arrived in town, but she'd darn well be fine from now on. With or without a man in her life.

"I'll take the number two."

She jotted it on her order pad. "Is that all?"

He waited a beat longer. "Yeah. And some coffee, please."

Without meeting his gaze—that she felt boring into her with every ounce of her being—she turned to the kitchen, placed the order, then hurried to wait on a family of six who had arrived in a noisy cluster of scolding parents, whining children, with stomps and chairs scraping until they were all seated. It was nice to see some disorder from others that matched the feelings churning inside her. She wanted to stomp, and whine, and scold herself, all at the same time.

After she'd placed their order, she gave Jake his coffee as she set his food in front of him. She couldn't—wouldn't—look at him. Glancing over at Cora, the other woman gave her a reassuring nod, making Melody feel better. She lifted her chin and planted a smile on her face that wasn't as stilted as she'd thought it would be. It seemed as if no time had passed before Jake had eaten and walked out the door, leaving a fifty-dollar bill for a seven-fifty meal.

The large tip made the empty spot in her heart deeper.

****

The normal noonday rush had passed with few people coming in for a late lunch, probably due to the warm day keeping everyone outdoors. By late afternoon, and well before closing time, Melody decided to give herself a break. She turned to Cora. "I'm going to check on Randi and visit for a bit. See if she has made any wedding plans yet."

"She's the woman who was abducted, right?"

Melody nodded.

"That was awful. How'd the guy sneak up on her, anyway? I thought there were all kinds of people around her place."

Shaking her head, she said, "There had been, but the cleanup crews had already left. She was on her porch when this guy jumped out of the shadows and grabbed her."

"Oh, no. How frightening! I think I would've peed my pants."

"You and me both. He put a cloth to her mouth and she passed out almost instantly."

"From a cloth? That doesn't sound right." Cora continued loading dirty dishes in the tub to take to the kitchen.

"She found out later it was soaked in chloroform."

"Wow. I thought that kind of stuff only happened in the movies, not in real life." Cora's hand had gone to her throat, and her brows had furrowed.

"That guy had watched a bunch of movies, then, because that's what he did. Randi and Wade are both lucky to be alive." She paused, thinking of her friend and how little she knew about her background. "I still can't believe Wade is her old boyfriend and now they're getting married."

"Anything is possible when you set your mind to it," Cora responded, the lilt and tone of her voice at odds with her previous concern.

Narrowing her eyes, she wondered about Cora. She had been distant all day. She might be thinking about her old boyfriend and how much courage it had taken to leave the abusive relationship. Or she could be thinking about Melody's folks coming back next week and wondering if she'd still have a job. As far as Melody was concerned, she would. She'd also continue to rent the house out back to her. If she'd stay. Come Monday, Melody would talk to her, reassure her about the job. But not right now. Right now, she needed to get out of there.

Grabbing her purse, she headed for the door. "Tell Roy where I've gone, okay? I'll be back in time to help close up."

"Don't worry. We've got it covered." Cora gave a reassuring nod before going back to cleaning the last few dirty tables.

Melody called Randi to make sure it was okay to come over. After Wade had gotten out of the hospital, he'd moved in with her and they'd been holed up. Not that Melody could blame them. They had years of separation to make up for. She didn't know if Randi planned to stay here or move to Kansas City where he was assigned. For selfish reasons, she wanted Randi to stay.

A few minutes later, she pulled up to Randi's

house, noting deep ruts going through the yard where the remains of the airplane had been hauled off the property. Trees had been cut down to allow access to the crash site, leaving a direct path, and a long-term reminder of the tragedy.

A shudder rippled down her spine as she recalled the events of that day. She hadn't seen what Randi had, but it had to have been horrific. *About as bad as seeing your husband murdered right in front of you.* Thankfully, Randi had Wade to help her through it, but sometimes you needed another woman to talk to. She would be there for her friend, like Randi had been there for her.

Before she reached the porch, Randi rushed out to greet her. Arm in arm they went inside, her worries forgotten. She looked forward to meeting the man who had saved Randi and stolen her heart.

****

Jake had talked to the commissioners behind closed doors earlier in the day. They didn't like it, but understood his situation. He gave a strong recommendation to appoint Deputy Larson in his stead if he were reinstated with the CPD. The man might be young, but he was eager, he knew the area, the town and its people. Discarding the fact his uncle mistakenly thought he could control the young officer, he'd make a good sheriff. Although Clay was about as happy as Melody had been about Jake leaving. The man didn't want the job but would reluctantly accept it.

Jake dug through his civvies and found a sports-jacket and trousers that would serve well for the interview. A pair of jeans, underwear, a couple of shirts, his shaving gear, and he was good to go. As he walked out of the little house, it dawned on him that it had become home. Boxes were still stacked everywhere, but somewhere along the way he'd settled in. He would miss not just the old house, but the town as well.

And Melody, his brain shouted.

He dropped his duffle bag into the back seat of the Firebird, climbed in and sat there, not bothering to put the key in the ignition. What was he doing? Granted, it looked like he might accomplish his goal of being reinstated. But giving up Melody? Was the job worth sacrificing her for? *Could* he walk away from her? The thought of being without her stabbed at him. She had slipped under his defenses and claimed a piece of his heart.

When he'd told her his news last night, the hurt and pain in her eyes had sliced through him as if he'd been shot. Intent on talking to her before he left, he jammed the key in the ignition and turned the motor over. But a glance at his watch told him he was running late. Silently cursing his bad timing, he pulled away from the house.

When he came to The Tangled Rose Café, he didn't get a glimpse of Melody as he rolled past the building. Disappointed, he stopped in the grocery store parking lot, letting the engine idle as he stared into space. Torn in two, he weighed his options. Every fiber of his being told him to stay, to stay with her. He felt like a better man when he was with her. The little town wasn't bad, and the people were nice. Yet, at the same time, he knew he had to clear his name. Finally, with an inward sigh, he put the car in gear and pulled back onto the road and headed out of town. If he was going to do this, then he'd better get going. It was over an hour and a half to the airport, and he didn't want to miss his flight. Plus, he'd like to be off the two-lane winding roads before he lost all daylight. It would have been much quicker if he could have gotten a flight out of Harrison, but had to settle for driving all the way to Fayetteville.

If only he could keep the auburn-haired woman who had impacted his life more than he'd thought possible off his mind.

****

Dusk had settled by the time Melody headed back to town. She hadn't meant to stay so long, but Randi was so excited she just couldn't leave. Bless his heart, Wade had left after meeting her, giving them time alone. And she did feel better. They moaned and cried about Jake, but quickly moved on to more pleasant subjects, like Randi and Wade's wedding. Melody smiled. She couldn't be happier for her friend.

When she got back to town, the café was already closed with the lights out. *Strange.* Roy always left a back light on for security purposes. It wasn't like him to forget. Maybe Cora had turned them all out before she'd left. Melody felt bad about not helping close up, but both of them were more than capable of handling the job. She was blessed to have such devoted friends and employees.

She unlocked the front door, flipped on the light, then stopped. Scorched coffee perfumed the air, dirty dishes still littered a few tables, chairs were pushed haphazardly away from some tables. Taking a step into the room, the hairs on the back of her neck stood on end. Where was everyone? Why hadn't Cora finished cleaning?

"Cora? Roy? Is anyone here?"

Silence.

Gingerly, she made her way past the dirty tables, the remains of a chicken fried steak on one, a half-eaten burger with soggy fries covered in ketchup on another. She even recalled who had sat at those tables. Were they okay? Had there been an accident? She glanced back out the window. The town was quiet. No emergency vehicles going anywhere. No one rushing around. Which made the scene inside the café all the more eerie.

The acrid smell of a burning pot reclaimed her attention and she rushed around the counter to shut off the coffee maker.

Did Roy get hurt in the kitchen and Cora had to take him to the hospital? What if Cora's ex had found her and kidnapped her? What if the guy Jake had in custody wasn't the vandal? What if the real vandal had escalated his activities, taking Cora and Roy? She debated about running outside and asking for help, but didn't want to look foolish if was a false alarm. There could be a perfectly simple explanation for why the café looked the way it did. Why no one was there. But no reasonable explanation came to mind. Pulling out her phone, she checked for missed calls or messages. None.

Her first instinct was to call Jake. *Oh, wait, I can't. The rat ran out on me.* But she could sure call Clay. Even if it did turn out everything was all right, he would take her concern seriously.

A faint sound drifted through the café. She moved to the kitchen doorway. "Hello? Is anyone in there?"

Hearing the sound again, she stepped through the swinging doors. It was pitch black so she turned on the light. She gasped. Roy was sprawled face down on the floor.

"Roy!" Melody rushed to his side. A small pool of blood lay under his head. Feeling for a pulse on his neck, she was relieved to find he was alive. What in the world had happened? And where was Cora?

"Don't worry. I'll get you help." Thankful she had her phone, she punched in 9-1-1 but hadn't hit Send yet when movement from the doorway caught her attention. Before she could turn, someone grabbed her from behind and held a sickeningly sweet-smelling cloth to her mouth.

Darkness overtook her.

Chapter Eighteen

A half hour down the road and Jake couldn't make himself drive any faster. Deep down, he didn't want to go. All he'd dreamed about for months, all he'd wanted, was to be reinstated as a CPD detective and have his name cleared. But he wasn't in a bigger hurry because of one person.

Melody.

Rolling down the window, he let the cool air whip through the car in hopes it would help clear the cobwebs out of his brain. He even leaned his head out the window...to no avail. Disgusted with himself, he rolled the window back up. Right, wrong, or indifferent he had to make this trip. After he turned onto Highway 412, he was able to pick up speed. Once the road turned into a four-lane, he'd be able to make up for lost time.

His cell phone rang. Matt. Pressing the speaker button, he said, "Hey, buddy. I'm on my way to the airport now."

"Good. Looking forward to getting all this settled and you back on the force. You've been missed."

"Thanks. I appreciate it." He'd missed them, too. Except lately he'd had other things—other people—on his mind. Enough to block out his life in the big city.

"After you land, want to grab a beer before heading to the house?"

"Sure. How about Halihan's?"

"Aw, naw, man. The place has gone downhill bad in the last few months. Nothing but crazies go there now."

Crazies? Why did that ring a bell? He'd heard something similar lately, but couldn't place where. Too much going on, too many sleepless nights, too much fuzz in his brain. It would come to him later.

"Hey, you there?" Matt's voice jerked him out of his thoughts.

"Oh. Yeah. I'll let you pick the spot, then." He needed to pull it together. Spacing out while driving down a winding highway wasn't smart.

"Man, I hope you haven't gone soft on me. You need to be at the top of your game when you walk in there Monday. Anything less and you can kiss your chances goodbye."

He mentally kicked himself...again. "Right. Is there anything you can give me to show them I haven't lost my touch?"

Matt paused. "There is this new piece of evidence from the case you were working before you got pulled off to do the witness protection detail."

The detail that had ended Jake's career, still leaving the other murder case unsolved. He flipped his lights at an oncoming car with their brights on, then refocused on the conversation.

"The murder in an alley with a female witness?" Yeah. He remembered all too well.

"That's the one. Get this. The woman who witnessed the shooting? Seems hers were the only fingerprints found at the scene."

"We knew that. We figured the perpetrator had worn gloves."

"Yeah, well, her DNA was the only other DNA at the scene besides the victim's."

He jerked as if he'd been sucker punched.

Matt continued. "There was a mix-up at the lab, so we didn't get the results until recently. You're not going to believe this, but the DNA showed up in at least three other cases."

"What?"

"Looks like we have a female serial killer."

He searched his memory for her name. Then it came to him. Pam Whitaker. "Where is she now?"

"That's the thing. She's dropped off the grid. Looks like she left town, and we don't have a clue where she's gone."

Jake balled his hand into a fist.

"We've sent her picture and info to every major city across the States. This woman won't stop. She'll keep killing."

He muttered a curse. Why couldn't he catch a break? The woman had come across as a professional businesswoman who happened to be at the wrong place at the wrong time. She'd later invited him to have a drink with her, and expressed a desire for a more physical relationship. He'd been tempted, but then the problems with the captain came up and he had to focus on saving his crumbling career. If he'd given in to his baser needs, would he have been her next victim?

"I found an overlooked scrap of paper stuffed in the victim's pocket with a message written on it. The guy had it folded so tiny we almost didn't see it."

"What'd it say?" His eyes were on the road, but his brain had already moved into analytical mode.

"Liar. You'll burn in hell."

He sucked in a ragged breath, jammed on the brakes, and pulled to the side of the road, grateful there was a shoulder. A car's horn blared as it zoomed past. A cold sweat broke out on his body. Several things clanged into place at once with an ominous thud in his mind. "That's what was overlooked?"

"Yeah, I know it isn't much, but—"

"Son of a...Right under my nose and I didn't see it!" He slammed his hand against the steering wheel.

"What are you talking about? Do you mean Whitaker?"

He wheeled the car around and headed back. "She changed her appearance. She's in Rock Ledge."

"What?"

"I gotta go." Jake disconnected and dialed Melody, then the café. No answer at either place. The café would've been closed by now, but where was Melody? He called Roy's number. Again, no answer. "Dammit!" He dialed the office.

Glenda picked up on the first ring. "Hey, boss."

"Where's Larson?"

"Getting ready to walk out the door."

"Put him on." A couple seconds later Larson came on the line. "We have a problem. Go check out the café. Make sure everything is all right. If the doors are locked, break in. I can't reach Melody or Roy. I'm on my way back, but it'll take me a while to get there. Keep me posted as to what you find."

"You got it."

"Oh, and Larson. If you see Cora, be careful. If she is who I think she is, she's a serial killer."

Jake could practically feel Larson coming to attention.

"As soon as I know something, I'll report in." He disconnected.

Jake felt powerless. Almost like when he'd been railroaded and lost his CPD job. Except that paled in comparison. No telling what Cora, aka Pam, would do. Especially if she felt threatened. If only he had checked out the woman like his gut had told him to, but he'd been so focused on the plane crash, and with Melody, he'd let it slide. Now his oversight could cost people their lives.

Melody's life.

He wanted to beat his head against the dashboard. Cursing the winding roads that slowed him down, he pressed the accelerator as far as he dared. Why hadn't he listened to those tiny warning bells?

A few minutes later, Larson called. Jake put the phone on speaker. "Talk to me." *Please say you found Melody safe and sound.*

"I found Roy on the kitchen floor at the café. He's been hit over the head and lost some blood. It looks bad, but I can't tell for sure. An ambulance is on its way. There's no sign of Melody or Cora."

Jake cursed. "Cora took her. Are there any signs of a struggle or any indication of where they might be?"

"Doesn't look like there was a struggle, but they were interrupted before the café was completely cleaned. Dirty dishes are still on some of the tables. Must have caught Roy unaware to have knocked him out like this. Found Melody's purse and cell phone lying next to him." He paused a minute, then added, "The EMT's are coming in the door now."

Jake heard the background noise of people coming inside, the muted voices as they checked Roy. Now what? Then he remembered what they'd found in Chicago. "Check his pockets before they take him to the hospital. See if there's a note of some kind." Pam had a pattern, and he hoped she hadn't broken it. He drummed his fingers, willing Larson to hurry.

Finally, Larson came back on the line. "I found a scrap of paper with a weird note on it."

"Read it."

"'Her sanctuary is now mine.' What does that mean?"

Jake mulled it over, trying to decipher the meaning. Then it hit him. Melody's spot by the stream. She'd called it her sanctuary. Maybe that was where Cora had taken her. Good thing he and Melody had done so much driving on the back roads, because he knew a short cut. If he could remember how to get to it from this direction. And in the dark.

"Tell the EMT's to write down anything he says if he comes to, then go over to the house where Cora has been living. See if you can find any other evidence."

"You got it. I'll also have Glenda put out a BOLO on her."

Jake disconnected and concentrated on his driving. Why hadn't he picked up on the clues sooner? Time slowed to a standstill as he wove around the winding roads. He was closer, but not close enough, not fast enough. Finally, his phone rang. Larson.

"What'd you find?"

"She's definitely the perpetrator. There are pictures of you and Melody all over her bedroom wall. She's been spying on you, both together and separately. I also found a body suit, like she wanted to come across as heavier than she really was, plus a wig." He paused.

"Looks like she changed her appearance so much I might not even know her if I saw her right now."

Jake cursed. So that was why he hadn't recognized her. Even her mannerisms were different. The woman must have had a good laugh at his expense. He slammed his hand against the steering wheel. What kind of detective was he that the woman had been right under his nose this entire time? And he hadn't realized it.

"I know where they are, but it'll be tricky getting there without being seen or heard. We can't take any chance on her killing Melody." Jake told him how to get there and where to wait until needed. Too much noise and Pam would hear them.

"Copy."

He started to hang up when his training finally kicked in. Damn. He had a hard time thinking when he was so emotionally involved. "Call the FBI and report the kidnapping. The perpetrator is Pam Whitaker, alias Cora Conway. The woman is armed and dangerous. With any luck, I'll have the situation under control before they can even get mobilized." At least he hoped so. With Pam, you never knew what to expect.

"Will do. And Jake? Be careful."

Easier said than done. "Just get out there as soon as you can."

"You can count on me," Larson replied. Both men knew if shots were fired, by the time Larson got there, it'd all be over.

One way or the other.

****

Melody awoke slowly, cold seeping through her cotton dress. She opened her eyes to find herself outside, by a stream from the sounds of it. What had happened? How'd she get here and who brought her? Then she remembered seeing Roy lying on the floor, blood around his head. She jerked upright but had to put her hand down to steady herself. Her head spun as her stomach threatened to lose its contents. Was he okay? Was he still alive? She knew head wounds bled a lot, but didn't know how much blood he'd lost, or how severe the injury. She had to get him help.

"Mel?" A voice came from somewhere in the darkness.

Cora. Fighting down nausea, Melody twisted around in an effort to see her friend. "What's going on? Did you see who did this?" She tested her hands and feet. They weren't tied or bound, which seemed strange.

Cora coughed, then spoke with a raspy voice. "Where are we?"

A flickering light behind her drew her attention. Several small candles sat on a large rock, giving off enough light for Melody to recognize the area. She gasped. Whoever had kidnapped them had brought them to *her* private spot where she went for solitude, where she'd brought Jake. Turning around, she saw Cora on the opposite side of the clearing. She couldn't make out much in the dark except for her jean-clad legs stretched out in front of her. Maybe they'd tied her up. If so, why not both of them? Questions buzzed around in her head. Still too groggy to think clearly, all she accomplished was to give herself a headache. She looked for their abductor, but didn't see or hear anyone.

"Cora, are you all right?" She wanted to go to her, but didn't think she could stand up yet.

"I will be in a little bit." Again, the raspy voice.

Whoever took them must have thought they'd be unconscious longer and had left them alone, assuming they wouldn't be able to escape. The flickering light drew her again. Maybe she could find something there to use as a weapon before they got back. Struggling to her feet, she stumbled toward the light, trying to be quiet yet hurry at the same time.

Finally, close to the rock, she found several objects scattered amongst the candles. A small jewelry box, a high school picture, an old necklace, a silver thimble. These were hers, keepsakes that had been in an old shoebox on the floor of her closet. She rubbed her hands up and down her arms to ward off the shiver threatening to envelope her. *Violation* blasted through her.

"This is my stuff," she whispered, afraid to speak too loudly. "Some psycho has been in my house, pawing through my things. And for what? Why kidnap us?"

Cora was silent for so long that Melody began to think she'd passed out. Finally, her voice floated across the clearing. "Have you ever loved anyone so much you can't see your life without him?"

What was wrong with her? There wasn't time to talk about romance. They had to escape. "Uh, yeah. Cora, we need to—"

"Of course you do. After all, that's what you did, isn't it?"

"What are you talking about?"

Cora laughed, the sound brittle. "You. After your husband died, you just stopped living. You holed up in that café with that shrine you claim you hate, and

248

watched the world go by from the window. How does it feel to go through life like a zombie?"

She froze. Tiny tingles of unease crept up her spine. This woman didn't sound like the person she knew, didn't sound like her friend. People reacted in different ways to stress, but this was beyond anything she would have expected from Cora. The woman had always been so kind and willing to do whatever it took to make a new life for herself.

"Know what I think? I think you wouldn't be able to breathe if someone took all those stupid little trinkets away and you didn't have that dead man to focus on."

She gasped. "Cora, I know you're upset, but that's no reason to be cruel."

"I'm just telling the truth, sweetie." She placed extra emphasis on the last word. "You're nothing but a weak, insipid female who can't take care of herself. You have to have a man to lean on. If you can't have the one you started out with, then you take someone else's."

Wh—what? That couldn't be Cora. Granted, it sounded like her, sort of. But the venom in her tone shocked Melody. As cold seeped into her bones, an atrocious thought occurred to her. What if it had been Cora who had thrown the rock through the window? Who had slashed her tires; written on the wall?

Who had abducted her?

So far, she hadn't heard anyone else out here. Wouldn't they have made themselves known by now? She glanced around the clearing, looking for the abductor to step out of the shadows. The only sound was a light rustling of leaves and the water bouncing over the rocks.

They were the only people there.

No. It wasn't possible. Melody couldn't reconcile that thought to the woman she knew; her friend and confidante. The woman had needed Melody's help so desperately and been so grateful when Melody had helped her out. She had worked tirelessly in the café.

Who seemed to know everything that went on around town.

The dire reality of the situation sent ice through Melody's veins and a shaft of fear spiked through her. She had thought she'd been afraid before, but right now her insides shook so hard she was on the verge of throwing up. She was alone. With a woman who was capable of who knew what. Trying to be as casual as possible, she headed toward the road.

Cora stood and stepped out of the shadows, blocking her path. Only this was a stranger. Dressed all in black, she was slim, her long blonde hair pulled into a ponytail, her makeup done to perfection. She walked with a swagger and had a cocky expression. How could this be the same woman? They looked, and acted, nothing alike. Melody wanted her friend back, but was sorely afraid that person had never existed. Petrified, she took a step back.

"You aren't going anywhere. Besides, he'll be here soon."

"Who?" To her dismay, her voice wobbled. She did *not* want to show weakness to this woman, for all the good it would do her.

"Jake, of course."

Of course? Her skin prickled. "I told you. He left."

"Oh, he'll be back. He'll come for me. It shouldn't be long now."

Another shard of ice slid up her back. She didn't want to know—really she didn't—but she had to ask, anyway. "How do you know Jake will come? And how does he know where to go?" She took a step back…toward the road…toward safety.

Cora tsked, shaking her head. "You have no imagination, you know that? You hate your life, yet you're not willing to do anything about it. All you had to do was tear your husband's stupid shrine apart, throw it in the trash where it belongs, and tell everyone to leave you the hell alone. But did you? Noooo. You go in there every single day and let the memories of how he always put you last rip you apart. You're lonely, have no friends, and no balls to do anything about it. You're nothing but a cowardly mouse."

Coward? Mouse? Did people see her that way? She didn't think so, but Cora's words made her doubtful. Either way, she wouldn't be anymore. She had grown enough that she had planned to make changes at the café. The next day, in fact. Thanks to Jake's encouragement.

Whom Cora seemed fixated on.

Chapter Nineteen

Melody straightened her back, lifting her chin. "What's your point?" Her voice now held a steely quality, one she used to have while Michael had been deployed, but had lost somewhere along the way since his death.

"Oooo. Listen to you getting all tough." Cora took a step forward. "My *point*, you spineless twit, is you aren't worthy of Jake Bennett and you never will be."

The sweet smiles Melody associated with Cora were replaced by a smug expression. But what scared her was the wild, almost mad gleam in the other woman's eyes. Without a word, she turned her back on Cora and ran toward the road. Too much distance and open space separated her from safety, though, and her flight ended all too soon when she was yanked to a stop from behind. Cora had moved so fast Melody hadn't heard her coming over the rushing in her ears.

"Uh-uh-uh. Not so fast."

Cora twirled her around, pointing a gun in her face. Her heart jolted to a stop. The blood drained from her head and her knees threatened to buckle. She couldn't take a deep breath. *No. Not again. I can't do this.*

Cora snorted. "See? I hold all the cards. *I* hold the power."

Melody shrank back from the weapon, and Cora let her go. Stumbling, she righted herself before being herded back toward the makeshift altar. Despite Cora's insistence that Jake would come, he wasn't here. The woman was delusional in thinking he would show up.

No, Melody was on her own.

Being a few feet away from the gun helped slow her thundering heart. She had to think. Surely there was a way out of this. Cora waved the barrel of the gun toward one of the rocks and Melody sank onto the hard, cold surface.

"It was you all along, wasn't it?" Knowing her so-called friend had done those things made it extra creepy. And disheartening.

"Give the woman a gold star. Who else around this dump of a town has the brains and skill to get in and out of all the places, and not leave a clue? Although, I will admit, you almost caught me the other morning while leaving my message on the café's wall. I barely had time to step back and drop the spray can and gloves in my bag before you rounded the corner. But you're so dumb and gullible you bought my act. You even begged me to stay."

Her condescending tone, her contemptuous sneer, drove another dagger into Melody. "You know, you meant a lot to me and I thought we had become good friends. We had a connection that, despite what you think, couldn't be faked."

Cora's eyes widened, and her expression softened with realization a moment before it was snuffed out, and the hard look returned. "Seriously?" Cora bent forward, eyebrows raised.

Yes, she had been gullible, but that didn't give Cora the right to do this.

"I had to see Jake in action again, you know. I had

to see him look at me like he used to." She paused to glare at Melody. "But he couldn't see me for you."

The venom in her voice made Melody cringe and draw back. Until what she said registered. "What do you mean, like he used to?"

Again, she scoffed. "In Chicago, where else? You don't think I came to this rinky-dink town because I wanted to, do you? We were an item. He couldn't take his eyes off me. He loved me!"

Yet he left you behind. That crazy gleam in your eye is probably the reason why. Melody was smart enough to keep the thought to herself, though. She looked around for a way to escape. But there wasn't any protection or cover.

It wasn't the smartest thing to do, but she had to ask. "Why did you attack Roy?"

"You are so dumb. As a diversion for you. Stupid man never knew what hit him. Literally." She threw her head back and laughed; sounding hysterical, and more than a little insane.

The sound made her skin crawl, as if dozens of cockroaches were scurrying all over her. She forced herself to not shudder. "You didn't have to hurt him."

"Oh, sure, I did. How else would my Jake know how to find me?"

Jake isn't coming, you ignorant woman. Struggling to keep her voice calm, even though she wanted to claw Cora's eyes out for hurting Roy, she said. "Cora, you're sick. We can get you help. It isn't too late. No one has been seriously injured and—"

"Shut up! You don't know anything. Of course people have been *seriously* injured. Not here, but they'll figure it all out eventually." She slowly walked around the clearing, looking into the darkness, the gun hanging loosely at her side.

Figure it out? What had Cora done before coming to Rock Ledge? Another icy wedge settled between her shoulder blades.

Cora had gone perfectly still, seemingly lost in thought. Melody took the opportunity to stand and take a few steps toward what she hoped was freedom. She couldn't make it to the road, but maybe she could reach the tree line. At least there would be a little cover. She didn't get far, though, before Cora stopped her.

"Don't. Just...don't." Cora glared at her, waving the gun in the air back and forth in front of her. "The party isn't complete without you."

Bile threatened to work its way up her throat at the implication. "Wh-what do you need me for? I'm nothing to Jake." Sadly, that was the truth. Otherwise, he wouldn't have gone to Chicago without her.

"He has to see you eliminated so he knows I'm the one he's supposed to be with."

"But he isn't here! Can't you get that through your thick head?" Her heart lurched as soon as she said the words. Cora wasn't stable by any stretch of the imagination. Antagonizing her wasn't a smart move.

Swinging the gun in Melody's direction, Cora narrowed her gaze. "Watch it. I can always adjust my plans. He'll think you drowned yourself while pining over him."

Oh, that was plain ridiculous. "With a bullet hole in me? Really, Cora?"

She glared. "Don't talk to me like I'm stupid, Mel, because I'm not. I fooled you and this entire town. I even fooled Jake. Guess he isn't as good as I thought."

Her lips twitched as she moved closer, then she suddenly wrapped an arm around Melody's shoulders and pressed the gun to her temple.

Taken by surprise, Melody stiffened when the cold metal touched her. *I won't panic. I won't panic.* She prayed saying the mantra would help her remain calm. It didn't work, but she refused to cower in front of this lunatic.

"Come on out, Jake. I know you're there."

Jake? Here? No way.

Then a movement caught her attention. Her heart sank and her knees went weak as Jake stepped out of the darkness.

Right into Cora's trap.

****

Jake's heart skipped several beats when Pam grabbed Melody, and pointed the gun at her head. One gentle squeeze on the trigger, and he'd lose Melody forever. There was no choice but to do as told. Leaving the safety of the trees, he moved into the open but stayed partially in the shadows. Melody gasped, but he couldn't focus on her right now. Not and have any chance of coming out of this alive. Why hadn't he seen the signs before? How had he let things go this far without a clue of Cora's true identity?

Shaking off the distracting thoughts, he stayed loose but kept his gun gripped in his hand. Now he wished he'd had Larson move in and take up a closer position. Between the two of them, perhaps they could take down Pam without Melody getting hurt, like they had with the escaped fugitive.

"Let her go, Pam. You don't need her anymore. Your beef is with me."

"Why, Jake Bennett. Of course I need her. She's pivotal to my plans, didn't you know? And don't forget, you're the one who made her important so it's way past the point where I could let her go," she said in a sing-song voice as she twisted Melody around so he didn't have a clear shot. "Step into the clearing."

He did as she said, itching to get the drop on her.

"Now, lay your gun on the rock over there and move away."

When he didn't immediately comply, she jammed the gun harder against Melody's head, causing her to whimper. He eased over to the rock, which held a collection of strange items, and laid his weapon where he could easily grab it if he stayed close enough. He took a couple steps away and halted.

Pam sneered. "Always the clever one, aren't you? I won't fall for your trick. I've studied you too long and know all your moves. None of them will work tonight. Move over by the stream."

Reluctantly, he did as she said. He glanced at Melody. Her chin trembled as, wide-eyed, she held his gaze. Yeah, he was terrified, too.

"Ah, that's better." She shoved Melody to the ground, shifting a few feet away from her, and trained the gun on him. "Oh, Jake. My darling Jake. If only you'd paid attention to me once I got to town."

"How could I do that when I didn't even know it was you?"

"I left you numerous hints, but you never picked up on them."

"Your appearance changed a lot since I last saw you in Chicago. The body suit was a nice disguise. Too good in fact."

"Testing your detective skills. Sadly, you failed."
She tsked.

"Something else is different." Why hadn't he
recognized her before? If he had, Melody's life
wouldn't be in jeopardy now. She remained on the
ground, but watched the exchange closely.

Pam ran her hand through her hair. "Besides the
wig and frumpy clothes, I also had my nose fixed to one
of those little pixie jobs you like." She beamed at him
as if he should be proud of her.

"Hate to burst your bubble, Pam, but I like the way
Cora looked and acted better."

Her smile slowly faded. Her entire demeanor
changed. "You like a frump like Cora, but you still
wouldn't look at *me*! All you saw was that spineless
twit over there."

He had to think. The last thing he wanted was her
focusing on Melody. "You said you were running from
an abusive boyfriend. I figured you wouldn't want to
get into another relationship right afterward. But I
noticed you."

She looked as if she might believe him.

Melody quietly stood, then inched toward the
woods, but she didn't get far.

"Stay where you are, Mouse. It isn't time for you
to leave the party yet." Pam didn't even turn her head,
simply pointed the gun in Melody's direction.

With a sigh, Melody changed direction, moving in
closer, and stopped not far from the rock, and his gun.
For all the good it would do. He'd seen her aversion to
weapons. But if she could pick it up and throw it to
him, he might get a shot off before Pam took them both
out. It was wishful thinking, though. "Pam—"

She swished her hair, cocking an eyebrow. "Cora.
I've decided I like that name better. Besides, Cora
Conway doesn't have a criminal record, doesn't look
anything like Pam Whitaker, and can go where she
pleases."

"You've put a lot of planning into this." He should
have done the same thing, instead of rushing in here
half-cocked.

She harrumphed, jutting out her chin. "Having a
meticulous plan is the only way to make sure things go
the way you want."

He squatted and plucked a blade of new grass—
toying with it—making himself appear subservient. If
she'd look away for even an instant, he could pull the
gun from his ankle holster.

"Can I ask you a question?" He kept his voice
calm.

"You can ask anything you like. Doesn't mean
you'll get the answer you want."

"Fair enough." He paused. "How did you find
me?"

"Plane crash. Pushy reporter. Ring a bell?" She
smirked.

He knew getting cornered by the reporter and
having his face splattered on national TV had been a
bad idea. Just not this bad. He needed to keep her
talking. "You're as smart as you are sexy. Why did you
focus on me in Chicago, then follow me here?"

She blinked, as if the answer were obvious. "That
first day in the alley? When you came to investigate
Albert's death? You were so kind and gentle, so
comforting, that I knew you were the one. From that
point on, I had to make you see how great we'd be

together. But then when you didn't, when you disappeared, I had to find you to give you another chance before I made you pay."

Taking a deep breath, he plunged ahead. Softly, he said, "All I did was touch your arm in consolation for having witnessed a murder."

"No. You touched me because you cared! It was love at first sight. I could tell."

He stared in disbelief. Just one touch and she thought they belonged together? The woman was definitely sick.

"Tell me about Albert."

She took a step backward. "What about him?"

"How did you happen to be with him in the alley?"

A hard expression came over her face as she narrowed her eyes. She grinned, but it was pure evil. "He wouldn't leave his wife. After all the time we'd spent together, after all we'd meant to each other, and he turned his back on me like I was nothing. I tricked him into coming, telling him I'd end it, but only after one last meet."

Like all the time we *didn't spend together?* "And once he was there?"

Pam blinked, wide-eyed. "Why, I shot him. But before I could get away, a stupid patrol car pulled up. I made up the story of the mugger. Then you came into my life and we fell in love."

She beamed at him. Which made him more nervous. The woman was definitely unhinged.

"So, you want me to run away with you? Live with you?"

She cocked her head. "Of course. We'll live right here." She waved her gun around the area.

"*Here?*" What the…?

"Yes. It's a lovely spot, don't you think? We can build a nice house, but not too big. We don't want people thinking they're overpaying you. I have a nice savings, so we'll use that."

"Will we have children?"

"Yes. No." She looked confused, then refocused on him. "How can I have you all to myself if there are a bunch of brats running around?"

"But what if I want kids? I'd like to pass on my name."

"No…no. You're too infatuated with me to worry about that. I'm all you need." She took half a step toward him. "Tell me I'm all you need, Jake."

He didn't say anything, letting her stew. Finally, he broke the silence that had settled over the little valley. "We'll have to take our time to make sure."

"But we've known from the beginning. You've always loved me, Jake." Her voice rose with each word.

Keeping his voice calm, he gave a little shrug. "When we met for drinks that one time?"

"Yes. Then and the other times."

There hadn't been any other times, except in her warped mind. "You're a fascinating and beautiful woman."

Initially, she seemed mesmerized, letting the gun droop. He started to reach for his backup piece, when she jerked and took a step back, her eyes clear.

"Stand up, Jake. And don't bother trying to pull your other gun." She raised her weapon and pointed it toward him.

He complied with the demand, glanced over at Melody and threw her a regretful look. He wished things could have been different. For the first time in his life, he'd found someone worth fighting for. He tensed his legs, ready to spring on Cora. He'd take a bullet, no doubt about it, but maybe he could disable her long enough for Melody to get away.

If he had to die, saving the woman he loved would be worth it. With sudden clarity, he realized it was true. Until this moment—this second—he hadn't known the depth of his feelings for Melody. He didn't want to profess his love in front of Cora, yet was afraid he'd never have another chance.

If he could just get close enough to disarm Cora before she put a bullet between his eyes. Or worse, kill Melody.

****

Melody plotted ways to distract Cora while listening to Jake try to reason with her. For the first time, she understood what Michael had been trying to do with the vets with PTSD. Her heart opened as a tear slid down her cheek. *I get it now,* she silently said to the heavens. There had been a purpose to his life, and yes, even his death. She accepted it all.

Including the importance of a firearm.

Cora was focused on Jake and didn't pay her any attention. Probably because she didn't consider Melody a threat. She moved to the boulder and looked at the gun lying there. At Jake's gun. Oddly enough, it looked exactly like the one pointed at her the day of the crash.

The conversation died away, and Cora's demeanor changed. Despite her earlier proclamation of her and Jake having a life together, she aimed her gun at him. *She's going to kill him!* Without hesitation Melody picked up Jake's weapon.

That garnered a look from Cora.

"Oh, puhleeze. You can't pull the trigger and we both know it," Cora taunted.

Melody was never more sure of anything in her life. "Don't push me."

Cora laughed. Not just a laugh, but a hysterical, shrilly laugh that spoke of how far over the edge the woman had gone. Melody almost felt as if she were standing in Michael's shoes that last day. He hadn't believed his friend would shoot him. He'd been dead wrong.

But Melody wouldn't make the same mistake. She'd been lucky enough to find not one, but two men to love in her life. She'd watched the first one die, and she had no intention of watching the second one do the same thing. Not when she had the power to do something about it this time.

"Stay out of my way, Mouse! I'll attend to you in a minute. Now Jake and I have to say our farewells." Cora refocused on Jake.

"You said we'd build a house together. Right here on this spot." Jake's voice rang with desperation.

"Don't try to play me for a fool, Jake. We both know that was never going to happen. I'm afraid this relationship will end the same way it did with poor Albert. Too bad because you sure are cute. Oh, well. All good things must end."

Melody pulled the trigger, the sound deafening. Cora screamed; the expression on her face twisted in shock and pain. Pulling the trigger had been harder than Melody thought, and her stomach rolled at the sight of Cora's blood, at the scream of pain when the bullet had cut through her shoulder. She'd shot Cora! Actually shot her. But she hadn't killed her. Thankful beyond words, she wanted to throw the gun she held into the creek...after she threw up. Except Cora still held hers.

Hatred and fury replaced the shock on Cora's face as she pointed her gun at Melody. "You bit—"

Jake had already retrieved his backup weapon and fired. Eyes wide, Cora looked down at the hole in her chest, then she crumbled to the ground.

Jake rushed to her and wrenched the gun out of her hand, tossing it a safe distance away. He checked her pulse, then shook his head. Cora was dead.

Melody had trusted her, had counted her as a blessing in her life and the betrayal cut her to the core of her being. The sights and sounds from tonight would haunt her dreams for a long time to come.

Jake took his gun from her, then wrapped her in a tight hug.

Pulling back, he brushed a strand of hair behind her ear. "I'm so proud of you. If you hadn't acted when you did, she would've killed us both. But I didn't know you knew how to handle a firearm."

She nodded. "Michael made sure I could take care of myself while he was gone."

"He was a good man."

"Yes, he was." She laid her head on Jake's chest.

Sirens wailed in the distance.

Before long, the little valley was flooded with vehicles. From Larson, to Malone, a crime scene unit, the state highway patrol and an ambulance. People swarmed everywhere as flood lights were set up and the area processed. Everything looked like a well-oiled machine.

Cora's body was loaded into the ME's van, Jake's

guns were collected as evidence, and Melody and Jake both gave official statements.

Deputy Larson came up to them. "I heard from the hospital. Roy took a hard hit and has a severe concussion. They'll keep him for a few days to make sure there isn't any excessive swelling of the brain. He'll be out of commission for a while, but he should be okay."

She sagged with relief. "Oh, thank goodness. I don't know what I would've done if…" She couldn't finish the thought.

"It'll take more than that to keep him down," he assured her.

"I appreciate you letting me know, Clay." She squeezed his hand before he turned and walked away.

"Are you all right?" Jake wrapped his arms around her.

She wasn't sure, but she refused to hide from life anymore. "I will be."

"I thought that was the end of us."

"For a while there I had my doubts, too." The vise grip around her heart dropped away. She hadn't thought they stood any chance of surviving Cora's carefully planned execution. But they had. Melody sank deeper into his arms, inhaling his scent, desperate to hang onto what little she could of him, while she could.

"This should secure your reinstatement." She said the words, trying to sound positive for him even as it ate her heart out to think of him leaving.

"I'm sure it would. *If* I went back."

The bleakness that had settled over her faded. With his arms still securely around her, she studied his face. "If? I thought that's what you wanted."

He gave her a rueful grin. "I'm pretty hardheaded. Took almost losing you to make me realize how important you are to me."

Her breath caught as hope began to bloom, one tiny rose petal at a time.

"I'll go back, but only to clear my name. While we're there, I'll show you everything the city has to offer. Then I want to make Rock Ledge my home...if you'll have me. I love you, Melody."

The thorns that had held her captive the last two years fell away, as if they'd never been there. The candles in Cora's shrine suddenly blazed brighter, and sparks burst into the night sky. Melody watched as they lifted upward. *Michael.* He'd been with her all along, just waiting for her to take the steps to live again. *I'll love you always.* Heart filled with love, she mentally blew her high school sweetheart a kiss as the last ember faded from sight. Then she brought her gaze back to the man she'd grow old with. "And I love you."

The crime scene people moved to the rock to collect all the items, but Melody barely noticed them. The only person she saw and heard was Jake.

He bent his head and captured her lips in a searing kiss that held promises of years of love and happiness.

"Think you can live in a small, boring town?"

He pulled her even closer. "There isn't anything boring about this town. And after the last couple of weeks, I could use some quiet."

Melody smiled as they turned toward the creek, toward the place where their hearts had first united. Toward a future where there were no entanglements beyond love, marriage, children, hope, home. The best of all worlds.

A word about the author...

An Award-Winning and Amazon paid Kindle sales top 25 Bestselling author, Oklahoma native Linda Trout loves Happily-Ever-Afters. When she isn't helping her husband remodel their home, she's outside trying to tame a small portion of their ten-acres (a losing battle). Between her numerous cats, who think they have to help her write, and traveling to various parts of the country, she's working on her next novel.

http://LindaTrout.com